THE PILOT

MICHAEL COLE

SEVERED PRESS
HOBART TASMANIA

THE PILOT

PROLOGUE

The universe is comprised of billions of stars, and amongst them, billions of planets. Whether through random occurrence, or divine intervention, each of them found their place in the infinite reaches. Each of these satellites began as a smoldering cinder, until time and distance transformed them into barren heaps. With gravity pulling equally from all sides, they formed into their common round structure. Some would be reduced to landscapes of ice, with temperatures of minus three hundred degrees Celsius. Others would become hellish landscapes, with volcanic fire blazing throughout the surface. Some would be reduced to gas, just a circular cloud held together by gravity, while others would become barren rocky masses. Then, few and far between, there became those baring a rare gift called life.

Between all of them is the empty clear black expanse. An invisible thing, with no texture or matter, yet containing a force of apocalyptic proportions. An unrelenting suction, continuously tearing apart anything without the protective shield of atmosphere. Moving about in this endless emptiness, portions of such "victims" floated about. Remnants of dead stars and planets, or just the leftovers from incomplete satellites, they became reduced to asteroids, meteors, and meteorites. All were in motion, either drifting in a large collective, or shooting through the endless black, driven by the unstoppable force within space.

Then, somewhere in the distance between galaxies, something traveled at unparalleled speed. Its direction was not random but deliberate. Its shape, like that of an arrowhead, contained a forward axis. Its interior was not compacted dust, but hollow. The exterior was a compact material made from a metal that only existed on a planet that had its gift of life stripped from it.

A blue light illuminated at the stern, and the object increased its speed, traveling past the speed of light to its next destination.

Standing at the cockpit, the Pilot patiently monitored the next destination. It had only a mathematical sense of time. It did not grow bored, nor did it experience thrill. There was only purpose.

Green lights brightened throughout the interior, mimicking the familiar atmosphere from the world in which it originated. A world it would never see again. The Pilot had no intentions of seeing its world again, nor did it desire to visit any planet any more than once. For once its purpose was complete, there was no need to return.

Vibrations on the "monitor" informed it of everything it needed to know. Waves projecting from the forward axis, like echolocation, informed it of everything in its trajectory. Objects traveling over the span of an entire galaxy were calculated. Each detail fed into the device, particularly distance, size, and trajectory. A near flawless technology, it prevented collision for precise and direct travel.

But no technology is flawless.

A sudden energy overload within a medium sized star instantly increased its mass a thousand times. Though millions of miles away, its gravitational pull was second only to that of a black hole. Planets and even other stars shifted from place, displacing thousands of miles in a moment.

Such an anomaly did not affect the vessel's course, as a slight adjustment by the pilot resisted the pull from the mass. However, the immense volume of matter shifting from all corners of space proved too much for the technology to calculate all at once.

What was once empty space had now become an asteroid field. With millions of miles of momentum, each piece of debris launched toward the newly enlarged star. One such rock, nearly a mile diameter, made of a crystalline carbon harder than diamonds, instantly became a shooting star.

The console had only the collision warning in a flash of yellow just as the object came into view. Even for a creature such as the pilot, there was no reaction time great enough to avoid the impact.

The rock broke the starboard section as easily as cracking an egg. Immediately, the vacuum of space went to work, tearing at the ship with unmatched force. Both interior and exterior portions broke away, zipping toward the dying star until eventually reaching a gravitational equilibrium. The cockpit sealed itself, giving the Pilot enough time to secure itself.

A pod, nearly the size of a car, unveiled like a flower. Its exterior shell was a bright silver, composed of layers of a barrier sheet made to protect the capsule from atmospheric entry should it find a suitable planet. The barrier would gradually dissolve into a powdery substance during the course of entry, leaving the capsule itself untouched.

The pod contained supplies, enough for the Pilot to survive, should it escape this predicament. The journey would not be as predictable as normally that of its vessel, as the pod did not contain the advanced navigational technology. It only contained a beacon for others of its species to collect it, should they ever travel within distance. That beacon, having mapped the paths of the ship during its travels, would now do so for the pod.

With the future now undetermined, there was only one thing remaining for the Pilot to do. It placed itself in the pod, and adjusted the limited navigation settings. With no suitable planets found within the scanner's reaches, the Pilot could do nothing else but simply set the course away from the star.

Unable to determine the length of the trip, the Pilot had only one other option. The interior of the capsule was a containment chamber, resembling a coffin in size and shape. The Pilot rested itself inside, prepping for stasis. The intent was not to escape years of boredom, as the creature had no such concept. Rather, it was merely to prolong its life through the uncertain number of years it would remain adrift.

Launch.

Like a bullet from a barrel, the capsule zipped through space, propelled by its aft thrusters. As it did, the suctioning power of space finished off the damaged forward section, reducing it to pieces of scrap, no more advanced than the rock that struck it.

Vibration settled inside the chamber, followed by an inflow of liquid. The chamber sealed with a high-pitched hiss. In a moment's time, the Pilot's consciousness paused, and its body settled into a state of suspended animation.

The capsule traveled endlessly. Despite its advanced technology, the passage of time would eventually drain its power, causing the pod to zip aimlessly in space. Its remaining energy would be dedicated to preserving the stasis, while preserving a minute amount should the navigation detect a suitable planet to land upon.

Like one of the directionless meteors traveling through the universe, the pod drifted. And like many of those meteors, its travels would eventually lead it somewhere.

CHAPTER
1

With the press of a touchscreen button came a loud booming sound rivaling that of Navy artillery. A booming sound echoed through the room, sparking a brief physical flutter from those inside. Rock music boomed from the small electronic device, wirelessly amplified by loud speakers set up in all corners of the room.

Tim Sutton cringed from the burst of sound, nearly spilling his beer onto his end of the large horseshoe-shaped sofa. He turned around, seeing his brother-in-arms adjusting the iPhone app on a tray table behind him.

"Jesus Christ, Charlie! You trying to put us all on disability?" he shouted, his voice barely audible over the classic rock. Glass bottles clang from the opposite side of the sofa, followed by obnoxious laughter. Sutton righted himself in his seat, looking directly at the two giants who sat across from him. Ivan and Rex, two soldiers who, by appearance, looked more as if they were trying out for *Mr. Olympia.* Muscles squeezed through shirts each a size too small.

"What's wrong there, Doc? Can't handle a little noise?" Rex said, before tilting his beer bottle completely upside down. Sutton shook his head as the brute drained his beverage, then attempted to balance the empty bottle with his tongue. *Lord help us,* Sutton thought. How two Lutheran pastors gave birth to this dog was a question he often asked God.

The bottle fell from his mouth, snatched up by a quick reaction by Rex. He balanced it briefly on his finger, verbalizing "whoa" obnoxiously before finally setting it down. He glanced at Ivan, who sat beside him, holding a half-full bottle.

"That's one for me, already," he said.

"Oh, for the love of…" Sutton said. "You guys are not seriously gonna make a competition out of THIS, are you?"

Ivan grinned. Each expression of disapproval by the doc always brought a repugnant joy to the duo. He finished the rest of his bottle, before tossing it up at the ceiling. The bottle flipped over-end multiple times before Ivan snatched it up and slammed it down on the table next to the competition's.

"One-for-one, *T,*" he said. Rex, who often felt the need to hyphen the letter "T" to his name for egotistical reasons, stood and reached into the cooler. Chunks of ice spilled onto the floor as he dug through the contents.

"Hey, hey," Craig Easley said as he entered from the kitchen hallway. Rex glanced over at the nerd, holding a tray of cheese and crackers in each hand. "You're getting ice all over my carpet there, *T.* Gosh, try and show at least a minuscule amount of respect."

Rex held up two beer bottles and looked at them with disgust, before turning his eyes back toward his host.

"You want to talk respect? How about serving something better than this crap." His thumbs pointed at the *Lite beer* logo on the bottle. Easley exhaled through his nose, while biting his lip.

"There's Weihestephaner in the garage fridge," he said.

"THANK YOU!" Rex shoved the lite beer back into the cooler and dashed past the much slimmer Easley. He slouched slightly as he balanced to keep his trays upright. He walked around the couch and placed the trays on the table.

"Alright, everyone dig in!" he announced. All at once, everyone in the room leaned toward the tray.

"Wait…this is it?" Ivan asked.

Charlie walked around from the back of the sofa. "That's all you've got? A cheese platter?" He looked at the other tray, which contained nothing but carrots, celery, and grape tomatoes. "WHAT THE FUCK?!"

"And this, gentlemen, is our reward for executing a flawless rescue of thirty hostages." Sarcasm radiated from Sutton's voice.

"Well shit, then," Easley said. "Next time you host, Doctor Holier-than-thou."

"Oh, believe me I will," Sutton said. He leaned back and looked around the large room. The walls were covered in movie and video game posters, several of which were signed by famous actors and developers. At the front of the room was a seventy-inch television, sitting atop a huge entertainment center loaded with multiple different video game consoles. As he always did, Sutton shook his head. *What a waste of time.* "Oh, good Lord, Craig. Even after working with you all these years, I still have a hard time seeing you as an Army Ranger."

"Oh, you're one to talk, Short Round," Ivan said with a large foamy belch. Sutton's face tightened. At barely five-foot-six, he was always picked on for his height, especially by the giants, Ivan and Rex.

"Here we go with this again," he said. "What about Nagamine over there? He's an inch shorter than me, and you never say anything to him!" Sutton pointed his thumb to the back corner of the room. Nagamine sat quietly by himself, not minding a word spoken by his fellow mercenaries. Ivan watched the former Japanese-Self-Defense-Force close-quarters combat instructor silently stroke a flat stone over the twenty-inch blade of his ninjato.

Ivan narrowed his gaze back at the ever-so-critical medic. "You want me to pick on *him?!* Look at him! You could send that guy to the moon, and all he'd do is spend his time looking for someone to kill." He shoved his hand into the tray, and grabbed a fistful of crackers and cheese, while blatantly ignoring the veggies.

"Oh, knock it off, gents," a female voice spoke from the hallway. All eyes turned straight to Terrie. She had emerged from the bathroom, having finally straightened her hair, which hung down to her shoulders. When off-mission, she was always quick to get rid of the tactical gear.

"I see you're dressed up there," Charlie said. "Going on a date?"

"If he ever responds to my text," Terrie said, her expression souring.

"You probably scared him away," Ivan said. "Fuck, you'd scare me away. Who'd want to date a lady who snipes people before blowing them up?"

"Me!" Rex rose his hand, clutching the German beer as he returned to the room.

"Fat chance," Terrie said, dodging to get out of the way as Rex moved around the sofa. Ivan reached out to accept a beer from him, only to see Rex had brought one only for himself.

"Hey, what the hell, man!"

"If you're gonna outdrink me, you'll have to get our own, fatass!" Rex said as he plopped down.

"Oh God." Terrie looked at Sutton. "Are they seriously keeping score of how many *BEERS* they're drinking?" Sutton quietly nodded.

"They do it with everything else, why not beers," Charlie chimed in.

"SPEAKING of which," Ivan stood and turned toward Rex, "where's that five-hundred bucks you owe me?" Rex nearly coughed up his beverage, and looked up at Ivan with eyes open wide.

"Excuse me?" he said. "Remember those two I bagged in the galley? I took down more uglies than you did. So, as I recall, it's you who owes *me* five hundred, pal."

"No, I took down the three pricks in the engine room!" Ivan argued.

"Oh, for Chrissake," Sutton said to himself. Terrie placed her palm against her forehead, plucked a carrot from the veggie tray, and mentally prepared for the inevitable debate.

"You said there were only two!" Rex argued. "So now you're lying!"

"No, it was three!" Ivan said. "I told you this before! So, pay up, man. You lost!"

"Can we just agree you guys took down an equal number of Somalis?" Sutton asked.

"Fuck that!" Rex said.

"If nothing else, you did find something we can agree on," Ivan cackled.

"You guys could settle it with a little *Call of Duty,*" Easley said, eating celery from the tray.

"For once, I agree with the nerd!" Sutton said in a high-pitched volume. The pounding of the rock music combined with the ridiculousness in front of him made him mentally pray for their leader to arrive. Once he was paid, he could go home.

"No need," Ivan said. "We already know how to settle this."

Rex snapped his fingers at Charlie. "Hey, Flyboy. You're the techno expert. Can you link up both of our recordings to make it a split-screen?"

"Recordings?" Easley said. "Wait, did you guys wear bodycams?" Both of the hulking guns-for-hire grinned, which in itself answered the question.

"You know the boss is gonna kill you if he finds out, right?" Sutton said.

"Oh, give it a rest, Doc. You'll give yourself a hernia," Rex said. He looked at Charlie again. "So...how 'bout it?" Charlie groaned, and stepped forward, realizing it would be quicker and less of a pain to simply do what they wanted.

"Give me your cams," he said. Both men thrust the round devices into his chest. Rex then pointed at Easley.

"Kid, turn on your tv! You're gonna witness firsthand how yours truly robbed this guy out of five-hundred bucks!"

Ivan held a middle-finger in front of Rex's face while Easley reluctantly turned the television on.

****

As Victor Seymour parked his truck into Craig Easley's garage, he could hear the rampant rumblings coming from the north side of the house. The team had gone into celebration, as they often did at the conclusion of every successful mission.

He didn't mind. A successful mission, especially one conducted as flawlessly as their recent rescue of thirty-five oil workers on board a hijacked tanker, deserved celebration. Much of the team was rejoicing in their payday. Seymour, however, took greater pleasure in preserving the innocent lives put at risk.

At least, he forced himself to assume they were innocent. One thing he had learned in the mercenary business, if clients are turning to him, rather than an official government service, likely there's something they want to hide. Despite seeing the worst in humanity during his service in the military, and even getting used to it, he found it best to be unaware of the underground details, as long as they didn't interfere with his team's ability to do the job.

He wrapped his fingers around the straps of the huge duffle bag sitting beside him, stocked with eight smaller duffle bags with divided cash. He stepped out of the truck, holding the bag effortlessly in one arm. He paused before entering the house. Through the music, he could hear the bantering of his team inside. Two booming voices stood out: Rex and Ivan.

They were good soldiers, both of them having served in the U.S. Marine Corps. And they were good reliable mercenaries. They followed orders, never arguing or questioning Seymour's authority. Despite this, they were troublemakers. And the louder their banter, the more Seymour knew they were up to no good.

He entered the house.

****

"Ah-ha!" Ivan pointed at the top of the split on the television. The video footage displayed the top of his HK416 rifle. Gunfire erupted through the audio, accompanied by cursing in Ivan's recording. "Oh, okay, not there...but..." the group watched the muzzle flash from his gun barrel as he emerged from cover, and neutralized the three enemy hostiles. "Ha! There!" he said, clapping his hands together.

Rex leaned forward, bitterly resting his jaw against a closed fist while watching the footage. "Well, fuck," he said, under his breath. Ivan turned to face him, his face glowing with excitement.

"That's right," he said. "Time for you to pay up!"

"You guys are sick," Terrie remarked.

"Hey, come on," Ivan said. "I even made you look good! Didn't you see? I caught the part where you sniped the ugly in the crow's nest." Terrie plucked a carrot from the tray and crunched it in her teeth, again shaking her head slowly at Ivan. He chuckled and looked at Rex. "You'd think she was our mother."

A deep, commanding voice reverberated in the room, "You're lucky your mother isn't here."

All eyes turned to the hallway entrance where Victor Seymour stood. Rex quickly grabbed the remote and shut off the television, then he and the rest of the team stood to their feet. With hands down at their sides and feet placed in a forty-five-degree angle, they stood silently in position of attention. Even Nagamine, who moments earlier seemed to have no care in the world, was suddenly alert and ready. Despite not being on active duty, they still operated like a military unit, and had such a respect for their commander.

Additionally, when caught in the act like this, they knew best to shut up and be quiet.

The room had gone completely silent. The music stopped, and the television was off, and each mercenary stood, staring directly ahead of them. Craig Easley did the same. The fact that he was in his own homemade no difference. In an instant, he was no longer the 'nerd'. He was a soldier. Terrie was no longer a dressed-up gal preparing for a date. She was a soldier. For Ivan and Rex, they were no longer obnoxious troublemakers. Tim Sutton was no longer the self-righteous, judgmental buzz-kill. Charlie was no longer the wannabe DJ techno-brat. They were all warriors showing respect for their commander.

Seymour stepped forward. First, as he always did, he scanned his eyes across the room, then stepped around the sofa. He could hear each shallow breath taken by the team members. Clearing the corner of the furniture, he scooted the table aside with his foot, careful not to spill the contents. He stood in the newly acquired space, staring at Rex and Ivan. Despite each of them standing six inches taller than Seymour, and weighing sixty extra pounds of pure muscle, Ivan and Rex knew better than to look into his eyes. First there was the respect of chain-of-command. Second, there was additional respect for his background. A SEAL was not one to be messed with.

Seymour picked up the remote and turned the television back on, bringing the split-screen imaging to view. He watched a few quick frames as the brutes stormed the catacombs within the oil tanker, eliminating hostile pirates along their path.

"Mind explaining this?" he said. Though quiet, his voice was sharp enough to cut through ice. A nervous grin creased Ivan's face.

"Just letting off steam, sir," he said.

"Letting off steam?" Seymour turned the tv off. "You like snuff films?"

Ivan's grin disappeared. "Hell no, sir."

"We just enjoy a little reminder of a job well done," Rex said.

"This should be plenty of a reminder," Seymour said, holding the large duffle bag. "You want to blow off steam, go to a comedy show."

"Yes sir!" Both brutes bellowed, revealing the inner Marine in both of them. Seymour opened the bag, reached in, and pulled out a smaller nylon bag.

"Don't let it happen again," he said, and thrust the bag into Ivan's chest. He did the same to Rex, then proceeded to toss shares to the other team members. Charlie caught his bag like an NFL linebacker. His share was heavier, as he was in charge of maintaining the ShinMaywa Us-2. Of course, Seymour took the largest share, perks of being the founder and manager of the team. After all, in addition to carrying out the operations, he was the one who conducted the business meetings, which in itself was occasionally a paramilitary operation. In this business, you never truly knew anyone's intent.

After finishing, he straightened out the table, remembering he was in another man's house. Everyone eased, taking their seats again. He glanced at Terrie.

"You look all set to go out," he said.

"Bastard just cancelled on me," she said, her voice sour.

"Told ya, she scares them away," Sutton remarked.

"Knock it off, before she scares *you* away," Seymour said. Sutton zipped his lip. He glanced back at Terrie. "It'll work out." He walked back around the sofa, making his way to the hall.

"Sir, feel free to stay," Craig Easley said. "I've got plenty of condiments here, enough for you to hang around."

"I wouldn't brag about that, sonny," Rex said, pointing at the trays.

"I appreciate it," Seymour said. "But I'll be taking off." He started walking out, but stopped and looked back at him. "One piece of advice though...damn, kid, put some meat on that table!"

The room erupted in laughter, and as if on cue, the music came bursting back on. Easley grinned and gave an informal two-finger salute to Seymour, who turned and left, exiting out the front door.

Taking his place in the driver's seat of his truck, Victor Seymour squeezed the steering wheel with both hands. For most servicemen returning home, being seated in their personal vehicle was a much-desired feeling. For Seymour though, all it brought him was a desire to clutch the handle of a GMV. Every time he returned home, it was his first emotional experience. He did not feel satisfaction, rather he felt a desire to do more.

Becoming a SEAL was something only the best-of-the-absolute-best could do. And Seymour considered himself as such. He was never one to turn down a challenge, or back down from a fight. In his time in the service, he fought alongside men whom he considered his brothers.

Together, they conducted missions of legend. Most of which, the public, and even much of the military, had no awareness of.

But it was what he was trained to do. Serving his country was worth more than any paycheck. Unfortunately, his medical officers wouldn't take his resume, nor his perseverance into consideration. With a few checkmarks and signatures, his military career ended abruptly. Not one to ever lose a fight, he beat the devastating illness that made others see him as unfit. But it didn't matter. To the doctors, his eligibility was no better than a man breathing his last. Re-enlisting was not an option for him.

Starting up his private business seemed like a way to keep the soldier in him alive. And doing so, he found new brothers and sisters-in-arms. He had a good team. But he quickly realized one thing was lacking: purpose. Each mission was in service of the almighty dollar. He had no problem making a living, but there was no greater good in what they were doing. Conducting missions for clients, two-thirds of which were shady in themselves, could not return the fulfillment he felt during his time in the service.

Gotta just let it go, he thought to himself. It was the same tired phrase he always repeated. It had no effect, other than to briefly cool his mood like a passing cloud shadow in burning sunlight. Its effect was momentary, and immediately forgotten. He loosened his grip on the wheel, and started the engine.

CHAPTER
2

Cassie Hawk smelled the salty ocean air as she stepped out of the black limo. The house they arrived at had an ocean view. Even in the nine o'clock twilight, she could see the waves breaking in the nearby docks, creating a mist that gave the air a wet texture. The house itself was a simple, single story building with a garage. Nothing bad, but not suitable for anything more than a single-person household. It was a tell that they had found the right person. The less connections, the better.

Three men stepped out of the vehicle. Two of them were in their mid-thirties, typical age for C.I.A. agents. At least, from what Hawk had seen so far in her early career. However, she thought the senior agent on her team, Agent Jim Lesher, looked more like a college professor than anything else. Like the other two, he was dressed in a suit and tie, the jacket concealing a loaded Sig Saur. He looked at the empty driveway, and the dark windows. He didn't need to knock to know nobody was home.

"Move the car onto the road," he said. "We don't want to take up his driveway."

"Sir," Hawk stepped alongside him. "May I suggest we go with another source. We don't have the luxury of waiting for…"

"I would rather sacrifice five minutes of timeframe than settle for a less valuable tool," he said. "Bravo-Unit said they saw him at the corner of Saint and Borjas, heading this way. He'll be here shortly."

Hawk knew it was best to shut up and comply. After all, she was chosen for a mission of extremely high importance. Pulling it off successfully would elevate her career to heights that would take others decades. She swallowed hard, fighting to keep from displaying her anxiety. She opened the tan folder she held, and silently read the file for the fifth time.

Subject: Victor Ryan Seymour.

Date of Birth: 09/22/1978. Age: 40. Place of Birth: Austin, Texas. Criminal record: N/A. High School Graduation. Anderson High   School, Class of 1996.

Entered United States Navy in Summer, 1996. Initiated SEAL training in October, 1998. Successful completion of BUD/s Third Phase in April, 1999.

Member of SEAL team 5.

Accolades:

- Silver Star, for gallantry in action during Invasion of Afghanistan.
- Three Purple Hearts.

Distinguished Operations:

- Operation Black Tower – Yugoslavia
- Operation Plain-Silver – Iraq
- Heart Diamond – Nigeria
- Battle of Mosul Dam – Iraq
- Unnamed anti-terrorism objective – Tripoli, Libya
- Operation Gravel-grain – Western Pacific.
- Leather coat – Panama.
- Glass Bottle – Benghazi, Libya.

Diagnosed with Acute Leukemia in May 2012. Released from service. Honorable discharge.
Declared cancer-free, July, 2017.

Hawk closed the folder, briefly thinking on Seymour's resume. Despite her position in the C.I.A., she knew there were more operations that were not listed on this particular file. Rarely did any one person know all the details. There was always some undisclosed operation that a select few were aware of.

Hell, look at what we're doing now. It was clear to her why Lesher wanted Seymour for the job. Highly trained and disposable, two key components for any useful tool.

****

From a block away, Seymour could see the limo's taillights. Even at this distance, he knew it was in front of his driveway. Calculating precise distance was one of a thousand techniques learned in SEAL training. However, it was clear these were not insurgents. When steering his truck up to his house, it became clear they were agents. The only question was: which agency?

He saw the three men and one woman standing in his driveway, waiting for him. Instinctively, he looked behind him. The road was clear. Whoever tipped them off that he was on his way had likely done so a mile back. Turning his eyes back toward the individuals, he quickly noticed the ever-so-slight bulge in the jacket, indicative of a concealed firearm. Even in the dark, he could still see the earpiece in each individual's right ear. Except the female. For whatever reason, she didn't have one.

He pulled his truck into the driveway and parked. He stepped out, leaving the keys in the ignition, and turned to face the group. The older member stepped forward, holding a thin tan envelope.

"Victor Seymour," the man said. He extended his hand. Seymour looked at it, then back at the man. He knew better. Shaking hands in this business wasn't just a greeting, rather an automatic acceptance of a proposal. With three additional agents ready to testify as witnesses, there'd be no way to back out.

"Not my first rodeo," Seymour said. Lesher withdrew his hand and smiled.

"My apologies," he said. "I'm Special Agent Jim Lesher. Clearly, you're already aware that we are in need of your services. Please examine these documents." He extended the envelope toward him. Seymour exhaled sharply. Of all clients, the government paid the best, but was often the first to stab you in the back. He reluctantly accepted the envelope.

The first page inside was a black and white photograph, featuring a man, roughly aged forty, dressed in khakis and a flannel shirt stepping off a helicopter. The foreground didn't offer many details, but from the perceived texture of the land he was stepping on, Seymour fathomed the man was on an island. He looked up at Lesher.

"Am I supposed to know who this is?"

"That is Dr. Martin Trevor," Lesher said. "He's a contractor on a special research project in the Pacific. We believe he and his team have been taken hostage, by a group called the *Ilgob Daelyug*. That's Korean, meaning…"

"Seven Continents," Seymour interrupted. Lesher nodded, revealing a very slight grin. He knew Seymour had thwarted some North Korean operations during his service, and became familiar with the language. Another reason he was a right fit for the job.

Seymour flipped to the next image, which was a satellite photograph of an island. Oval-shaped, with a jagged peninsula in the southeast corner, the small island appeared to be about eight miles in diameter. A second photograph showed the island's position on a map, positioning it several miles northeast of the Philippine Sea.

"What is this place?"

"That island is called Kuretasando," Lesher said. He didn't bother translating, as he knew Seymour was up-to-date on his foreign language.

"Crater Sands." Seymour had briefly heard of it during his travels. If memory served him correctly, it was one of many islands that the U.S. invaded during the Pacific Theater.

"There's an old Japanese command post left over on that island from World War 2. A rather large bunker. We believe it was mainly used as a Communications station," Lesher said.

"What does a North Korean want with a Japanese Island?" the former SEAL asked.

"We believe they're using it as a testing site," Lesher said.

"A testing site, huh?" Seymour said, crossing his arms. "Aren't we in the middle of making peace with that country? I thought ceasing their testing sites was part of the package?"

"Correct," Lesher said. "As you know, North Korea is a military regime. However, what most people don't know, there's often an internal power struggle going on within the government. There are high ranking officials who would like to see Kim Jung-Un out of power. A general in particular, who formed the *Ilgob Daelyug*. General Rhee is his name. He has his own private command of soldiers, loyal specifically to him and his cause. Because of ties to arms dealers worldwide, he's got the resources to run this operation." Lesher allowed a small chuckle to slip through. "From what we know, he calls himself the Supreme General."

"Classy title," Seymour said. He looked back to the photo of Dr. Trevor. He lifted it up and held it in front of the C.I.A. agent. "Obviously it's best I don't know the precise details...but I need to, at least, know the gist. A weapons testing site on a Japanese Island most people haven't heard of; a Ph. D that the government wants back...I'm assuming this guy has the goods to some new tech or something that you don't want anyone else to have, and you're worried that these goons will force him into working for them."

"Let's say yes," Lesher said.

"One thing I do want to ask," Seymour said, closing the folder, "this is a very delicate matter, and I can already tell you want it handled immediately."

"Correct..." Lesher said.

"Okay, so why me? Why not send in an actual SEAL team?" Seymour said. He noticed one of the other agents snickering. "Care to answer that?" Seymour raised his voice.

"Because we said so," the agent said.

"Meier!" Lesher looked to the agent, who took a step back and quietly looked away.

"You guys think I'm sending my team in there to collect some Top-Secret tech and a scientist, just to be erased in the end by you guys?"

Lesher swiftly turned his eyes back toward Seymour. "Absolutely not!"

"Then I'll ask again, why me?"

"Our intelligence reports that the group is fronting as a Chinese Research Group called..." he paused, as he couldn't remember the correct Mandarin pronunciation, "Deepwater Nine."

"A research operation?" Seymour said.

"Correct." Lesher straightened his tie. "I'll assure you, these people are not researchers. They're common terrorists, hellbent on unleashing chaos on South Korea, and eventually the Western World. However, General Rhee has connections with China, and might use this front as a ploy to declare an international incident. Should they do that, our Government wants to maintain total deniability. Hence, we'd rather go with a private contractor."

Seymour reopened the file, looking at a third photo. It was another map of the island, only with hand-drawn x's marked in various areas.

"Care to tell me what these are?" he asked.

"Those are approximate locations to guard shacks scattered throughout the island perimeter," Lesher said. "If you look at the one on the peninsula, we believe that's the area they're using as a docking station. It's the flattest region of the island."

"*Approximate.* Excellent reconnaissance work," Seymour remarked. He looked at a marking on the island interior. "What about this one?"

"That's the location of the main command post," Lesher said. "You need to go in there, collect Dr. Trevor, and get the hell out. If you can eliminate the hostile forces, that'll be a bonus."

"Don't see how we'll have a choice," Seymour said. "They're certainly going to have this place heavily guarded." He closed the file again. "I have to ask, what happens if they've killed this guy?"

"Then collect any and all material you can find," Lesher said. "Trevor has been making hundreds of pages worth of notes regarding his...work. Bring back anything you find."

"How will I know?"

"You probably won't," he said. "But she will." He tilted his head toward the female agent. Cassie Hawk stepped forward, maintaining a blank expression while staring Seymour in the eye. He gazed at her, as if studying her. She could feel him reading every inch of her, taking in what details he could.

"Great," he said. "Just what I need."

"Would you rather you try to identify all the material yourself?" Hawk spoke up.

"YES, actually," Seymour said. He narrowed his eyes at Lesher. "You realize you're asking me to take one of your lackies into a hot zone, infested with God-knows how many militarized combatants eager to blow holes in anyone who steps foot on that island." Seymour clenched his teeth and stared angrily at Lesher. For private contractors shadowing an operating official, should the client representative be killed in the operation, they would likely disappear. "Thanks, but no thanks. Have a good evening." He turned around to walk to his house.

Lesher anticipated Seymour's hesitation.

"I suggest you wait a moment," he said. Seymour ignored him. The two male agents suddenly approached, taking large strides to catch up with him. Within seconds, they were right behind him. One made the mistake of putting a hand on his shoulder.

An elbow struck the agent square in the nose. In that same instant, Seymour snatched his wrist, bending it counter-clockwise. The agent had two choices: go with the motion, or let his wrist snap. He went with the motion, flipping head-over-heels before landing hard on the pavement.

The second agent drew his firearm from his jacket, only to feel it snatched from his grip. Seymour grabbed a fistful of the agent's sleeve with one hand, while grabbing the collar of the suit jacket with the other. Turning his hips sharply, Seymour lifted the agent over his shoulder, and dropped him to the pavement. The agent felt his head bounce against the concrete, and everything went blurry.

Hawk instinctively reached for her weapon, only for Lesher to hold up his hand, signaling for her to stand down. Seymour kicked the dropped sidearm to the side, then crossed his arms while staring at Lesher.

"I'll need to bring along new field agents," he said aloud. "Forgive me, these boys were a bit too rash..."

"Stupid's the better word," Seymour said.

"That's plenty accurate," Lesher said. He glanced at Hawk. "Grab the other folder from the car." She opened the rear passenger door, reached inside, and returned with another tan envelope. She handed it directly to Seymour. She could hear the air hissing from his nose as he eyeballed it, before taking it out of her hand.

You guys should be a postal service. He opened it, revealing photographs of a Caucasian man in a suit-and-tie shaking hands with the leader of what appeared to be a paramilitary group. He recognized the man in the suit. He was Seymour's most recent client.

"Yeah, so your customer is into more than just oil," Lesher said. "He's been selling weapons to Boko Haram in Nigeria. And you, sir, officially helped his most recent shipment reach its destination." Seymour closed the folder. Lesher slowly walked up to him, extending his hand to take the folder back. "Successful completion of this job will bring substantial payment….and in addition, we'll drop this matter."

"Seven Mil," Seymour said. "Half up front."

Lesher creased a satisfied smile. He turned and started walking back to the car.

"Agent Hawk will go over the details of the plan," he said. "I trust she's in good hands." He opened the trunk and brought out a small duffle bag. Hawk caught it in her arms, and held it by the straps at her side. He brought a second back to Seymour, unzipped it to reveal the blocks of cash, then set it down at his feet. "You're getting a bonus…I figured you'd negotiate up to ten." He walked to the limo.

Seymour stood silently as the two agents struggled to their feet. One pressed a handkerchief to his broken nose to control the bleeding, while helping the other one up. They collected their weapons and made their way to the limo, walking past Hawk.

The engine started up, and the vehicle quickly disappeared into the darkness. Hawk walked toward Seymour's truck.

"You're driving," she said. Seymour kept his expression blank. However, inside he was raging. However, there was no way out of it. Either they do the job, and keep this hotshot from getting herself killed, or face dire consequences. Prison would be a best-case scenario.

Terrie's gonna be pissed.

CHAPTER
3

Cassie Hawk quickly pressed her hand over her equipment, keeping it from falling over onto the floor of the ShinMaywa US-2. Since piercing the storm, the aircraft had entered some turbulence. The shaking eased up, and she released her grip on the vial holder. The sealed glass vials juddered in their slots, stirring their contents. Hawk pressed her eyes back into the microscope, gently applying the syringe to the glass platter.

Creating a vaccine was difficult enough under normal circumstances. On board a moving plane, traveling at over three hundred miles per hour, inside a storm, proved to be a whole new endeavor.

It had been a long, ten-hour trip, after leaving the coast at Twenty-two-thirty hours. Six hours later, they landed on a Nimitz-class Aircraft Carrier for refueling. Thirty minutes later, they launched again, this time traveling north of the Philippine Sea.

Now they were less than an hour's flight time from their destination.

Hawk could hear Seymour and Charlie in the cockpit, discussing several avionic details of which she had no knowledge of their meaning. The only part of the conversation she understood was the mentioning of windspeed decreasing to thirty-eight miles per hour. They were approaching the edge of the storm.

Then there was the nonstop interchange coming from the inner cabin.

"Eighty-six! Eighty-seven! Eighty-eight!" Ivan counted out loud. He and Rex were doing pushups on the floor, the latter slowing down considerably. Both men were wearing sleeveless combat vests, exposing biceps the size of footballs. Ivan paused and looked at his competitor. "Getting tired there, buddy? I'm five ahead of you, and still going strong!" Rex leaned on his right hand, and used his free arm to wipe beads of sweat off his brow. All it did, however, was smear it everywhere and add extra grime to his face.

"Only coming up halfway will do that," he said. Rather than continue, he allowed himself to rest on his knees. Ivan sprang to his feet and started reaching into the side pocket of his camouflage tactical pants, pulling out a tin container of chewing tobacco. He shoveled his fingers into it, and scooped a black ball of tobacco into his mouth. Ivan noticed Hawk watching him, and extended the container toward her.

"Want some, Miss Agent Lady?" He smiled, baring brown stained teeth.

"Uh...no, thanks," Hawk said. It was all she could do to keep from wincing. Her gaze briefly trailed further into the cabin. It was a spacious area for a team of eight, nine including her. The plane, which had previously been a medical search-and-rescue vehicle, had been converted into a military transport. The large cabin and cargo area had been converted into sections.

The first section was where she stood. It was directly behind the cockpit, and was considered the tech area. Several computers and maps lined the walls, and overhead were storage chambers for other electronics.

The next section was the personnel quarters. The stretchers and gurneys had been removed, replaced by bunks. In the wall space between the bunks were seats with harnesses, in case of major turbulence. With a twenty-foot width, the mercenaries had plenty of room to stretch out.

As Ivan and Rex were exercising, Craig Easley was doing the complete opposite. He was stretched out on his bunk, passed out, with an open comic on his chest. Across from him was Nagamine, fully dressed in his tactical gear. An inch behind his head was the handle to his ninjato, freshly sharpened. He sat upright, with the tranquility of a praying mantis. Hawk was uncertain whether he was awake, despite the fact that his eyes were open.

"You get used to it," Terrie said. She sat in the bunk next to Nagamine's. Her hair was up in a bun, hidden under a dark green ballcap. She had just finished cleaning and reassembling her McMillan TAC-338 sniper rifle.

Hawk realized Terrie was speaking to her, after staring at Nagamine for a moment.

"Yeah?" Hawk pointed to Rex and Ivan, who kneeled by one of the chairs to arm wrestle. "What about that?" Terrie looked at the duo, smiled and shook her head.

"Never," she said.

Hawk nodded. Before looking away, she couldn't help but notice Tim Sutton. He glared at her and her microscope. Hawk stared back, envisioning the imaginary bubble over his head.

"Is there a problem?"

"Do you even know what you're doing there?" Sutton said, pointing at the vials. Hawk leaned in toward the microscope, finishing the mixture.

"Being on this island will bring exposure to certain types of viruses…" she started to explain.

"Oh, believe me, I know." Sutton stood up.

"Doc, leave it be," Terrie said.

"Fat chance," he said. He walked to the table and reached past Hawk for the vials. Hawk stood straight and swatted his hand away.

"Don't touch!" she said in a loud commanding voice. Everyone's attention was now on them. Easley snorted while waking up from a deep sleep, dropping his comic on the floor as he sat up. He scrubbed his sleeve over his eyes, and eagerly watched the spat. Even Nagamine turned to watch, while maintaining the same blank expression.

Sutton raised his hand, warning Hawk back.

"Let's see, you've got Typhim Vi and RTS,S. Those make enough sense," he said. He then pointed to the vials at the far end of the vial holder. "But what the hell are those?"

"It's classified," Hawk said.

"Oh, hell no," Sutton said, holding both hands up. "I'm not having any experimental junk injected into me."

"Forgive the Doc…Doc, he just gets a little paranoid," Rex said.

"*Doc*." Sutton looked at the floor, shaking his head. He looked at Hawk again. "Are you a doctor?"

"Yes," Hawk answered.

"A doctor of what, may I ask?" Sutton said. Everyone waited patiently, wanting an answer. Hawk was used to having Lesher, or another senior official to back her up. But now, she was on her own, and had to remember by heart what info she could and could not distribute.

"Bio-chemistry and toxicology," she said. A crack of thunder echoed around them, and the plane shuttered, causing her to tense up. *Damn it.*

"Damn," Ivan bellowed. "And we're rescuing another Doc…who's supposedly making weapons! We're told this island is used for weapons testing. And we're getting vaccinated…by a doctor specializing in bio-toxicology!"

"Bio-*chemistry*…and toxicology," Sutton corrected him, immediately realizing the effort was useless. However, he agreed with Ivan's point.

"Listen, it's just a precaution." Hawk said, growing defensive. Everyone stared at her with questioning eyes. Terrie and Easley stood up, suddenly feeling uneasy.

A shadow cast over her as Seymour stepped in from the cockpit.

"Ease up, everyone," he said. The group looked at him and quietly returned to their bunks. Sutton walked into the last section, which contained the armory. He looked at the weapons, each carefully stored in a rack along the wall.

Seymour stood alongside Hawk. She simultaneously was grateful and resentful of his presence. She was aware he despised this assignment, despite the pay, and detested her presence.

"Listen up, everyone," he said. "We'll be touching down in fifteen. Get geared up and stand by to inflate the Zodiac."

"Fifteen?" Hawk asked. Seymour glared back at her.

"We need to set down a minimum of ten miles away," he said. "If these assholes are as equipped as you guys might suggest, they'll detect this plane if it gets any closer. We need to approach by water." He removed a folded piece of paper from his vest, unfolded it, and slammed it down on the table. The impact rattled Hawk's equipment, and she quickly steadied the vials. She looked at the paper, which was the map of the island. Seymour was studying it, examining the markings of the known guard shacks.

"I suggest we make landing there," Hawk said, pointing to a region along the southeast side. "It's shallow there, with a lot of canopy. We can hide the boat there…"

"No," Seymour said. "We're making landfall here." He pointed to a red marking on the south side of the island. Hawk shook her head.

"That area's nothing but a big cliff overlooking the Pacific," she said. "Plus, there's a guard post right nearby! That's insane."

"Listen, Agent," Seymour said, "this is MY command. I was hired as the combat professional, and my team will execute the job the way I see fit." Hawk shut her mouth. One perk of her previous Army training, she knew when to keep quiet. Seymour pointed to the map, running his finger along the eastern perimeter. "Now, they're likely patrolling these other areas more tightly, because…AS YOU POINTED OUT…it would be easier to dock landing craft. However, if we come up the cliffside, under the cover of night, in this weather, we'll have better luck making landfall here. We'll climb up, eliminate the guards, and then move on to the peninsula and eliminate all personnel there. That way, nobody'll get off the island except us."

Hawk nodded, taking in Seymour's reasoning. "Okay. What about the Zodiac?"

"Do you know how to drive it?" Seymour asked.

"Yes," she answered.

"Good, because you're gonna stay in it," he said.

"HEY!" She raised her voice. "I'm more than capable of handling myself in a combat situation."

"Yeah, yeah," Seymour said. "I know what you are. Army infantry, blah blah blah…not impressed. You spent most of your service in the lab, kid." Hawk bit her lip, growing agitated. Seymour turned and walked toward the armory while continuing his lecture. "You get capped out there, your pal Lesher will have my head. When we disembark, you'll wait in the Zodiac. When we clear the dock, we'll radio you to come ashore. Then you can tag along, since we'll need you to identify the goods." He reached toward the rack, grabbing an HK-G36c from the rack. He grabbed several loaded magazines, inspecting each one before placing it in his vest. He reached above the rack, pulling a locked box from a storage compartment. He opened it, revealing an eight-shot S&W R8 revolver. He inserted it into his thigh holder, strapping it tightly. Holding his rifle properly pointing toward the floor, he walked back toward Hawk. He stood in front of her and turned to the right.

"You gonna give me the vaccine, or should I?" he said.

"Oh!" Hawk said. She grabbed a vial, placed it into the jet injector, and inserted the needle into his arm. With the press of a trigger, the injection was complete. "Okay, all set."

Seymour stepped away. "Alright, team, go see the doctor and get your shot."

Rex stood up first. "Do I get a lollipop?!"

CHAPTER
4

The plane had come to a full stop after landing in the water. Hawk looked at the window, looking at the thrashing waves outside. She watched as a swell rolled toward them, gaining height with each passing moment until it was as tall as a man. It hit the hull, breaking apart over the side of the plane. She grabbed a bar handle on the wall, keeping herself upright as the plane rocked to starboard.

She heard Ivan and Rex laughing. Still holding on to the bar, she looked over her right shoulder. Sure enough, they were laughing at her.

"Look out! WHOAAAA" Ivan held both arms out on each side of him, tilting to his right to mimic a boat capsizing. "Splash!!!!"

"I think I saw a movie where that happens!" Rex said. "Boat tried to ride up a wave, only to fall backwards and…"

"Stow it, you two," Seymour said.

Rex cleared his throat, "Yes sir." Seymour walked toward the cockpit, where Charlie stood at the table where Hawk had been working on her vaccine. Several computer monitors lit the compartment. A two-foot long drone, shaped like a little airplane, rested on the table. Its body was equipped with several small cameras, each linked to the various monitors.

"Everything all set with you?" Seymour asked.

"Ready to go," Charlie said. He picked up the drone, and with a click of a couple of buttons, the rear propeller began to rotate. Holding it by the bottom as one would to a paper plane, he brought it to the side door. Seymour opened it for him, allowing a swell of water to wash inside. Charlie released the drone, which took off like a bird, immediately disappearing into the stormy night. Charlie shut the door and quickly returned to his computers. He tapped a few keys, and the monitors came to life. One monitor was like a dark, murky green. He zoomed that camera in.

Hawk stared at that monitor, seeing a fuzzy, cross shape in the middle of the screen. After a moment, she realized she was staring at an aerial view of their plane in night vision.

"Alright, you have eyes in the sky," Charlie said to Seymour. He handed him a small metal briefcase. Inside was a computer, linked to the video feeds, in case Seymour needed his own visual perspective.

"Thanks, Charlie," Seymour said. He walked to the cargo doors, where the Zodiac had been inflated. Its metal hull was unbalanced on the floor, and the boat teetered to the side. Once in the water, it would be correctly positioned. Everyone boarded the vessel, with Easley at the helm.

For this mission, Seymour would prefer one of the Navy's stealth speedboats. However, they had to make do with what they had. He stepped into the boat and took a seat next to Hawk. She was fully strapped in, one hand gripping her vest, another resting on the grip of her Beretta M9.

"You do realize you won't need that just yet," he quipped. She looked down at her hand.

"Habit, I guess," she said.

"Habit, or ego?" Seymour said. It was more of a remark than a question. During his many years of combat, he'd seen plenty of the John Wayne types: men and women who wanted to believe they were tough enough to handle the cruel life of war. Those people were often the types who felt they had something to prove, and therefore were often more of a threat to themselves and their own team than the enemy.

Of course, it always led Seymour to question himself, *which one am I?* Here he was, a former SEAL, now a mercenary leader constantly picking and choosing his missions, not just trying to make a buck, but actually make a difference, trying to relive that glorified satisfaction he had when he was in the service. The reality was, during those times, he was fighting for freedom. Now, he was just fighting for money, no matter how he bent the truth in his mind. What was that, if not ego?

"You sure this boat can handle this weather?" Hawk's voice brought Seymour back into reality.

"It'll be bumpy, but it'll do the job," he said. "We need to move before the weather dies down, otherwise we'll lose our cover."

"Hope you took your Dramamine, babe!" Ivan shouted back to her. Hawk simply answered with a thumbs up.

She didn't.

Charlie hit a lever, and the cargo bay doors lowered into the sea. Ivan and Rex started cheering as the boat started moving down the ramp, as if they were on a roller coaster ride. Hawk swallowed hard, watching the swirling water grow larger and more intense as the hull touched down.

"Good luck, guys," Charlie said.

"Don't fall asleep," Seymour replied.

"Must be nice to get paid more and have the easy job," Ivan shouted.

"Perks of going to college!" Charlie said. Ivan held up a middle finger as the boat splashed down entirely. Immediately, the ocean began pounding the fifteen-foot vessel.

Easley leaned on the throttle. Water sprayed behind the boat as the propellers pushed it forward. As the Zodiac accelerated, the rocking of the boat was reduced to more of a shake. Within seconds, her outfit was drenched. Salty mist permeated the air. Hawk relaxed herself with long, deep breaths, closing her eyes for several moments at a time.

She opened them, just as a large wave approached the bow. She gulped.

"Hang on, ladies and gents," Easley said. The boat met the developing swell, and began its climb.

"You know what happened when Clooney tried this?!" Rex shouted.

"Shut up, Rex," Terrie said, while holding back her own laughter. Every so often, the duo's obnoxiousness was genuinely amusing. The boat rounded over the top, and started its way down. The hull hit the water, causing the Zodiac to bounce upward.

"Whoa!" Easley cheered. The nerd was now on adrenaline junkie mode. Even Seymour allowed a small smile to expose itself. He glanced over at the C.I.A. liaison seated beside him. She was holding her breath, her skin pale white.

"You gonna make it?" he said.

"I'm fine," she said. She crossed her arms, trying to create the illusion she was relaxed. In reality, she was hugging herself. Another swell approached.

Fuck this.

CHAPTER
5

"—my papa said 'son, don't let the man getcha, Do what he done to me!'" Singing along to Creedence, Charlie sat at his computer module. He pinched the joystick, tilting it to-and-fro to remotely control the drone. In low winds, he would set a course and allow it to fly on autopilot. However, the present conditions forced him to manually control it, otherwise the winds would force the drone into the Pacific. Losing a delicate piece of tech would greatly displease his boss.

Charlie didn't sweat it. An accomplished pilot and software engineer, he had previously handled worse conditions than this. He saw this job as a run-of-the-mill mission, only for a much more important client.

Ding!

He looked to his left. His portable pizza oven had timed out. He could smell the aroma of slightly burnt pepperoni, cheese, and pizza sauce.

"Dinner time!" he said. "Or would this be breakfast…" He thought about the time change, then shrugged it off. Twisting the knob, he ascended the drone several feet, giving himself a few seconds before the autopilot would issue a turbulence alert. He hurried to the oven and removed the pizza. Putting it onto a plate, he hurried back to the controls.

Eating food and working on a computer. Just like being at home. The shifting of the ShinMaywa didn't bother him, except to keep his equipment from falling over.

He lifted the pizza to take a bite. His eyes went toward the night vision camera. He paused, struggling to see what he was looking at. Placing his food back down, the mercenary adjusted the drone to circle back and descend. He stood up to look at the radar screen in the cockpit.

"Well shit…" he said. He snatched up a radio. "Hatchling, this is Eagle Nest. Come in…"

****

"We've only been out for thirty minutes, and already he's lonely," Rex joked after hearing Charlie's transmission. Water sprayed the team as Seymour clutched his radio.

He pressed the transmitter, "Go ahead."

"*About half-a-click north of you is a vessel, moving away from your destination,*" Charlie said.

Each mercenary looked back at Seymour. They each felt the same immediate concern: Had they been detected?

"Intercept course?" Seymour asked.

"*Uh...hang on.*" A few moments' silence filled the air. "*Negative. It appears to be moving in a northeasterly direction. Going from its path, it came from that port on the southeast peninsula. I, uh...it almost looks like they're working their way around the island, like they're trying to turn around to go mainland.*"

"How big?"

"*One hundred eighty feet,*" Charlie said. "*Research vessel. It's got some sort of Chinese lettering on the side.*"

Seymour opened the case, revealing a small monitor. "Charlie, link me the feed, and get a closer view on the ship. I want to see who's on it."

"*Roger.*"

"They might be using it as a patrol boat," Terrie said, spitting out a mouthful of rainwater.

"Not likely," Hawk said. "If they're trying to move around the island, it's likely they're moving material and personnel back to their country."

"You think Dr. Trevor might be on that boat?" Seymour asked.

"It's possible," Hawk said. "It's also possible they are transporting material off the island."

"What material?" Sutton said. Hawk looked at him and said nothing. He rolled his eyes. "Right...I forgot...Classified."

"You aren't being paid to learn, you're being paid to eliminate the threat, and recover Dr. Trevor, his staff, and any-and-all findings pertaining to his research." Hawk turned to face Seymour. "I need you and your team to intercept and board that vessel."

"Uh, Boss?" Easley raised his hand to gain Seymour's attention. "Uh, forgive me for asking, but how can we be sure these aren't actually researchers aboard this boat?"

"The *Ilgob Daelyug* are fronting as a research division," Hawk said. "Didn't you pay attention during your briefing?"

"Oh, he did," Sutton said. "Whether he believes it, is a different story. Same with me."

Hawk felt her blood pressure rising. "These individuals provide a threat to our national security and…"

"Right...." Sutton said. "'Cause our government would *never* murder anyone and steal their stuff."

"Can it," Seymour said. The green light from the monitor reflected off his face as he examined the camera feed. The drone passed over the vessel. He pressed his radio transmitter. "Charlie, get a closer view of the bow deck." It took a moment for the drone to circle back. Once in place, it zoomed in, capturing images of two men hurrying across the deck. "Zoom in on the one on the right as best you can." The camera zoomed in, and Seymour froze the image. He used the computer to get an even closer view.

"Don't worry," he said to his team. "I don't think Type 58 Assault Rifles are standard issue research equipment." He zoomed in on the individual's neck. "Also, see that?" He turned the monitor toward each member, pointing at a tattoo of what appeared to be a star on the man's neck. Except, it wasn't a star, but a symbol of an explosion. "This guy is a member of a death squad, by the good ol' North." He switched off the monitor and closed the case.

"Nice picture quality," Rex joked. Seymour ignored him.

"Easley, turn starboard. Everyone, fasten suppressors to your weapons. The more quietly we can take this thing, the better."

"Awe, man," Ivan said, stroking the barrel of his M60E3 Machine Gun like a pet cat.

"I said "quietly,'" Seymour said. Ivan sighed and placed his signature weapon down, settling for a much smaller HK416 Carbine. The team members attached suppressors to their weapons and applied night-vision goggles to their headsets.

Hawk sat quietly, as she did not have a suppressor for her Beretta. Seymour tapped her on the shoulder, sensing her concern.

"Don't worry about it," he said. "You're not coming aboard until we've secured it." She grimaced, but didn't argue.

CHAPTER
6

The team waited in darkness and silence as their Zodiac approached the ship. With their lights out, the small black boat was invisible in the thrashing sea. The team huddled down, carefully watching the 180-foot boat rocking in the waves. Golden streaks of light stretched from the decks, fading into the night air. The bow rocked up and down as swells of water bombarded it. Interior lights helped mark the pilothouse and lower decks, giving Seymour further knowledge to construct an assault plan. Where there were lights, there would certainly be personnel.

"*You got two guys on the trawl deck, and two on the forward deck,*" Charlie's voice came through the comm.

"Terrie, you have a visual?" Seymour asked, waiting left of the helm, never taking his eyes off the boat. On the starboard side of the console, Terrie stood on one knee, resting her rifle on the edge of the boat. She pressed her eye into the night-vision scoop, confirming the two hostiles on the trawl deck. Each of them carried a rifle, as they moved to-and-fro across the deck. They stopped periodically, checking under tarps and opening unsecured crates, as if searching for stowaways.

"Affirmative," she said. "Not sure what it is they're doing."

"Perhaps a hostage got away?" Easley said.

"We'll figure it out," Seymour said. "Easley, take us around. We'll board from the stern." Easley rotated the helm and throttled the boat, the moan of the engine lost in the sound of screeching wind. In two minutes, Easley had the bow pointed at the stern.

"Hold this distance," Seymour said to Easley, then snapped his fingers at Terrie. "Take those two out..." he looked to the rest of the team, "...then we'll make our approach. Nagamine...you and I will go first and secure the trawl deck. After that, the rest of you come in groups. Rex and Ivan, accompany us to the structure. Easley, Terrie...move around to the forward deck. Wait for Nagamine and me to secure the pilothouse...otherwise, those inside will see you and alert the remaining crew. When we give you the all clear, eliminate your targets and secure forward deck.

"Once the topside is taken, we'll proceed inside. The corridors should split into two main sections, one fore, the other aft. Nagamine and I will go aft, and secure the galley, mess area, and Captain's quarters...assuming there is a Captain. Ivan, Rex, take the fore section. That should have the crew's quarters and chart room. Check each target before disposal, we don't want any dead friendlies. And no cowboy shit. Keep it quiet and smooth."

"Oh...allllllright," Ivan said, making a pouty face.

Sutton shook his head. *Children!* Seymour pointed a finger at him.

"Doc...stay with the boat, and provide backup if needed. Terrie, Easley, keep the deck secured while we're down there, should any of them get past us." Seymour paused and gazed at the team, allowing for any questions. There were none. He looked to Terrie, who positioned her rifle.

It took several seconds to focus the first of the two targets within the crosshairs of her scope. She measured the distance and windspeed, which blew constant at thirty-eight miles per hour. She adjusted the rifle position to accommodate the rocking of the Zodiac, as well as the motion of the research ship.

She kept the target in her crosshairs, following him along as he moved toward the port side. He stopped. The bow of the ship bounced up, causing the stern to dip down nearly five feet. This gave her a clearer view.

She aimed twenty-eight inches north of him, and five feet over his head. She squeezed the trigger. The suppressed weapon shuttered in recoil. The bullet zipped through the air, pushed south by the unrelenting wind. The ship rocked back upward, elevating the target to the bullet's trajectory.

Terrie watched through her scope, as a black misty cloud burst around the target's center mass. The guard fell backward, sprawled out on the deck. She panned her rifle slightly, bringing the second target into sight. Hearing the sound of something hitting the deck, the guard had turned. He paused, seeing his comrade laying in a pool of his own blood. It was the last thing he would see.

Terrie squeezed the trigger. The bullet pierced the guard above the left ribcage, exiting his right shoulder after displacing the heart. He fell forward, dead before his face slammed against the steel deck.

Easley throttled the Zodiac. Waves pounded the hull as the small boat raced to catch up with the larger vessel. Nagamine stood, gripping the edge of the boat for balance. Seymour moved near him, watching the vessel grow seemingly larger as they neared it.

The Zodiac climbed a wave, accelerating speed on the way down until it completely closed the distance. Easley throttled back and cut the wheel to port, barely keeping the boat from bumping into the transom. Nagamine reached out, grabbing a bar on the stern platform. He pulled himself up, then turned and reached out to Seymour. Taking his hand, he helped lift his commander onto the platform. They climbed a ladder, leading up to the trawl deck. Nagamine peeked over the side, confirming nobody other than the deceased guards were on the deck. He waved a hand to the team, signaling all clear, then pulled himself up. Seymour followed and took cover in shadows provided by the towering gantry. Terrie and Easley came up next. The sniper had switched to her suppressed H&K. She knelt in shadow, eyeballing the deck. It was covered with loose crates and other equipment left unsecured. Tools and weapons were scattered about, carelessly left unattended.

Almost looks like they left in a hurry, she thought.

Seymour noticed the oddities as well, but knew there was no time to waste analyzing. Staying close to the side, he and Nagamine moved fore, reaching the steps leading to the superstructure's main entrance. With rifles in hand, he and Nagamine took position on opposite sides of the door. Terrie and Easley spread apart, moving onto opposite sides of the structure. Both of them kneeling down, they inched their way to the forward deck, where their oblivious targets waited.

Ivan and Rex moved at a faster pace. Being the size of linebackers, they couldn't conceal quite as easily as the others. In addition, they were eager to get to action. They made their way to the entrance.

Seymour held up an open hand, signaling for them to hold position. He then grabbed the handle, and opened the door in a swift and silent motion. Nagamine immediately entered, the sights of his submachine gun raised at eye level. Scanning the stairs, he confirmed nobody was in sight. He moved upward, followed by Seymour.

They could see a door at the top of the small row of stairs. There was no window, but through the tiny gaps around the edges, they saw that the lights were on. Carefully, they walked up the stairs, keeping their weapons pointed at the door. There, they listened intently. A voice sounded inside, speaking in Korean. Another voice overlapped, confirming the existence of a second pilot.

Nagamine looked to Seymour, who gave him a nod. Understanding the instruction, Fujiwara Clan's descendant strapped his firearm. He drew his Ninjato, holding it at waist level, pointing the blade down.

Seymour reached for his vest, drawing a three-inch throwing knife. Holding it by the blade, he tapped his hand on the door.

One of the voices shouted, "Geugeos-eun mueos-inga?"

"Mun-I maghyeossda!" Seymour mimicked, shaking the handle to imply the door was stuck. They listened to the footsteps. Seymour backed down a step. The door swung open, revealing the pilot. His initial expression was irritation to the incompetence of what he thought was a crew member. A breath later, he was alarmed. Before his hand could reach for his sidearm placed at his belt, Nagamine slashed the blade of his sword across his throat. The pilot fell backward, bleeding onto the floor. The other pilot stood from his seat, caught completely off guard by the invasion. A rifle leaned against the dashboard. His hand was halfway to the barrel when Seymour launched his knife. The knife and handle completed a single rotation before the blade plunged three inches into the pilot's neck. Blood seeped through the wound, and the hand pressed against it. The pilot fell to his knees, still attempting to grab his weapon. His fingers just barely managed to touch the barrel grip when the life drained from his body. His arm dropped away from the weapon, and his body hit the floor.

****

Waiting along the narrow pathways along the structure, Terrie and Easley watched their targets from their separate position.

"*Pilothouse clear. Proceed to forward deck,*" Seymour's voice whispered through the comms. Terrie moved first, shouldering her firearm. She moved seven paces ahead, stopping just short of light cast by a spotlight on the structure deck. The guard turned, momentarily seeing her silhouette moving again in the darkness. He paused, initially believing his visitor to be one of his comrades. Terrie positioned her sights on his center mass. With her weapon set on semi-auto, she double tapped, placing two 5.56x45mm NATO rounds into his sternum.

As the Korean fell backward, Easley fired two rounds into the other one, silently ending his life. Both mercenaries quietly moved out onto the deck, briefly checking their targets' vitals. Terrie clicked her transmitter.

"Clear," she whispered.

****

Seymour and Nagamine descended the small flight of stairs, meeting Ivan and Rex at the main entrance. Seymour took point, leading the way to C-Deck. The stair ramp led them down twelve feet, where they found a door leading into a hallway. Seymour glanced to Ivan and Rex, then pointed to the left of the hallway.

Nagamine sheathed his sword and clutched his MP5. Seymour pressed his ear to the door, listening for any chatter. He glanced through the window. The hallway was well lit. They wouldn't be able to camouflage. They would need to instantly identify their targets and neutralize them immediately.

Nothing they haven't done before.

Seymour slowly turned the handle, then opened the door a crack. Nobody. He stepped out, checking both directions. Clear. He led the way, rifle raised, as he and Nagamine continued aft. Ivan shut the door then followed Rex to the fore section of the ship.

Seymour saw the mess hall doors ahead. Both double doors opened, and three Koreans walked through. Each was dripping wet and covered in mud, as if they had just undergone trench warfare. Each carried a 58 Assault Rifle and seemed nearly out of breath.

Seymour squeezed the trigger. NATO rounds cracked the skull of the nearest soldier, instantly ending his life. In that same moment, Seymour fired a second burst, dropping the one right behind him, while Nagamine fired a three-round burst into the third.

They pushed forward, approaching the galley.

****

Ivan and Rex hugged the walls on opposite sides of the corridor as they drew near the quarters. Brief, shallow breaths, they listened to the chatter amongst the crew they approached.

Though not able to understand the Korean dialect, they took notice of the tone. The exchange between the unseen crew sounded panicked. The mercs knew they hadn't been discovered, as the crew would be mobilizing for a counterattack. Plus, their voices lacked the particular urgency of an active assault.

Whatever it was, they were unnerved.

The only thing that mattered to the mercs was that they heard no English speech. They burst through the door, causing five crew members to jump from their bunks.

Ivan took the right, while Rex took the left. They released an onslaught of bullets, peppering all five crew before any of them could snatch up a weapon.

Ivan looked to his friend, mouthing the words, "Three-to-two," before grinning.

34

The door on the opposite side swung open. Two Koreans paused in the doorway, seeing the massacre and the two armed brutes. They jolted with surprise. Exclaiming in Korean, they raised their weapons.

Rex fired from the hip, putting a round through each combatant's forehead. Their skulls burst in showers of red. Their corpses fell backward, twitching uncontrollably from muscular reflex. Rex looked at Ivan.

"Four-to-three, bitch," he mouthed.

****

Seymour proceeded past the dead crew, gently pushing the double doors open. He peeked into the mess hall. Five Korean crew sat inside. Like the ones he'd just put down, these personnel were all dripping wet, and covered in grime. Each of them wore tactical gear, complete with automatic rifles.

Seymour and Nagamine burst through the doors. The small group spun around in surprise. Before they could react further, each one felt his torso torn open by a barrage of strategically placed bullets. The bodies hit the floor with a thudding sound. Positioning near the entry of the next corridor, Nagamine ejected his empty magazine.

As he reached for a fresh one, an alarmed soldier jumped from the galley entrance. He gripped a semi-automatic pistol in his hands. In one motion, Seymour turned, rose his rifle, and squeezed the trigger. The combatant's head ruptured as the bullet entered his torso, instantly killing him.

Nagamine lifted a thumbs up as a 'thank you.' As he did, another crew member burst in from the nearby entrance, rifle in hand. His speed was second only to Nagamine's, who drew his Ninjato. In a flash, he swung downward, striking the blade atop the rifle, which fell from its owner's grip. The merc thrust the blade forward, driving it through the soldier's chest cavity.

Seymour slammed a fresh magazine into his weapon and stepped into the hall, while Nagamine sheathed his sword.

Two more soldiers approached, drawn by the sound of a struggle. They entered the corridor, only to be met with bullets fired from the two mercs. As their bodies hit the floor, the sound of a door echoed through the hallway.

Seymour moved to the end of the corridor, where the captain's quarters was located. He heard the soldier inside yelling on the radio, attempting to make contact with his fellow comrades. There was no answer, as Ivan and Rex had completed their sweep.

Seymour and Nagamine stood on opposite sides of the door, staying clear of the frame. Keeping himself standing off to the side, he slapped his hand hard against the door, just hard enough to make the Korean believe he was trying to break it down.

The ploy worked. Deafening gunshots cracked through the room as bits of wood burst from the door. Ten shots rang off, followed by an empty click.

Seymour stepped in front of the door and put all his weight into a powerful kick, breaking the door off of its hinges.

The Korean soldier quickly slammed a fresh magazine into his pistol. He pointed the gun at the intruder.

In a lightning fast motion, Seymour grabbed his wrist with his right hand, maneuvering the soldier's extended arm upward like a lever. Three rounds pierced the ceiling before the former SEAL grabbed a handful of the soldier's hair on the back of his head. Turning his hips clockwise, he slammed the soldier's head into the doorframe.

The gun dropped from his hand, and the unconscious soldier slid down the wall, until he was sitting upright, his head hanging to the left. Nagamine quickly checked him for other weapons, while Seymour checked the hallway again for any more stragglers.

He clicked his transmitter, "Mess hall and galley secured."

"*Crew quarters secured. Engine room checked and secured,*" Ivan responded.

"Any hostages?"

"*Negative.*"

Seymour took a breath. All he could do was hope that the hostages were somewhere on the island.

"Alright. Good work everybody. Agent Hawk, the vessel is secured. You may come aboard."

CHAPTER
7

Hawk tapped several keys on her tablet, linked by cable to the ship's main computer. Clicking 'enter' she uploaded her bypass, allowing her access into the files.

The lab room's floor was smothered with paper files, all cast aside while she looked through everything. What little was there was nothing other than old research printouts from the ship's previous ownership. Printouts on water temperatures, fish species, sodium levels, etc. The only knowledge she gained were clues as to how the Koreans likely acquired the ship. Odds being it belonged to a Chinese institute who sold it for quick cash. Either that, or the black market.

With her computer able to translate any data, she downloaded the computer documents. The translator swept each page within a few minutes. Like the printouts, the computer contained nothing of relevance. It almost seemed as if the Koreans hadn't even used it yet.

"Damn it," she slammed her fist against the computer desk. She cooled her temper and thought for a moment. She searched for any flash drives or discs, only to find nothing.

The data must still be in the bunker.

The echoes of voices traveled down the corridor, drawing her attention. She stepped out through the doorway in time to hear the Korean captive yell in pain.

"That was to ensure we have an understanding," Seymour said, tapping the butt of his knife against his palm. The Korean captive slumped facedown over a table, held in place by Rex and Ivan. Blood dripped from the gash in his forehead, and his right index finger swelled where Seymour had crushed it with his knife handle. The remaining mercenaries continued roaming the corridors, securing weapons and supplies.

Rex grabbed the Korean by the hair, forcing him to look up at Seymour, while Ivan kept his hand pinned to the table. Bathed in his own sweat and blood, he grimaced at his captor, enraged by his defeat and the humiliation of his torture.

Seymour put a foot up on a chair and leaned in toward the Korean, "Make this easy. Where are you holding Dr. Trevor?" The Korean glared at him for several tense moments, then spat in his face. Seymour straightened his posture, brushed his sleeve over his face, then rose his knife high above his head. He slammed the butt of the handle hard over the middle finger, crushing the knuckle into gravel. The Korean yelled out, cursing at Seymour in his native language.

"I'd talk man," Rex said. "You'll save yourself a lot of pain." The soldier turned his head, looking at the leviathan of a man who held him in place. His snarl gradually turned into a smile.

"Neoui eomeoniga amsoleul yeosmeog yeossni?" he said, laughing maniacally. Rex could sense verbal abrasion through the tone.

"What'd you say?" He looked toward Seymour. "What'd he say?"

Seymour knew telling him would only incite anger, and doing so would waste valuable time. "He's just trying to get under your skin," he said.

"I say...did your mother...fuck with...cow?" The Korean hollered. Rex's face stiffened with anger, while meanwhile, Ivan struggled not to grin with glee.

"Oh, you're funny!" Rex said, drawing a large knife from his vest. He pressed the tip of it against the captive's throat, barely keeping it from puncturing. Exactly why Seymour didn't translate.

"Rex, chill," he said. Rex hesitated a moment, then withdrew the blade. Seymour leaned in once again. "So, you speak English. Good...that saves me the trouble of translating." He dug into a pocket in his vest, unfolding the photo of Dr. Trevor. "Where is he? Where are you holding this man?" The Korean stared at Seymour, appearing bewildered. "Yes...we know you have him hostage. Now you have five seconds to tell us where." He folded the picture back up, and held the blade of his knife to the swelling fingers.

The Korean looked at the blade, then back to Seymour. His bewildered expression lit into a large grin. He started chuckling.

"Dr. Trevor..." he said.

"SEYMOUR!" Hawk yelled as she entered the mess hall. "You are not to speak with this individual." Seymour stepped away from the table, his eyes a fiery blaze.

"Agent, we're in the middle of something called "acquiring intelligence." We need to find out how many soldiers are on the island, and where the hostages are being held."

"This man may hold classified information," Hawk said. "He may only be interrogated by an Agent with special clearance."

"Oh! Like you?" Ivan blurted.

"Agent, we don't have time for you to conduct an interview," Seymour said. "We need to move before we lose the cover of night and weather. This storm won't last much longer."

"Fine," Hawk said. "If we have to move now, then why don't we take him with us? We can tie him down and secure him in the first outpost until we're finished."

Ivan noticed all color leave the Korean's face upon hearing the Agent's suggestion. The captive's amused expression instantly became one of intense anxiety. Keeping quiet, Ivan glanced at Rex, who made eye contact with a shared puzzled look. He also had noticed the soldier's shift in demeanor.

Seymour briefly thought about it, then nodded. It seemed like a plan suitable for both parties. Seymour would see to it that the soldier would not be able to escape the guard shack and alert his comrades. This would entail breaking both his legs and at least one of his arms, leaving one available to allow him to drink water. Cruel, but it was less than what a member of Pogoung Death Squad deserved.

Seymour turned to look at Ivan and Rex. "Get him up. We'll make him talk on the boat."

The Korean's eyes widened. Panic overtook him. "No...NO!"

"Oh, yep yep!" Ivan said.

"NO!" he was screaming now. Ivan reached for a rag to gag him.

With veins bulging from his face, the soldier glanced down to the left. Rex still held the knife, its tip pointed directly at his neck. With Ivan having released one of his grips, there was a little leverage.

He dry-heaved and hyperventilated. Through clenched teeth he wailed, then threw his weight downward, slipping his arm from Ivan's grasp. With his remaining digits, he grabbed Rex's wrist.

"Hey!" Rex prepared to outmuscle the soldier. Before he could react, he felt the warm sensation of blood smother his hand. The Korean pressed his throat against the blade, pushing upward on Rex's hand. The knife plunged four inches deep. "Holy shit!" Rex yelled, instinctively withdrawing the knife. Blood filled the trachea like water down a drain. The soldier collapsed onto the floor, gagging and squirming in a puddle of red.

"Doc, double-time it to the mess hall!" Seymour yelled in his transmitter as he jumped over the table. Withdrawing gauze pulled from a small first-aid pouch in his vest, he applied pressure to the soldier's throat.

The soldier's trembling slowed, and the repeated clicking of his jaw ceased. His eyelids closed halfway and froze in place. The dead soldier lay on the floor, still as a billboard, containing equally as much life. The effort was fruitless. Seymour stood up, hands covered in blood.

"Well, you got your wish. He won't be spilling any "classified data" to us." He looked to Agent Hawk. She stood perplexed from what she had just witnessed. Staring at the dead body, she tried to utter a response.

"I...he...I didn't..." she could only stutter. "Why did he..."

"Eh, it's not too uncommon for captured soldiers to off themselves," Ivan said. He reached into one of his many pockets and pulled a Kit-Kat bar. He stuffed it into his mouth and munched. "Hell, I hear prison food tastes like shit. Probably why he did it."

Hawk stared at him, jaw agape, simultaneously appalled and amazed by the brute's casual indifference. She took control of herself, remembering she was in a position of authority, and did not want to appear feeble in the presence of the combat-hardened veterans.

She cleared her throat.

"He seemed fairly confident a minute ago," she said.

"For some reason, he didn't want to go back to the island," Seymour said.

"For fear of punishment from the other units?" she asked. Seymour looked at the body and shook his head.

"Doubt it," he said. "He had no qualms with taking himself out."

"He killed himself?" Sutton said, hurrying into the room followed by Terrie and Easley.

"Yep," Rex said. "Stuck his own neck into my knife!" He looked over at Ivan, who pointed at him and smirked.

"Oh no!" Ivan said. "That one does not count!"

"Fine," Rex said.

"Damn, Boss," Sutton said. "There's a lot on this boat that doesn't quite add up. I mean, how many personnel did we eliminate?"

"Probably around thirty," Seymour said.

"Are we aware of any other vessels in the area?" Hawk asked.

"Charlie's monitoring the waters," Seymour said. "He'd let us know if there was."

"Another thing..." Terrie chimed in. She held up one of the enemy rifles taken from a dead soldier in the crew quarters. "I checked some of the weapons..." she removed the mag, "...this thing is half full. These weapons have been fired."

"Well yeah," Hawk said. "You'd expect that in a firefight."

"Except we popped those chinks before they could get a shot off," Rex said. He noticed a glare from Nagamine, who sat at one of the tables. "My bad."

"They had shot at somebody," Terrie said. "Then there's the cargo. They had nothing battened down. They had equipment scattered all over the deck...."

"Doesn't seem like they had much in the way of rations, either," Easley said, stepping out of the kitchen.

"Seems like they left in a hurry," Seymour said. He looked at Hawk. "You have any insight?"

"No," she said. "And they have nothing pertaining to the research. No sign of the team."

A crack of thunder echoed. Seymour glanced at the ceiling, seemingly looking through the steel barrier into the night sky.

"Right now, the only way we'll find out where they are, is to get on the island and find out," he said. "We'll proceed with the original plan." He raised his voice, conveying authority to his team. "Let's move! Storm won't last much longer." He led the way down the corridor, followed by his team in single-file.

Hawk hesitated, looking down at the dead Korean. Staring at him, she pondered. A chill struck her spine like lightning, and a deep dread caused her stomach to ache.

The footsteps from the team grew evermore faint, and she snapped into reality. She dashed down the corridor to catch up.

CHAPTER
8

Coming in from the ocean, Crater Sands looked like a huge mountain in the dark stormy cast. In truth, while the terrain did contain many steep hills, the elevation did not excel over 1,430 feet above sea level. However, the island was teeming with enormous Cryptomeria trees. With the island left predominantly undisturbed over the decades, many of the trees grew to record heights, many exceeding 250 feet. The vast groupings of trees, and the thick interior jungle, gave the island a towering appearance.

The whole side of the island seemed to quiver as the winds caused the exterior layer of trees to sway. Like fireworks without the sparks, loud crackling echoed from deep in the forest, as smaller trees succumbed to the force of the storm.

The surrounding waters were steadily calming as the storm moved off. The large five-foot swells reduced in size, climbing no higher than three. Still, the ocean appeared like one huge enraged beast, stretching its anger out for miles. Waves rolled one after another, hurling themselves toward the island.

A swell of water, thickening with each inch in momentum, hit the south side of the island. Hitting the rocks, it broke apart into a thousand fragments of water that sprayed in all directions.

One of them splattered all over Hawk's face. Standing inside the Zodiac, she winced as the salt stung her eyes. The boat, secured by two cords that were strung on the rocks, bounced in the water. Rubbing her wrists over her eyes, she looked back up at the towering cliff. With each flash of lightning, she shook at the sight of the steep, jagged wall.

The seven mercenaries took a foothold on a group of shallow rocks that acted as a platform for their landing. Seymour clipped his harness together, stringing the cable through his carabiner. Standing near him was Terrie and Ivan, both of them secure in their harnesses, holding loops of cables to serve as belayers.

Hawk looked back up at the cliff, then back down at the rocky shore. One slip, one screw-up, and the climber would be at the mercy of the equipment. If one were to fall several feet down on these rocks, death would be a merciful conclusion.

"You…" Hawk's voice was lost in the wind. She took a breath, "You sure about this?!"

She saw the incensed look on Seymour's face. He pinched his index finger and thumb together, then brushed them over his mouth.

"You *trying* to give away our position?" Hawk couldn't hear him, but she understood.

Ivan stepped toward her, stretching his shoulders. "Don't worry, Agent-chick," he said. "This is no more than a hundred-eighty-feet. This is nuttin." He moved back, accepting a harness from Sutton.

Seymour held his drill and bolts, ready to initiate his climb. His weapon was strung over his shoulder, overtop his harness. Standing next to him was Nagamine, equally ready to climb. Seymour turned toward the team. Hawk saw his lips moving, but couldn't hear a word over the wind.

God, how can they hear him?

The realization immediately came to her. She looked down at the console and located her headphones. She placed them over her ears, and Seymour's commanding voice boomed from the pads.

"When he and I give the all-clear, the rest of you will ascend. The outpost should be less than half a click that way." He held his hand out toward the south. "We're gonna hit that first. When we do, we'll move on to the harbor." He turned his gaze towards the Zodiac. "Agent Hawk?"

"Yes?'

"Good, you can hear me," he said. "Right now, your job is to keep out of sight. Keep your radio on. We will contact you when the harbor is secure. When it is, bring the boat and meet us there. We'll find a place to secure it and keep it hidden." Hawk simply nodded. She begrudged his instruction, and felt an intense urge to argue back. She wanted to reference her arms training and tactical knowledge. However, that same knowledge informed her that, at this point, arguing would do nothing but compromise the mission. She gave a thumbs-up, signaling her understanding.

Seymour looked to his team. "Any questions?" Ivan raised his hand.

"How come he always gets to go first?" he said, pointing at Nagamine. Seymour rolled his eyes and turned around.

Imagine the drop-out rate if SEAL trainees suffered constant exposure to this guy.

He and Nagamine initiated their climbs. They studied the wall with their hands, looking for an initial hold. Digging his gloved fingers into a rift, Seymour lifted himself, pressing his boots into small ledges. He found his next hold and elevated another six inches. At ten feet, he held position. He held his drill to the rock and paused. A large crack of thunder sounded, and he initiated the drill. The drill bit rotated, digging into the rock. After a few more cracks of thunder, Seymour had the hole deep enough, and inserted a bolt with an attached carabiner. Stringing the cord through it, he pressed upward.

At thirty feet, he repeated, creating a route for the rest of the team to follow. Down below, the team secured their equipment in large black bags. Each would be hauled up by cable. With nothing else to do, Hawk watched as Seymour and Nagamine climbed the steep cliff. With every few feet of ascension, the duo grew smaller in view.

Seymour placed a new bolt in the rock. As he continued his next climb, he glanced over to his partner. Nagamine was nearly twenty feet ahead of him. Seymour smiled to himself.

Only because he's smaller.

With a focus as concentrated as diamonds, Nagamine located each hold with ease. Each movement he made was concealed in darkness, visible only to his leader. He checked each rock before drilling, checking to make sure it was hollow enough for drilling without compromising the structure. If the layer was too weak, then the weight from the next climber would cause the bolt to break free.

Seymour felt the wind gradually dying. He checked the time. They had just over a half-hour until sunrise. They would need to take the first outpost by then.

Rain pummeling his face, he climbed further. The ledge of the cliff was only a few meters away. He drilled a hole, inserted the bolt, then proceeded to the ledge. As he looked again, he saw Nagamine holding position under the ledge, waiting for him to catch up.

"Yeah, yeah, showoff," he whispered into his microphone. He climbed to the ledge, holding place beside Nagamine. They looked at each other, taking hold of their sidearms with a free hand, holding to the ledge with another. In unison, they peeked over the ledge.

The ledge led to a thirty foot plain of tall grass, leading up to a gathering of trees. The outer layer of plants formed a wall of green that shifted in form as the wind tore into the jungle.

"Clear left," Seymour said.

"Clear right," Nagamine said. Holstering his revolver, Seymour pulled himself over the ledge. Immediately, he positioned onto one knee and scanned the area through the sights of his rifle. Other than the swaying plants, there was no movement. He held out a hand and helped Nagamine over the edge. Nagamine braced his hands on his weapon, serving as a lookout while Seymour secured the final posts for each cable route.

"Alright," Seymour spoke into his transmitter, "Initiate ascent."

Terrie and Sutton were the first to climb. With the aid of the cable, their climb was much faster than the first ascenders. Next were Ivan and Rex, with Easley coming up last, along with the supplies.

Sitting inside the Zodiac, Hawk watched each of them disappear over the edge of the cliff, listening to the various chatter over the comm. Soon, she was alone near the rocky shoreline. Tapping the helm, she grew increasingly impatient. Being told to wait behind felt humiliating, and she questioned whether Seymour was actually concerned for her safety, or if he considered her a hinderance. The more she pondered, the more irritable she became. As the C.I.A. liaison, she was supposed to have command of this operation, and here she was taking orders from the contractor.

She checked the time. Sunrise was in eleven minutes.

"You guys better hurry up," she said aloud.

CHAPTER
9

The wind slowed to a strong breeze. The overcast gradually moved on, reducing the downpour to a drizzle. The southeast horizon turned a shadowy gold as the storm pushed east.

Seymour crouched low in the trees, seamlessly blending in with the wilderness as he neared the outpost. He gazed through an opening in the angular tree line, measuring the outpost. Behind him were Rex and Ivan, both huddled in the dense forest, soaking in rain, mud, and grit. As the winds died down, the local insect life emerged. Flies and mosquitos buzzed around the brutes, landing on their bare arms and inserting their proboscis into the skin. All they could do was slowly rub their hands over their skin to help keep them off. Anything else would risk giving away their position.

From his view, Seymour could see the rear of the outpost, as well as a shed to the left. Two Jeeps were parked in front of the shed, indicating the building could have as many as eight personnel. Behind the building was a generator, which rested in the grass. From what he could see there were no power cables hooked up to the building.

"Terrie, report," he whispered.

Two hundred meters west, Terrie was huddled down in the brush behind the tree line. The disjointed trunks from two banyan trees formed an "X" shape in front of her. Behind it were two more trees with grass standing three feet high. It was the only decent sniping position she could find, where she could have a decent view and remain camouflaged. Looking through her scope, she gazed under the crossed trees, looking at the side of the outpost.

Through the crosshairs, she examined the side of the building. The lights were off, and from her angle, there was no movement. She steadily panned left, putting the open door in her sights. It swayed to-and-fro with the wind, revealing an empty interior.

"No movement," she whispered. "No lights. Crew might be asleep."

"They should have at least one on lookout," Seymour whispered back. The cover of darkness started fading away with the sunrise. He shouldered his rifle, ready to stand. "Team Two, move in on west exterior. We'll take the southeast...on three...two...one...move!"

Seymour exited the tree line first, swiftly moving toward the open door. Ivan and Red followed suit, eager to unleash their M60 machine guns on the unsuspecting squad. To the east, Easley, Sutton, and Nagamine emerged from a different point in the tree line. Easley stopped near the shed, peeking inside to confirm nobody was inside, then waited to provide backup. Easley and Nagamine stopped alongside the door.

Positioned behind the open door, Seymour removed the pin to a stun grenade. He tossed it inside. An exploding flash illuminated the entire interior. The next instant, both teams rushed inside, guns pointed.

Seymour and Rex burst into the main lookout chamber. Nobody. They immediately kicked down the next door, ready to unload a barrage of bullets. Stepping through, they found themselves inside the personnel quarters. Several empty bunks lay in rows, their occupants nowhere to be seen. Seymour turned and re-entered the lookout chamber.

"Clear!"

"Clear," Sutton said. He entered the lookout chamber, lowering his weapon. Seymour walked about the large room. Three empty chairs were pushed away from the control panel, where several computer panels were powered off. The console was comprised of radar equipment, as well as long-range binoculars looking out toward the vast ocean. A radio unit lay on the floor. Two feet away, a Makarov pistol lay on its side.

Sutton picked it up, removing the magazine. It was full. Nagamine entered the room.

"Go scout ahead," Seymour said to him. "I doubt they know we're here, but I don't want them laying any surprises for us." Nagamine nodded and hurriedly moved out. Seymour pressed his transmitter. "Terrie, all clear. Scout ahead with Nagamine."

"*Yes, sir.*"

Seymour noticed Sutton looking at him.

"What's going on here, Boss?" he said. Seymour shrugged.

"That's what we're figuring out, Doc," he said. "It appears they abandoned this outpost."

"Why? There's no sign of a firefight. The only sign of conflict is that!" Sutton pointed at the Makarov. "And look at this." He led Seymour around to the back through another doorway.

It was a small armory, packed with several high powered automatic weapons and several explosives. However many men this outpost housed, they were armed well enough to repel a larger force. Several tables held bazookas and grenade launchers, with crates of ammo everywhere.

Seymour stepped outside. The drizzle continued, though not for much longer as the clouds were beginning to scatter. The morning sunlight had fully lit the side of the island. The roaring jungle stilled as the wind calmed.

Seymour looked to the Jeeps. There were no recent tread tracks around the building. The vehicles themselves didn't look like they had been used in a while.

Why would they leave all of this unattended? It was clear the military force was worried about an operation to counter whatever it was they were doing. All he could surmise was that this may have been part of the group that had departed on the ship.

"Charlie?" he said into his microphone.

"*I see you guys,*" Charlie responded. "*So, there's nobody?*"

"Negative," Seymour said. "What about the harbor?"

"*I flew the drone that way, and I don't see anybody,*" Charlie said. "*However, there's canopy in that area, so I cannot confirm.*"

"So much for that college education," Ivan said.

"Should we let the Agent know about this?" Easley said.

"Negative," Seymour said. "Right now, I want to focus on securing the harbor. As you can see, they've trimmed out a half-assed trail for their vehicles there." He pointed toward the opening in the trees. Several of the plants had been flattened down or removed completely, forming a five-foot wide path barely wide enough for the Jeeps. "We'll stick to the jungle, out of sight, but keep that trail in sight. If we come across anybody, we'll want to question one."

"Is it possible they knew we were coming?"

"Maybe that's why those other soldiers took off," Rex said, chuckling.

"I mean, they did look ready to piss their pants," Ivan interjected.

"Knock it off," Seymour said. He grew tired of repeating the phrase. *If you guys weren't good soldiers...*

Seymour looked at the mud near the nearest entrance. There were no signs of footprints leaving the outpost. Even if there were, the torrential downpour would've severely impaired any physical evidence in the dirt. Seymour narrowed his gaze. Something in the mud had caught his eye. A single imprint near the entrance, like that from a stake that had been pounded into the ground. Only this was only an inch or two deep. Seymour scanned the mud with his eyes, but couldn't see any more due to the prints left by his team.

"Sir, we're ready to move out," Sutton said. Seymour studied the ground a moment more.

"There's nothing here," he said. "The harbor is roughly a mile-and-a-half away. Let's get moving."

In seconds, the team disappeared into the thick jungle, quickly becoming invisible among the plant life.

CHAPTER
10

Ivan took point, with Rex trailing twelve feet behind. Being the towering man that he was, moving quietly in the dense jungle didn't come as naturally. Leaves as large as road signs blocked every square foot of view. Trees crowded the landscapes, with smaller plants and vines hugging their trunks throughout the forest floor. For the mercenaries, this thick wilderness provided both an excellent cover, and a hazard. The slightest inevitable movement of plants could give away their position, meaning the team had to spread out. Brush moving in isolation, if seen by the enemy, would likely be written off as an animal passing by. However, if movement was detected in a large gathering, it would lead to suspicion of an intrusive force.

A large mosquito made its landing. Like a tiny power drill, it plunged its proboscis into the back of Ivan's ear.

A piercing sting lit his nerves.

"Dick-fuck!" he nearly yelled. He slapped his hand over his ear, smothering the insect over the side of his neck. He looked at his hand, then wiped it over his vest. "Little bastard."

"Big baby," Sutton muttered.

"Coming from the guy wearing all the bug cream," Ivan said.

"Stow it, guys," Seymour said.

"My bad, Boss," Ivan said. Keeping his M60 pointed downward, he pushed through a blockade of plants. Several insects leapt from the leaves toward Ivan, who casually brushed them off. He glanced behind him, seeing Rex trailing behind him. He wore a smirk on his face. "What are you laughing at?" he whispered into his mic.

"Dude, quit asking like you don't know," Rex said. "You're freaking terrified of bugs."

"*Guys...*" Seymour's voice came through their headsets. It was just one word. As usual, it was softly spoken, but it was enough to convey his annoyance. Ivan continued forward, entering a small clearing between two huge trees. Three steps ahead were another wall of plants. Small trees with dual trunks stretched out in crooked formations, reaching any sunlight that crept through the elevated canopy.

Ivan stepped around the tree. He pointed his elbow to push through a large display of leaves. A grasshopper, green with red lining throughout its body, launched himself inches past his face. Ivan jerked his head back, his senses heightened. He exhaled, then grinned.

"Fucking-afraid-of-bugs-my-ass," he muttered through a shark-like grin.

Two large plants were bunched up in front of him. Their vines were entangled five feet off the ground. Ivan tried to gently pull them apart, but was unable to do so without creating too much ruckus. Underneath the vines was a small opening. He ducked down and slipped through it.

He stood up. "Je---" he nearly shouted. The spider poised on a branch, inches from his face. Its legs were bent, as if it were ready to leap at him. Its abdomen was a yellow-green oval shape, its head perfectly round.

Ivan scurried several feet backward until his boot hit something hard and stiff, his gun raised at the spider. Rex slipped under the vines. He looked at the spider, then over at his buddy. He shook his head.

"My point exactly," he whispered.

"Fuck your mother," Ivan muttered. Rex pressed his fist to his mouth, trying to keep his laughter contained. Sutton emerged from the plants. He looked at the spider.

"It's a fucking orb spider," he whispered. "They're not even deadly."

"Listen, Doctor Douche," Ivan hissed. He pointed his finger at the arachnid. "That thing was poised and ready to come at me!"

By now, Rex was shaking with repressed laughter. "Look how far it made him jump," he said, pointing at Ivan's boots. Sutton smiled. His eyes narrowed past Ivan's feet. The smile faded.

"What is that?" he muttered. Ivan squinted, barely able to hear him. Following the medic's gaze, he realized he wasn't looking at him. Ivan turned around.

"…the hell?"

He had assumed his boot had hit a log when he stepped back. Laying on the ground near his feet was a boar. Over four feet in length and weighing two hundred pounds, the animal lay in the mud, stiff as a brick. Red blood trickled from its mouth, forming a tiny red stream.

Seymour emerged from the wall of plants. His face was tense, almost demonic.

"You assholes are on my last nerve," he said.

"Sorry, Boss," Sutton whispered. He nudged his elbow toward the spider. "We've discovered Ivan's worst enemy."

"Hey guys," Ivan whispered. They quietly walked over. Sutton shook his head.

"It's a boar," he said.

"I know it's a fucking *boar!*" Ivan said through clenched teeth. "But what's that?" Seymour gazed at the creature's bulk. From the center of its thick hump was a strange bulge. Though it appeared like a large infectious lump, it wasn't part of the animal itself. Shaped like a mushroom cap, the bulge appeared to have several veins running through it. Where it connected to the flesh, the veins were red, but as they moved further up, they took on a greenish color.

Sutton studied it quietly, then looked at its trunk. "It looks dead, but its blood is free-flowing..."

"Yeah, okay..." Ivan said. "But what is that?" He knelt down, pointing at the strange lump.

"Hey boss?" Terrie's voice came through the radio. Ivan twitched again. Even Seymour had difficulty hiding his amusement. A rare smile creased his face.

"Go ahead," he said.

"We've located the harbor."

"Any movement?"

"Negative, sir. From what we can see, there's not a soul here. But it looks like something went down. You'll want to take a look at this."

"Copy that. Stand by, we're on our way," he said.

"Oh, and sir?"

"Yes?"

"Let Ivan know he can borrow my dress, since he's being such a girl."

Ivan grunted. *Bitch.*

"He'll take a raincheck," Seymour said. He stepped away from the boar. "Alright, gentlemen, let's get a-moving. I'm getting tired of saying it...keep it quiet. Easley, why don't you take point."

"Aye-aye," Easley said. The nerd gripped his rifle and disappeared into the jungle. The rest of the team followed, maintaining fifteen feet of distance.

CHAPTER
11

Seymour knelt six feet away from Nagamine, concealed in tall grass. The team spread out along the edge of a steep hill overlooking the harbor. The harbor was located in a cove, which indented into the inner side of the peninsula. Several trees around it had been chopped down, making room for three helipads. From the shore, three docks extended fifty feet into the water. Thirty feet inland, between the docks and the helipads, was the outpost. It was a similar design as the abandoned one on the southside cliffs, but much larger. And like the other, it had a propane generator.

"Jesus," Seymour said. They could see the charred remains from a sixty-foot vessel, docked near the furthest deck. It remained afloat, but the top portion was riddled with burns and impact craters, as if it had taken hits from RPG's. Two hundred feet out in the water was another boat, half submerged. Its bow pointed upward at a forty-five-degree angle, the stern lodged into the reef.

The two helicopters were in even worse shape. The cockpits were smashed inward, the rotors fragmented in countless pieces spread all over the cove. Even from afar, the team could see traces of a large fire that ignited from what they speculated to be two crashes.

"Don't know about you guys, but I'd say these fellas had themselves a fiasco," Rex said.

Seymour studied the area through his binoculars.

"No movement," he said.

Terrie looked up from her sniper scope. "Nothing that I can see."

"Alright," Seymour said. "Let's check it out. But don't drop your guard. Keep low. Rex, Ivan--take the left near the shore. Sutton, Nagamine--move out to the right. Terrie, provide sniper cover. Easley, move down the middle with me. Move!"

The team crouched down to blend in with their surroundings. Each movement between open space had to be swift and silent as they moved down the hill.

Terrie ignored the ants that sprawled toward her from the ground as she consistently moved her crosshairs along the harbor. Having spent time in both Iraq and Afghanistan, she understood the cost of dropping her guard.

Several trees in the area made a clean line of sight impossible. She kept her main focus on the building. She could see one entrance, but not the other. As with the previous outpost, the lights appeared to have been turned off.

Seymour and Easley kneeled several meters within the last thick group of trees.

"Ivan, Rex, provide cover," he said. He pointed his rifle and hustled, followed by Easley. Sutton and Nagamine moved in from the right. They pointed their weapons toward the downed aircraft, and checked the open cabins. Confirming nobody was inside, they proceeded to the building.

"Damn," Sutton muttered to himself. The side of the building was charred. Entire portions, each roughly the size of a car tire, had been blown away, exposing charred edges. Shell fragments and bullet casings littered the ground. They hurried around the corner, finding the second doorway.

The door was completely torn from its frame. The hinges had been bent into jagged, irregular shapes. Sutton looked at the ground. Two feet past the door, an arm lay in the dirt, torn off above the elbow. The hand still clutched the M58 assault rifle, the index finger pressed tightly against the trigger.

Further along the outside wall was an assortment of other body parts. Blood, dried and charred, smothered the entire side of the building. All Sutton could identify was a boot. The rest had been completely mangled.

Standing outside the doorway, he ignited the flashlight on his rifle. After a quick breath, he entered the building. Smears of blood, turned a light brown, covered the small hallway. He entered the radio room. Several computer consoles, all powered down, lined the dashboard.

Sutton turned off his light, as the daylight seeping through the window provided enough illumination. He looked about the room.

Three semi-automatic pistols lay on the floor, each with the slide locked back.

Seymour and Easley entered, having already checked the armory. Seymour tapped his mic.

"Building's all clear," he said. "Team three, anything?"

"*All clear out here, Boss,*" Ivan said. Seymour examined the computer consoles.

"The generator is out," Sutton said.

"I don't think that's why these are powered down," Seymour said. He shined a flashlight under the dashboard, where the hard drives were located. Each one was riddled with bullet holes. Judging by the placement, Seymour knew it was done deliberately, and not in the midst of blind gunfire. "The generator was shot too," he said.

"Obviously, they didn't want anyone to know they were downloading porn!" Rex shouted from outside.

"Friggin apes," Sutton whispered. He looked at the radio units. Like the computers, they had been shot repeatedly. He glanced back at the hard drives. "Can these be used for messaging?"

"Probably, yes. Most likely, that's what their purpose was," Seymour said.

"I mean, I doubt they would store important files in these computers. The only logic in destroying them is..." he paused and looked out the window at the ships and choppers, "...to cut everybody off from the outside."

"I know someone who might know," Seymour said. He lifted his microphone to his lips. "Agent Hawk?"

"*I read you,*" Hawk responded.

"Bring the boat in," he said. "Harbor is secure."

"*Coming in,*" she said. Seymour moved the mic away.

"Frankly, I'm shocked she even followed my instructions," he said. Sutton looked all over the room, then peered through the open window. He stared at the ships, then back at the choppers.

"I don't like this, man," he said. "I'm tellin' you; something's not right."

"Yeah, man," Easley said. "I mean, where are the bodies? All we saw was one...or what was left of one...splattered outside over there."

They led Seymour through the door frame. He quickly noticed how the door had been pulled off the hinges, then looked at the charred body pieces.

"There were no bodies in the choppers?"

"No sir, not a one," Sutton said. Seymour walked to the bloodstained wall. Through the layer of blood, he could see scorched markings on the wall directly behind the human remains.

Ivan stepped around the front of the building. "They did a number on him, whoever they were." Seymour didn't respond and continued examining. He looked at the other damage along the side. Chunks of wall had been completely blown away, in near perfect circles, leaving behind burnt edges.

"What do you think did this?" Sutton said. "Couldn't have been an RPG."

"No, that would've done more damage," Seymour said. "But these certainly are impact craters."

"Impact crater from what?" Sutton asked. "I don't see any shrapnel in any of these blast points." Seymour looked around. The doc was right. It almost appeared as if a fire had somehow burnt away these precise portions of the wall without spreading. However, looking at the remains of the exposed frames, it was clear they were bent inward. Something had definitely hit the wall, without leaving any physical evidence.

"I see some in these choppers," Ivan called out. Seymour turned around. The choppers lay twenty yards from each other. One was still on its helipad, the other embedded in the mound, turned over on its side. Ivan stood near the standing chopper, pointing out the fifty-caliber bullet marks. "This one didn't even manage to take off," he said.

"Clearly the other one did," Seymour said. Its cabin and cockpit had crumpled inward as the craft landed and rolled. Bullet holes were riddled throughout its hull. "Those guys we encountered on the ship fled from here," he said. "Whatever happened here, we just missed it."

"Oh, it gets weirder," Ivan said. He stuck his head inside the open hatch, and waved Seymour over to do the same. "Look at this." Seymour poked his head inside and shined a light. The entire interior was charred black, and smelled of smoke.

"Damn," he said. "They took a flamethrower to this thing."

"Yeah man," Ivan said. "Had to stick the nozzle right through this door. They really wanted to smoke out whoever was in here."

"At this close range? They probably caught themselves on fire in the process," Seymour said. He backed away from it. He looked out toward the hill, seeing nothing but a thick blanket of green throughout. *Whoever they are, they could be anywhere.* He picked up his long-range radio. "Eagle nest?"

"Go ahead, Hatchling."

"Is there any other point on this island where someone could make landfall?"

"All I've been able to see are shallow areas along the east, and a couple of small areas to the west. I don't see any vessels other than those in your location."

"You sure?"

"Boss, I've been spending this whole time studying the terrain and layout. The north and south sides of the island are nothing but rocks and cliffs. The jungle is so dense, you can't really land a chopper, except a grass plain over on the northeast. But I see nothing there."

"Alright, keep looking. Hatchling, out." Seymour switched frequencies. "Terrie, scout ahead along the shoreline. I want to know of any signs of anyone moving in and out of here. Nagamine, you go as well."

"Hai!" Without hesitation, Nagamine took off toward the jungle.

****

As instructed by Seymour, Hawk hid the Zodiac in another small cove further up along the peninsula. Thick bushes and dense trees created a perfect cover for it. Ivan and Rex had met her at the landing point, and guided her back to the outpost. During the trip, she endured the endless banter and innuendo between the two towering mercenaries.

Upon reaching the outpost, she felt as though a whirlwind was twirling in her stomach. Her heart started racing. The hundred-degree heat, which had hardly fazed her, suddenly felt nearly unbearable.

"Did you guys..."

"Nope," Rex interrupted her. "We found it like this."

"Oh, no." She looked at the boats and choppers. Waiting by the outpost was Seymour, standing with his arms crossed. She quickened her pace, walking toward him. "Seymour..."

"Agent, has the C.I.A. sent any other strike team to this island that you're aware of?"

"No," she said. "They really wanted to keep this as quiet as possible."

"Are you guys aware of any other countries after...whatever it is they were working on here?"

"Not that we're aware of," Hawk said. She stared past Seymour, looking at the damage along the outpost exterior. Seymour stood quietly, watching her examine the damage. She placed a glove on her hand and ran her fingers over the cavity.

Ivan and Rex both started grinning.

"Oh, for the love of..." Sutton placed a hand over his face. Hawk took no notice of the immature mockery. Her expression was stone cold as she observed each impact crater.

Oh, Doctor Trevor, I hope you didn't...

"Agent?" Seymour's voice broke her concentration. She turned around. Seymour was growing impatient. "You know what did that?" She held her breath, maintaining complete silence. Seymour kicked a small mound of mud. "*Classified.* I get it," he said. He turned and walked around the building, moving toward the shoreline.

He looked out into the ocean. The storm had completely moved off, unveiling a bright, beautiful horizon. The majestic, distant view contrasted sharply with that of the cove, which was now a murky, discolored lagoon of death. Metal groaned under the water as the bow of the sunken ship swayed a few feet toward the shore and back, pushed by the tide.

The four remaining team members stood silent, each staring at Hawk with questioning eyes. Hawk grew anxious, but tried to maintain a calm, commanding presence. It was clear they felt uneasy about this assignment. With the C.I.A. forcing Seymour into taking the assignment, the classified info, the strange disappearances, the entire scenario reeked of some sort of set-up.

Her visibly increased anxiety only strengthened their suspicions.

CHAPTER
12

Even up to the shoreline, the jungle was intensely thick. Even moving a thousand yards out proved a challenge in itself, as the terrain did not allow for easy movement. Terrie stepped atop a fallen tree and leaned down against her own knee. She opened her canteen and guzzled a small mouthful. The humid air felt heavy and thick as did the jungle itself, like an invisible weight clinging to her.

Nagamine approached from the right, stopping to make sure she was aware of his presence. A quiet whistle from him drew her attention. She held a hand up, acknowledging his presence. Exhaling sharply, she put away her canteen and stepped over the dead tree.

There were no traces of footsteps or machinery. The portion of jungle appeared undisturbed. Whoever stormed the harbor did not come in from this direction. She whistled at Nagamine. With his attention on her, she pointed at herself, then pointed to her left, indicating she would proceed north. Nagamine nodded, and continued east.

Ducking under vines and enormous plants, Terrie walked a hundred yards. So far, there was no sign anyone had come through here. A mild wind brushed through the jungle. Terrie stopped and embraced the cooling sensation, listening to the leaves rustle in the canopy high above. That thirst irritated her throat again.

Damn, she thought. She felt mildly dehydrated. With the ocean splashing her face as the team approached the island, she believed to have inadvertently swallowed a mouthful or two of saltwater. *Just one more.* She leaned against a tree and unscrewed the lid to her canteen.

The crackling sound of a snapping branch burst through the air, immediately followed by the rustling of leaves. Mud splashed as something heavy fell to the earth. Terrie snatched her rifle, completely alarmed. She looked toward the sound, keeping the barrel of the gun pointed forward. The wind died down.

She figured it was probably just a tree branch damaged in the storm that gave in to the wind. However, she knew better to be sure. She slung the rifle to her back and drew her PM-84 Glauberyt Machine Pistol. She walked a hundred feet, coming to another downed tree. This one was fresh, having possibly fallen during the worst of the storm. She peeked through the wall of leaves.

She saw nothing but black. However, it wasn't darkness. Because of the fallen tree, a stream of light had managed to burst through the upper layer of forest. Two hundred feet of land had been burnt. Ash from trees and other plants had crumpled down into the earth, creating a large open area.

Terrie looked to the ground. Cartridge casings had peppered the dirt. She looked to her right, seeing several assault rifles in the mud. Terrie squinted as she gazed past the rifles.

"What the—"

Two large canisters, each encased with mud from hours of exposure, lay in the mud. They were strapped together, linked to a single hose that hooked to an ignition valve. It was a flamethrower.

Maintaining awareness of her surroundings, she slowly approached the weapons. Empty magazines surrounded the rifles. She knelt to check the gauges on the canisters. They were empty.

She stood straight, ready to alert Seymour.

As she adjusted her mic, she found herself staring at the maze of plants ahead. Many of them were dead, but not from fire. They appeared withered, as though the life had been sucked from them entirely. Their natural green pigment had darkened to a wet charcoal color. A thick oily fluid dripped from the withered leaves. She moved over, noticing several feet of jungle in the background, with the same bizarre color and texture.

She carefully brushed the plants aside, and gazed at the dying area of jungle.

"Oh…Jesus," she said. She prepped her mic. "Seymour…"

"*Terrie, go ahead.*"

"You'll want to check this out."

CHAPTER 13

Seymour gazed at the open area. For several hundred feet, bodies of North Korean *Ilgob Daelyug* lay motionless, smothered in a mixture of mud and the bizarre slimy substance growing on the surrounding plants. Some lay on their sides, others on their backs. A horrified, final expression was frozen on each of their faces. Seymour counted at least thirty human corpses.

Scattered amongst the dead soldiers were the bodies of several hundred animals. Different species of all shapes and sizes, indigenous to the island, lay frozen in the dying wilderness. White cranes, now grey from the strange substance in their feathers. Giant salamanders, racoon dogs, wild boar, Sika deer, monkeys, and various other species lay still as ice.

A strange object protruded from the center torso from each corpse. Each was charcoal-colored, and had an organic appearance. Some were small, resembling a charcoal-colored bulge, with red veins lining the skin. Others were in a different state of growth. Like a plant growing from a pod, the strange orb retained a roundish appearance, protruding upwards from a stem embedded in its host.

Easley glared at a particularly large pod, whose stem was rooted in the chest of one of the soldiers. It stood like a small tree, four feet tall, which led him to assume this thing, whatever it was, was a more mature version of the strange 'bulge.' Though having an odd appearance, its shape and method of growth reminded Easley of mushrooms. He looked down at the body from which it grew. It was shrunken, the soldier having lost all identity. It shriveled into its clothes, which were now two sizes too big. The jaw stretched open, two inches past the joint limit, the eyes shriveled, like dark yellow grapes that had been crushed.

He gulped as he held in his bile, and looked away.

The team spread out, maintaining a perimeter. Each member grew increasingly unnerved. Even Rex and Ivan, the two macho touch guys of the group, were now antsy. It was clear these bodies did not randomly end up here, but had been deliberately moved to this location. Both men clutched their machine guns, while constantly looking out into the surrounding jungle. Every whistle of the wind, each sway of a branch generated shadows of some silent unknown killer. They couldn't help but suspect they were being watched.

Nagamine emerged from the depths of the woods, having scouted nearly a half mile. He looked at Seymour and shook his head. There were no tracks, other than a few faint ones leading to the burnt area. Rex huffed, hoping that the tracker would be able to dig up some answers. He clenched his teeth together, balancing on the toes of his boots, eager to move.

"It's a fucking gravesite," Rex remarked. Ivan started nodding his head.

"Yeah...mission accomplished. Clearly, nobody left for us to kill. I say we get the hell out of dodge," Ivan remarked. "Boss, whattaya say? Look, even the Agent lady looks like she's gonna be sick!"

Hawk had stepped further into the jungle. With rubber gloves on her hands, she approached one of the trees. It was withered and discolored, the bark flaking off its trunk like greyish-brown dandruff. She pinched a six-inch piece of bark and pulled it free. She tipped it, dripping several drops of the strange fluid into a vial. She capped the vial and placed it into her pack.

"Everybody, maintain focus," Seymour said. His voice was tranquil. He knelt down by one of the bodies. The Korean lay flat on his back, his arms bent at the elbows, fingers crooked as though he was still holding an assault rifle. He looked to the dead man's chest. The black uniform shirt was torn open.

"You know about this, Agent?" he asked, pointing to the strange round substance. Hawk was silent as she knelt nearby to examine the oddity. It resembled the cap on a mushroom, even containing a stem that embedded itself deep in the soldier's flesh. Veiny lines reached about, red in color along the bottom of its stem. She looked up at the vast gravesite. Every corpse had something growing from it. Each were in different stages of growth. The larger ones took a form resembling pod plants; the corpses from which they grew were withered and shrunken.

"It's like that thing we saw on that boar," Rex said. To his right, he watched Sutton kneel by a dead walrus. Several pods grew from its enormous hide, each bulky in its own shape. A small wound opened up along its shoulder. He removed a q-tip from his pouch and inserted one end into the wound. The blood was red and thin. "Doc...I'm not sure I'd be messing with that," Rex said.

Sutton stood up. "I think, for the first time ever, I agree with you." He looked at Seymour, his eyes expressing urgency. "Sir, I think we ought to go." Hawk whipped herself around.

"No! We leave after we've secured the bunker and the data," she said.

"Sir...we're either dealing with a new species, or these scientists have cooked something up here on this island."

"Seymour," Hawk raised her voice, "once we've secured the facility then..."

"What do you mean, Doc?" Seymour said to Sutton, cutting Hawk off.

"Sir, this could be a viral infection, or the result of some bio-organic, or chemical experiment...I don't know. Whatever the case, these things are growing from their hosts. On that note...I'm not even sure everyone...everything...here, is dead."

"The fuck you talking about?" Rex said.

"I checked the blood on that walrus. It's red and oxygenated. By the looks of it, it's flowing through its body. Dead blood would not look like that. By all accounts, it's technically alive. Though, probably not for long, as you can see in some cases." He pointed to the shrunken bodies. "I don't know how it happened, don't think I *want* to know. But frankly, we're not equipped to handle it."

"That's enough!" Hawk said, pointing a finger at Sutton's face. He squared up, showing no intimidation. Hawk turned and looked to Seymour. "We are not leaving until we've secured the bunker, and collected the data."

"You do realize, Agent Pigeon," Ivan said. Fuming, Hawk turned toward him. "...these guys were taken out, and clearly they had a lot more manpower. What makes you think the same thing won't happen to us?"

"Here-here," Rex said.

"We're here to save hostages," Hawk said.

"How do we know there's any hostages to save?" Rex said.

"Who exactly is this Dr. Trevor?" Sutton said.

"Yeah...and if this is so "Top-Secret," how the hell did North Korea get wind of it?" Ivan said.

Sutton nodded. *Wow! For once, he shows intelligence.*

"I'd say we're covering up a hot mess," Terrie said. Hawk stuttered, immediately hating herself for doing so. She felt a mutiny billowing amongst the team. Everyone gathered in on her. Seymour stood silent, allowing it all to happen. Even Terrie, the one member who showed her a sliver of respect, had now turned against her.

"I can't..." She stuttered again. She grew tired of repeating the word classified. She became increasingly overwhelmed. With the pushback from the team, adjoined to her own increased fear stemming from her worries and suspicions regarding the situation, Hawk's mind became frantic.

She squared up against Seymour. "Seymour, if you don't see this mission through to completion, I will assure you the C.I.A. will crack down hard on you. That's not me threatening. I'm just letting you know the reality of it."

"I'm starting to think I'll take my chances," Rex said, eyeballing one of the shriveled corpses.

Several moments of silence followed.

"*Hatchling? Hatchling, come in.*" Charlie's voice broke the silence.

"Go ahead," Seymour answered.

"*Boss, I've been trying to get ahold of you. I'm uploading a feed to your monitor. You'll want to see this.*" Rex approached and turned, allowing Seymour to access the computer from his pack. Seymour turned it on. The monitor came to life.

The image was grainy for several seconds. It finally cleared, revealing an overhead view of the jungle. The high layer of jungle was a bright green, which sharply contrasted to the dead zone where they stood. As the drone moved, it captured an opening in the blanket of green. It was a paved trail. The drone followed the trail, coming to a bend.

Two Jeeps had parked at the bend, almost concealed by the canopy. Three soldiers, dressed in black tactical gear, had run up ahead, catching up with two others. Two other people, dressed in casual clothing, were lying face down. One had propped himself to his knees, only to be struck by the butt of a soldier's rifle.

"Those are two of the scientists," Hawk said.

The soldiers looked to one another, appearing to be in the midst of discussion. After a few seconds, they aimed their rifles downward, and opened fire. Even at the drone's altitude, they could see the bullets tearing into the backs of the two helpless scientists. The soldiers quickly boarded their Jeeps. The tires kicked up gravel as they floored the accelerators.

"Damn!" Easley said. Hawk put a hand over her forehead, angered and disgusted at what she had just witnessed. The mercenaries showed equal displeasure. Ivan and Rex held their M60s, winking toward Seymour.

"Well, well," Terrie said, unstrapping her sniper rifle. Seymour looked to his team. They were clearly ready to continue the mission.

"Eagle Nest," he said, "keep track of those Jeeps as best you can. Let us know where they go."

"*Yes sir,*" Charlie answered. Seymour switched off the monitor, and stuffed it back into Rex's pack.

Seymour looked at Agent Hawk. She was sweating, and breathing shallowly to maintain control. He looked at the gravesite, gazing over the strange pods, then back at the agent. "You're not completely sure what happened, are you?"

"I only have suspicions," she said. "I can't say for sure until we get to that command post." Seymour nodded, then reached for his backup weapon.

"Can you handle one of these?" he said. He held a submachine gun by the barrel, extending it toward her. She slowly accepted it, not intimidated by the weapon, but confused by the gesture.

"You're damn right I can," she said.

"Good," Seymour said. "I'd rather you be able to hold your own, now that you're stuck on this shithole with us."

"You got it," she said.

"Alright," Seymour said to his team. "We've got ourselves a bit of a stroll ahead of us," he said. "Keep a five-meter spread. We'll eliminate the hostiles, then continue toward the bunker. There, we'll let Agent Hawk collect what she needs, then we're out of here."

"Yes sir," they responded in unison.

"Keep low and move quiet," he said. He gestured toward Nagamine, who took point. In seconds, he vanished into the untouched jungle. Seymour was next, followed by Hawk and the rest of the unit.

Ivan and Rex, the last to move, took one final glance. "Fucked up shit...but then again, could've happened to better people," Rex whispered.

"Well..." Ivan switched the barrel on his M60 to full auto, "at least there's leftovers."

CHAPTER 14

Back up alarms sounded in loud beeps, echoing into the jungle, preceding the deep roar of the engine. Two large bulldozers plowed the area, sinking the cutting edge of their blades deep into the ground. The tracks rotated as the bulldozers pushed the dirt into enormous mounts.

Loud cracks sounded over the groaning engines. Men, with chainsaws in hand, rushed out of the way as the huge tree gave in to the deep slice they cut into its lower trunk. The tree smacked down into the earth, landing near two others which had shared the same fate. Sunlight poured through newly created holes in the canopy, shining down on the construction zone.

The guard stopped and looked toward the site as the tree touched down. He listened as his superior barked orders to his fellow troops. Remembering to not allow himself to get distracted, he continued his patrol. He clutched his rifle, ready to fire on anything that moved. It wasn't just training, nor was it instinct. It was a rare display of fear.

During his years of military training and indoctrination, he had been taught that his life had no value, other than to serve his superiors. There was no purpose other than to fight for his country, and eliminate the evil influence of western culture. He was not to fear injury or death. He was not to fear at all.

Only now did the soldier fail to live to that example. Looking into the jungle, unable to see anything over ten feet away, that forbidden emotion encompassed him. He slowly patrolled, watching out for any movement, ready to alert the remaining men.

His path led him to a posted guard, who rested in a machine gunner's nest atop a hill. The guard looked out to the jungle, and like the patroller, he kept watch. The guard made brief eye contact with the approaching patroller, then tilted his head left, instructing him to keep moving.

The patroller moved, constantly pointing his rifle whichever direction he looked. The guard stood, stiff as a statue, following the patroller with his eyes. As the patroller crossed over to the other side of his post, the guard kept his eyes planted on the seemingly infinite jungle. He registered every sight and sound; each tremor from the leaves, each sway of the tree branches, drips of rain water, the whistling from the breeze.

And amongst all these sounds; a faint rustling. It was a precise vibration, however feeble, off to the right. The guard turned to look.

Nagamine slashed his Ninjato. The blade effortlessly cut the throat just below the jawline, spilling blood down his shirt. The guard's body collapsed over the side of the gunner's nest, landing in the soft mud below.

Hearing a soft splash behind him, the patroller turned. He saw his comrade laying still beside the post where he stood. On the other side of that post, he saw a faint black blur of motion as Nagamine ducked.

The guard lifted his rifle, and opened his mouth to shout to the other troops. His shouts came out as nothing more than a muffle, as a hand reached from behind him, cupping his mouth.

Like a blowtorch through butter, the freshly sharpened blade entered his neck.

Seymour held the Korean tightly, twisting the elite SEAL knife, severing the vocals, blood vessels, and trachea. He gently lowered the dead patroller to the ground. Kneeling, he turned around and waved.

The rest of the team emerged from hiding and gathered around their leader. With a closed fist, he signaled for them to wait. He took his time, climbing into the gunner's nest. It gave him a view of the site, while keeping him obstructed from view. He pressed binoculars to his eyes and studied the area.

Charlie's drone had tracked the vehicles to a construction site, where Trevor had planned to build a new, high-tech facility. The North Koreans operated two bulldozers, which were actively clearing out a flat, open area. As they pushed, the dirt piled into high mounds, reaching heights of ten feet. Soldiers scattered about the work zone, each carrying an assault rifle. Many of them worked on the mounds with shovels, embedding other debris into the huge piles.

Others worked around the fallen trees, using a third bulldozer to away the fallen trees. Kicking up dirt with its tracks, the bulldozer slowly rolled the tree along, after soldiers had trimmed the branches. Seymour estimated they had cleared out nearly two hundred yards of open space so far. Several meters off to the right, a backhoe sat in the muck, twenty feet from the tree line. Nobody sat in its platform.

Looking to the center of the site, Seymour identified three temper tents. He aimed the glasses inside, hoping to possibly identify a hostage.

However, he could not see. The tents were spread out several meters apart, two of them near the upper side of the site, the third isolated further down. Near that one was a much smaller tent, covering a large long-range radio unit. The two Jeeps seen in the monitor were parked near the two tents on the upper side, unoccupied.

Seymour glanced at the opening they had created in the tree line, then at the clearing of jungle within the site.

Son of a bitch. They're trying to radio for rescue. They're making space for a chopper to touch down.

A solder stood at the radio unit, actively attempting to make a call. Seymour could hear the faint static, indicative that the signal was not making it through the trees.

After making a rough count of the soldiers hurrying about, he scanned the glasses to the other side. On two corners on the opposite side of the site were guard posts, one to the northeast, one southeast near the unmanned backhoe. After studying further, he determined those were the only two.

He lowered himself down behind the gunner's nest, and looked to his team. They huddled around him, awaiting instructions.

"They have two guard posts on the other side," he said. "We'll have to take those out first. Nagamine, you take the one on the northeast corner, I'll take the southeast one.

"Ivan, Rex, work your way toward the mounds. Keep out of sight. When Nagamine and I are done, I'm gonna light up the loggers and draw their fire. Nobody fire until their attention is on me. Once they are, you two light them up with the M60s. Terrie, pick off the radio man and the bulldozers. Craig, Easley, Hawk, use those as cover and move in. Don't fire on the tents unless necessary. Our objective may still be inside. Move."

The team spread. Seymour and Nagamine moved right, moving around the north side of the perimeter to the guard post. Ivan and Rex went left to take their position to the southwest mounds.

Hidden by the leaves and shadows, Terrie perched along the side of the gunner's nest. She planted the stilts over a thick branch, and adjusted her sights. The position gave her excellent view, while keeping her hidden. Hawk waited behind the nest with Sutton and Easley, waiting for the signal to attack.

Terrie glanced back at the anxious agent, worried that she was about to lose her cool. To Terrie's surprise, Hawk appeared relaxed and ready. Perhaps she had spent more time on the frontlines than the team suspected. They could only hope.

CHAPTER
15

Nagamine pressed his stomach to the ground as the unsuspecting guard turned his gaze. Like a snake in a flowerbed, the merc lay still. Several seconds passed, and the guard finally looked away, scanning another direction. Nagamine pushed up on his toes and fingertips, keeping low as he approached.

The guard post was a wooden platform resting high on a compacted dirt mound, resting against the thick trunk of a two-hundred-foot tree. The mound itself was about eight feet high. It would be difficult for Nagamine to climb that height and take out the guard without creating noise and a struggle.

He reached along his vest, pulling out two small knives. Clutching one in each hand, he inched closer, careful not to disturb the plants around him. He kept his eyes locked on the target, observing his every move. The guard seemed to have a routine, looking in various directions for several seconds at a time. As Nagamine observed, the guard checked each area in the same order, looking to his right, his left, then looking back toward the site. Each time he glanced right, Nagamine froze, resuming approach when the guard looked away.

He rested on his elbows and knees underneath a bamboo bush. Peeking between the leaves, he watched the guard, determining the right moment to strike. He didn't want him to fire and alert the other soldiers. Also, he didn't want him to yell out, or fall off the platform, which would draw attention. He waited, watching the guard turn left. After a few seconds, he turned around to look at the site.

Nagamine had his chance. He lifted himself onto his knees, and launched both knives at his target. The guard started turning, just as Nagamine calculated. In the midst of his turn, the blades simultaneously embedded into his neck. One struck below the left ear, severing the carotid artery; the other through his trachea, preventing him from calling out.

After a brief gag, the soldier slumped down against the tree, hardly making a sound.

Nagamine glanced behind him. Seymour emerged from behind another bush, and nodded to his fellow warrior.

That guy's good. He waved his finger toward the post, instructing Nagamine to take position and wait for his signal to attack. As he did, Seymour began sneaking toward the next post.

Rex spat out a mouthful of dirt. Lying flat on his stomach, he crawled under bushes and over anthills, ignoring the bites from the little critters as he moved toward the southeast corner.

Ivan trailed behind him, following along the same path. Two large men built like Greek warriors, they had no choice but to keep low to remain undetected. In his mind, Ivan cursed Nagamine and Terrie, briefly envying their smaller statures which allowed for stealthier movements.

The mounds cast giant shadows into the already murky jungle, helping the two giants to blend in. Having reached their destinations just past the mounds, Ivan and Rex distanced themselves from each other, peeking through the vines at the several huge tree trunks. They listened to the groaning engines as the bulldozers pushed more dirt into the piles. With the position of the mounds and the trees pushed into the southern perimeter, Ivan came to a realization.

These guys are creating barricades.

Seymour gradually worked his way around the perimeter, calculating every step as he neared the final guard post. The soldier stood high on his platform, carefully keeping track of any movement coming from the jungle. Seymour froze and waited for his watchful gaze to turn elsewhere.

This guard was not stupid, nor lazy. He was thoroughly observant. Hidden in the brush, Seymour watched his target. This guard's uniform was not clean. Dried mud was caked all over him, leading Seymour to believe he had recently encountered some type of skirmish. To sneak up on this lookout undetected, Seymour would have to move fast and accurately.

Nothing he hadn't done before.

He held his SOG knife, pointing the blade down. With his free hand, he touched along the dirt, looking for anything to distract the guard. He located a chunk of bark, then looked for a place to put it. Seeing the paranoid appearance, he determined that throwing the decoy into a pile of bushes might illicit a nervous, accidental discharge.

Seymour gradually moved left, drawing closer to the perimeter. He eyed a clear opening near the backhoe, where no guards were present. With the guard looking into the jungle, Seymour tossed the heavy piece of wood behind the post. It landed and split.

The guard turned toward the sound, now looking toward the site.

No longer in the line of sight, Seymour stood and rushed the post. The guard turned back, just in time to feel the blade enter his throat. Seymour lowered the guard down off the post. He sheathed his knife and held his HK 416. He moved around the guard post and studied the site once more, ready to begin shooting.

He eyeballed the backhoe, then the scattered soldiers working along the mounds and trees. Looking past the barricades, he knew Ivan and Rex were in position. However, he knew it was unlikely the soldiers would bunch up in a crowd.

He decided to adjust his plan.

He emerged from the tree line. Though in the open, he was unseen by the unsuspecting soldiers as they were focused on their work. He hurried to the backhoe, taking cover behind it. He snatched two of his C-4 blocks from his vest. After activating the sensors, he placed them into the platform.

The nearby rumbling from one of the bulldozers caused him to duck behind the backhoe. The huge construction vehicle moved on its tracks, passing nearby the backhoe. Seymour peeked around the front. He watched it push a large collection of grit into the perimeter on the other side of the fallen trees, then back up to start another round.

Seymour moved toward the back of the backhoe, again watching the soldiers to make sure nobody was looking toward him. He waited as the bulldozer backed past the backhoe. As it did, Seymour sprinted toward it. He leapt onto the moving tracks, immediately pulling himself onto the platform.

He whipped the cab enclosure door open and burst inside. The driver shuddered with shock and reached for his firearm. Seymour plunged his knife into his chest, inflating his lung. Seymour repeatedly stabbed the driver in the torso, then into the throat. With the driver dead, his foot lifted from the hydraulic accelerator, stopping the vehicle.

"What the fuck's he doing?" Terrie whispered to herself, watching Seymour through her sniper scope. She observed as he planted two more blocks of C-4 onto the bulldozer's converter. He disappeared behind the hidden side. Scanning left, she saw two soldiers slowly stepping toward the bulldozer, shouting for the driver to move.

Knowing Seymour, he has a plan.

Holding their rifles down, the soldiers could only see the soldier slumped in the cab enclosure. A moment prior, he had been driving fine. They suspected he was tired and taking a rest, something they would not permit. Angry from his lack of response, they marched forward.

A green blinking light gave them pause. A small object, the size of a coffee cup, rested on the converter. A tiny bulb was at its center.

They had only just begun to realize what it was, when they saw Seymour step out between the backhoe and bulldozer. His HK416 was shouldered. The suppressor was detached.

Seymour cracked a grin.

"Good morning!" He squeezed the trigger. Three-round bursts ruptured the skulls of both soldiers, their bodies falling hard against the ground.

CHAPTER 16

All eyes turned toward the sound of gunfire. Two of their men were down, with a single shooter standing before them. Shouts of directives echoed through the air, and the soldiers opened fire.

Firing back blindly, Seymour dashed back into the woods, taking cover behind the tree near the guard post. An endless barrage of bullets tore through the air around him, forcing him to keep as low as possible.

Dozens of soldiers rushed the perimeter, firing their assault rifles toward the jungle in which the assailant disappeared. They spread out to avoid bunching up, tearing the jungle apart with their munitions.

Bullets passing around him and splintering the thick tree, Seymour dug for the remote trigger. He extended the antennae, igniting a green light. He pressed the trigger.

The backhoe and bulldozer erupted into massive balls of flame. The thunderous boom of the blasts ripped across the site. Glass from the other bulldozers shattered. Caught in the blast, several North Korean soldiers rolled along the ground, completely ablaze. As the fire stretched out, it forced several soldiers away from the blast zone, grouping them together near the fallen trees.

With their machine guns mounted over the trunks, Ivan and Rex opened fire. Bullets soared from the two M60s, mowing down the gathered platoon. Blood and body parts flew in one large gory fountain.

"Like fish in a fucking barrel!" Ivan yelled, grinning ear to ear as he blasted the enemy soldiers.

"Ten! Eleven! Fourteen…" Rex counted out loud.

"Those last three were mine!" Ivan shouted. They continued hitting the platoon, all while endlessly bickering about their "scores."

With the enemy fire drawn off, Seymour burst from the tree line. Two soldiers took cover from the M60s behind the burning backhoe. They saw Seymour and turned to fire. He shot first, putting several rounds center mass in each of them. After they dropped dead, he rushed past the burning backhoes.

A soldier hurried to the radio tent. He had just clutched his radio when his torso exploded into pink mist.

Terrie watched her target collapse and scanned the scope left. The soldiers were moving the remaining bulldozers to provide cover from the M60s.

"Oh, no you don't," she said. She squeezed the trigger, sending a bullet into one of the cab enclosures. Blood sprayed onto the dashboard as it passed through the driver. The vehicle came to a halt. After adjusting her sights, Terrie sniped the second driver.

Sutton and Easley began their run, tearing toward the nearest tent. Several soldiers backtracked to the north, while others were still grabbing weapons from the tents.

Sutton fired on the retreating soldiers, dropping several, while Easley focused on those emerging from the nearest tent.

At the same time, Nagamine rushed the opposite tent, dodging fire from several soldiers. He took cover behind a large stump from one of the fallen trees. The shooting died down, and the soldiers started reloading. Nagamine emerged from cover, pointing his MP5 forward. A spray of bullets launched from his weapon, tearing into the three enemy soldiers. After reloading, he entered the first tent, immediately shooting down two more soldiers.

The tent was comprised mostly of makeshift beds, rations, and some weapons. No hostages. He tore through the opposite entrance. To his right, a soldier saw him and aimed his rifle.

Like an airbag going off, his chest suddenly ripped open. Blood sprayed from his front and back, and the soldier fell to the ground, dead.

Terrie's voice came through the comm. *"Saved your ass."* Nagamine looked toward her post, knowing she could see him through her sights. He smiled for her, and continued to press on.

With most of the soldiers retreating to the north side, Ivan and Rex picked up their M60s and moved inward.

Three soldiers took cover behind one of the nearby bulldozers. Believing they had the drop on the two brutes, they emerged to open fire.

Ivan, aware of their presence, had his M60 already pointed. Bullets ripped from the barrel into the soldiers, tearing their chests into minced meat. The third, realizing he wouldn't be able to hold his position against them, dashed toward the jungle. Ivan squeezed his finger on the trigger, sending a five-round burst after the runner.

The bullets pierced the runner's neck, tearing through the spinal column and muscles. As the soldier fell, his head detached from his body and rolled several inches away like a bowling ball.

"Oh, MAN! That's just wrong," Ivan said in a fit of laughter.

Sutton and Easley spread out, as a group of soldiers burst from the tent. They fired at the two mercs, narrowly missing as they both ducked for cover.

Two of them, moving side-by-side, pursued Sutton, who was in the midst of reloading.

"Shit," he said to himself as he ran toward one of the surviving trees on the site. A soldier, who had retreated from Rex and Ivan, had already taken refuge there. He saw the Doc approach. Alarmed, he whipped around and began firing.

Sutton drew his Beretta M9 and emptied half of the mag into the soldier's chest. As the Korean fell, Sutton aimed his pistol past the tree, where another armed soldier approached. Depressing the trigger rapidly, he emptied the mag. The bullets pierced the soldier's belly, doubling him over as he squeezed the trigger of his rifle. Several shots rang from the gun and tore up the ground as he fell on his face, dead. Sutton looked back over his shoulder. The other two soldiers closed in, their weapons pointed right at him. He turned to aim his pistol, but saw the slide locked back.

"Fuck."

With the nearest soldier centered in her crosshairs, Terrie squeezed the trigger. The round zipped from the barrel or her rifle. It entered the soldier's left ribcage, ripping through his lungs and stomach before exiting out the right ribcage and piercing the second soldier.

Both dropped dead in their tracks. Sutton breathed a grateful sigh of relief and quickly reloaded.

Easley dove into the jungle as four soldiers pursued him. As he disappeared, they hurried toward the Jeeps. They boarded them two-by-two. The engines came on with a roar.

Flesh, blood, and clothing covered the interior of the Jeeps, as Agent Hawk ambushed the group. She emptied the magazine of her submachine gun into the four soldiers, who all slumped dead in their seats. She reloaded, then moved into the tent.

Two soldiers stood up, having just assembled a large machine gun. They shouted in Korean, and picked up the gun to fire on her. Already aiming, she fired a burst, tearing open the triggerman's upper torso. She fired at the other, putting two rounds in his stomach. He knelt over. Though in severe agony, he was still determined to fight. As he drew his sidearm, Hawk put a round in his head, splitting his skull like a ripe melon.

Two soldiers rushed from the southern tent, only to be gunned down by Seymour. After they fell to the dirt, he sprinted to the entrance. Several soldiers, having retreated from both the northern side and the M60 fire, had rushed this way for reloading. Seymour dropped to one knee and began firing, taking out the nearest soldier first.

"No hostages," he yelled out, gunning down another soldier.

The walls of the tent juddered violently as a storm of bullets ripped through. Firing from outside the tent, Ivan and Rex yelled obscenities. Their bullets shredded soldiers and the structures. With nothing to hold it up, the tent collapsed over a half-dozen dead troops.

Seymour backed away from the downed tent, examining his surroundings. Several bodies littered the construction zone. Smoke billowed into the sky. All shooting had ceased. His mercenary team spread over the site, securing the area.

A rustling of green drew Seymour's attention. He looked to the west, seeing several swaying plants. Behind them, he could hear the cracking of twigs and brush.

"Nine o'clock!" he shouted. He sprinted into the tree line. Dodging trees left and right, he followed the sound of running footsteps.

A gunshot rang, and chunks of bark exploded from a nearby tree. Seymour dropped and rolled as several more bullets passed by. He came up to one knee, with his rifle pointed. One of the soldiers stepped around a tree, unsuspectingly into his line of sight.

Seymour double-tapped, killing him. Two other soldiers emerged and returned fire. Seymour took cover behind a tree. The soldiers continued firing, pelting the trunk with projectiles. Seymour crouched low. Realizing they were not about to let up, he blindly pointed his rifle around the tree and shot back.

The soldiers withdrew deeper into the woods. Seymour emerged from cover and continued his chase. The soldiers ran, stumbling over the jumbled landscape. Each turn led them into another tree, another bush, another hill.

Confused, overwhelmed, and exhausted, the soldiers stopped. They turned around to fire their weapons at their pursuer. Seymour, already in position, squeezed the trigger. Two bullets struck one of the soldiers square in the shoulder, knocking him down in a pool of his own blood. The magazine emptied.

Seymour dropped the weapon and drew his revolver. With no time to aim, he fired from the hip. Each .357 round caused a heavy jolt as they fatally pierced the other soldier's center mass.

As his target fell, Seymour allowed himself a relaxing breath. He glanced down to his rifle. As he leaned down to pick it up, he noticed the footprints left by the soldiers. Two sets led to the ones he just encountered.

Then there was a third set, not belonging to either of the parties he had just neutralized, which banked to the right. Like a bolt of lightning through his body, Seymour's defensive instincts kicked in.

The third soldier jumped from around a tree. He pointed the barrel of his rifle at Seymour's head to shoot him point blank.

Seymour grabbed the weapon by the barrel, forcing it towards the sky just as the soldier pulled the trigger. Bullets ripped into the canopy as the men fought. The Korean struggled, fighting to regain control of the weapon. Looking his enemy in the eye, Seymour thrust the weapon forward, cracking the barrel against the soldier's forehead. Seymour yanked back on the gun, pulling it free from the dazed soldier's grip. With a swift kick, he planted his right boot square in the soldier's chest, knocking him back several feet.

Just the distance he needed.

Seymour pointed the rifle and fired, killing the soldier with his own gun. Seymour tossed the weapon aside and began looking for the revolver which had been dropped in the scuffle.

Another rustling in the ground alerted him. One of the soldiers he had shot was still alive.

"Oh, for crying out loud," Seymour said to himself. The soldier grunted as he slowly got on his knees, holding his rifle in his left arm.

Seymour's eyes located the revolver. As he was about to sprint, machine gun fire tore through the jungle, finding their way to the soldier. Bullets chopped through his torso, shoulders, legs, and even his face, erasing any and all identity. The soldier rolled backwards, reduced to nothing but a shredded blood bag.

Seymour picked up his revolver and turned around. Holding their machine guns, Ivan and Rex strolled from the blockade of trees.

"I hit him first," Rex said.

"My ass!" Ivan said. "That counts as mine!"

"Your mother's ass!" Rex barked.

Seymour shook his head. *If they weren't good soldiers... I swear...*

CHAPTER
17

The jungle was an endless maze of green, seemingly leading to nothing other than more green. The soldier kept his rifle shouldered as he ran, resting his finger on the trigger. Saliva and bile built up in his throat, and his mind was a whirlwind of tactical planning.

After seeing his fellow comrades overtaken by the strike team leader, the soldier realized he was no match and had chosen to flee. He knew three others had made it out of the site, and he hoped to regroup.

Blinded by the dense jungle, he ran faster than he ever had. Leaves and branches scratched his face and uniform, constantly slowing him down. His lungs burned, his eyes watered, and his mouth dried. He tore under a bamboo bush, closing his eyes as the leaves slapped the ridge along his nose.

Temporarily blinded, he was completely unaware that his foot had landed in a bed of vines.

His rifle launched from his hands and the soldier tumbled forward. Propelled by a thousand yards of momentum, the soldier bounced along the terrain, rolling along the downward slope of a hill. Shouts of foul language rang from his vocals as his legs hit a tree, causing his body to turn like a lever as a combination of force and gravity pulled him down the slope.

Laying on his back, he opened his eyes. All he saw was one giant green blur. The world spun around him. His stomach churned and his legs ached. His energy nearly spent, he pushed himself up onto his hands and knees. Taking in deep breaths, he collected his wits. With his vision back in focus, he looked around him. He needed to locate his weapon. Otherwise, venturing further into the jungle was suicide.

Or would it make any difference?

The threat of the strike suddenly subsided from his mind, replaced by the realization of his situation. He wasn't concerned with pursuit from the enemy soldiers.

His heart raced, driven not by the intense physical activity, but from the comprehension of his vulnerability. He thought of what his platoon was trying to barricade before the surprise attack. No longer did he have the visibility from the newly cleared perimeter. He no longer had access to the remaining explosives and flamethrowers, and the assistance of the forty-three remaining comrades.

He whipped himself around. He slouched slightly, ready to run. Something in the distance had rustled the trees. The soldier backed away. He turned, deciding on a path. Every direction offered no visibility. The canopy blocked the sun, leaving him in a dark ravine. Every so often, the wind would sweep through the trees, offering brief streams of light.

Every shadow was full of menace. Every plant served as a screen, concealing the presence beyond. The soldier silently breathed through his nose, taking in the sounds of the surrounding jungle. He was being watched.

He suddenly regretted his decision to retreat into the jungle, and not combat the strike team. In the midst of battle, being overwhelmed by a superior force, he did not consider that death from gunfire was a preferable alternative to what waited for him.

Echoes from within taunted him. Another small gust of wind brushed through the trees. Shimmers of light broke through, briefly illuminating the murky floor. A speck of light caught the soldier's eye. A reflection, looking like a star in the dirt.

The soldier rushed toward the reflection. He had found his rifle, laying against a large root. He snatched it up, and began brushing the dirt from the slide. He removed the mag and checked for dirt in the barrel of the gun.

The light faded away, taken over by a shadow. Moments later, another breeze swept the trees. The soldier froze. He was still shrouded in shadow. Something else was blocking the light.

The soldier slowly turned. He looked up.

It stood two feet taller than him, gazing at him with an eyeless face.

Like a jolt of lightning, he felt its barb puncture his stomach.

Involuntary muscle twitches overtook his body. His jaw clicked, and his throat tightened. He tried to raise his rifle, but his arms failed to move. Foam filled his mouth and poured from his lips. The weapon dropped from his grip, his hands still frozen as if ready to aim.

He fell on his back. Paralyzed in the dirt, he stared upward into the canopy. The only thing he was in control of was his mind, which was a whirlwind of terror. He was silently screaming.

It lifted its barb from the inferior victim, and stood silently. Blending into the trees, it felt the vibrations from within the jungle.

It heard the thunder of battle raging nearby. The disturbance had stopped, and thus many of its quarry were now dead. However, new vibrations entered into its nervous system.

New prey now lurked within the island. New hosts for its seed. New potential for its species to spread.

CHAPTER
18

The fire died down, exposing blackened metal from the ravaged remains from the construction vehicles. The black smoke turned a faded grey, which faded through the opening in the canopy.

The mercenaries ransacked the tents, looking for any possible clues for the whereabouts of the remaining scientists.

"Remember, I got the three by the bulldozers, so that puts me ahead by five," Ivan said to Rex.

"Yeah, but when we first lit them up, I was the first to shoot. I took down at least five before you even got cracking."

"Bull-SHIT!" Ivan said. "I got to shooting right as you did."

"Oh, for crying out loud!" Sutton said. "Give it a rest, why don't you?"

"Eh," Ivan said, waving him off. "We'll determine this later."

"Fine," Rex said. Sutton glared at them. His mind swelled with suspicion. *Please, God, tell me they weren't using body cams.* He tried to ignore the banter as he continued searching the south temper tent. It had been completely shredded by the machine gun fire. Underneath its collapsed walls were the bodies of several enemy soldiers. He went through their pockets, looking for any notes Hawk could find of use.

"Nothing here," he called out.

"Damn it," Hawk grunted, throwing a pile of papers aside. They scattered like leaves in autumn. She knelt by the body of another soldier and began digging through his pockets, hoping to find any written notes regarding the research of Dr. Trevor's team. Each failed attempt elevated her frustration.

Seymour had his team collect any munitions compatible with their weapons. Being a career soldier, whether private-sector or military, he developed a certain sixth sense. He wasn't worried so much about any possible remaining military force on the island. Rather, his mind kept wandering back to the strange gravesite, the abandoned outpost at the southside cliff, and the devastation at the harbor. Though they had eliminated the hostile force, responsible for the abduction and murder of scientists, U.S. citizens no less, that sixth sense of his was sounding off in his mind like an air-raid siren.

The presence of threat was not what troubled Seymour. It was that he wasn't sure what the threat was. Initially, after investigating the harbor, he believed it to be a secondary strike team sent by a rival nation. Then they came across the "dead jungle," and the resulting effects wrought on the soldiers and wildlife.

He began to feel something he rarely felt since completing his first SEAL mission; a small degree of apprehension.

"There's nothing here," he said. He stood up, having checked the contents of the tent.

"I think you're right," Hawk said. She stood up. Seymour couldn't help but notice the mild twitches in her body. She leaned on a table, appearing notably exhausted.

"It's been a while, hasn't it?" he said.

"Beg your pardon?"

"Since your last firefight," Seymour said.

"Oh," Hawk said. She looked at the submachine gun, still strapped over her shoulder. "I guess I'm a little rusty." She unstrapped her weapon and held it back to Seymour. He glanced at it and shook his head.

"Hang on to it," he said. "And by the way, you did fine."

Terrie's voice echoed from the jungle. "Coming out!" Seymour stepped from the tent, meeting Terrie and Nagamine as they emerged from the northwest perimeter.

"Did you find anything?" he asked.

"He found two sets of tracks," Terrie said. "A single individual made it off to the southwest. Then another set, retreating to the north."

"How many?" Seymour asked. Nagamine held up three fingers.

"Oh, come on!" Rex said, looking at the Japanese tracker. "We KNOW you can speak English! What? Do you just like to let the lady do the talking?"

"At least he thinks of me as a lady," Terrie remarked.

"You're complicated. You're like…your own breed. You like macho stuff like shooting people, then you get back to the world and want to go salsa dancing and be taken out for dinner," Rex said. He looked back to Nagamine. "Just say one English word. Just ONE."

Nagamine stared at him. "Prick."

"How 'bout *clowns*," Sutton whispered.

"Alright, enough with the nonsense," Seymour said. Recognizing the authority in his voice, the group silenced the banter. Seymour dug out his map. "Hawk, where would you estimate our position to be?" Hawk glanced at it.

"We're here," she said, marking an X on the map with a pen. "That's where the team had left their construction vehicles. The terrain matches the description. The bunker is over a click to the northwest."

"That's the direction the three remaining soldiers went," he said. "Good. Two birds, one stone." He turned toward Terrie and Nagamine. "What about the fourth?"

"We...don't know," she said. "The trail...it just stopped at a certain point." Nagamine nodded.

"Stopped?" Seymour said.

"Just stopped. Like he had just vanished," Terrie said.

"Look, it's a thick jungle," Hawk said. "It's very easy to lose track of anyone here."

"Not for Nagamine," Seymour said. "He could track a termite through an anthill."

"...tell you whether it screwed the queen," Rex chimed in.

"POINT is..." Seymour glared at Rex, who promptly shut up, "...we still have hostiles in the area. We need to keep our wits about. We're gonna secure the bunker, let the doctor do her thing, then vacate this island."

"Wait, uh, Boss...if I may?" Ivan raised his hand. Sutton perked his head, surprised at the rare display of civility. Seymour nodded to him. "Frankly, sir, why aren't *these* guys at the bunker?" Ivan pointed to all the slain soldiers. "What I mean is, look around. The mounds! The trees! These guys weren't just trying to make a landing zone. They were barricading themselves against something."

"Something?" Easley said, expressing a smile. "Not *someone?*"

"After seeing all 'em dead soldiers and animals with the weird stuff growing out of 'em, I don't know," Ivan said. "I don't know if visiting that bunker is a good idea."

"Whether it's a good idea or not is out of the question," Hawk said. "One thing it's not, is a choice. We HAVE to go there." Ivan stared at her, then looked to Seymour.

"Then let's stop wasting time," Seymour said. "Maintain awareness. We still have hostiles in the area. We'll finish this then move back to the harbor, and have Charlie extract us."

It watched the team follow their leader out of the construction zone, leaving the devastation behind them. Perched high in a tree, blending into the surrounding colors, it gazed upon the carnage.

So many potential hosts lay in the dirt, now inadequate to its needs. However, new hosts now lurked about. It had watched them, studying their vocals as they conversed. The creature, while incapable of producing speech or sound, contained an advanced intelligence allowing it to discern languages. During light-years of travels, it learned of the cultures of various species, whether advanced or primitive. On this new planet, the various human languages it had been exposed to was by far the simplest of intelligent beings.

It knew where they were going. More importantly, it now had access to further hosts. A new plan took shape.

Driven by its biological imperative, it lowered itself from the tree, following the trail set by its new prey.

CHAPTER
19

The team came around to a patch of trees ranging between forty and sixty feet in height. They were much younger than the other trees spread throughout the island. Hawk gazed up at the decreased canopy.

"We're close," she said to Seymour.

They pushed through another two hundred feet of jungle, until finally a small clearing opened up. A slight hill rested in the middle of that clearing, leading to the Japanese bunker. Seymour and the mercenaries kneeled in the bushes, keeping their rifles raised as they looked upon the cement structure. The trees and plants around it had been cleared for a twenty-foot distance. Scattered all over the ground were the rusted remains of Type 92 machine guns and other weaponry left over by Imperial Japan after World War 2. Most of the weapons were in pieces, scattered across the terrain amongst shell casings and spent cartridges. The grass was littered by a greenish-grey dust, with chunks of gravel littered about.

A remnant of a nation's dark past, the bunker stood at thirty feet high, with a width of a hundred-and-fifty feet. The exterior had worn over the years. Small cracks formed throughout the foundation, though not enough to compromise its stability. The cement had turned a shade of yellow, and moss had gained years of growth onto the structure. Multiple orange cables stretched out from the open doorway, connecting to a large generator unit.

Behind the command post was an incomplete trench. Nearly eight feet deep, it extended from the building in a jagged line, stopping at a dead end near the trees.

"We're in position," Ivan whispered over the comm.

"In position," Terrie said.

"Myself and Easley are in position," Sutton said. The team had made a perimeter around the bunker, maintaining a visibility on all corners.

Seymour and Nagamine were the first to step out of cover. Seymour took position near the generator, while the tracker checked for signs. Nagamine made his way along the building, gradually checking the ground. The soil was covered with old prints of soldiers moving away from the building. Tire tracks led out to an open trail. They too, were at least a day old. Nagamine made his way back to the main entrance. He looked to Seymour and shook his head. There were no prints leading toward the bunker. The remaining soldiers had not returned.

"All units move in," Seymour said. Quick and silent as fleeting shadows, the team moved in toward the bunker. Ivan and Rex took positions on each corner of the front entrance, while the rest regrouped with Seymour. Like a SWAT team ready to commence a drug bust, they converged on the door.

"Ivan, Rex, Easley, you three maintain a perimeter, and cover our backs. The rest of you, on me," Seymour said. He pushed against the steel door, which opened with a loud clunking noise. Placing a night-vision goggle over his right eye, Seymour entered, followed immediately by Terrie, who substituted her sniper rifle for her H&K. The door led to a dark hallway which immediately turned left for ten feet, leading to a right turn. They passed by another open doorway, entering a large open space. Streams of sunlight passed through machine gun loopholes in the wall, enough to provide visibility without the goggles. They removed their night vision, they looked at the several computer panels lined across the south wall. On the opposite side, several communication patch panels, covered in dust and grit, remained in place.

Sutton and Nagamine entered, followed by Hawk. Sutton gazed at the old panels. For seventy years they sat untouched in this room.

"This was the operation room. Damn, they really did use this as a communications station," he said.

"This deep into the jungle?" Terrie said. "How would they get a signal out?"

"Well, the trees were shorter," Seymour said. "Clearly, when this place was built, they landscaped the surrounding area. Everything's been growing back gradually since." He looked at the modern computers. "Agent, would these contain your data?"

"Not those," she said. She pointed to the far wall. "That one."

"Oh shit!" Terrie exclaimed. The "far wall" was not a wall at all. It was one massive supercomputer, nearly twenty feet in length. In the dim light, it simply appeared as though it was the wall itself. "Damn...what does a computer like that even do?"

"Configurates data," Hawk said.

"My iPhone configurates data," Terrie said, amazement still in her voice. "What the hell kind-of-data does that thing configure?" Hawk didn't answer, and followed Seymour. There were two doorways at the corner of the room. He checked the first, which led to a vacant office. It contained leftover armaments, and a machine gun loophole. He pushed the second one open and entered into another large room. It was the bunker's planning room, which was converted into another computer lab. Pieces of old tables, broken down by age, had been pushed into the corner, making space for modern equipment. More monitors lined the inside wall. On the opposite wall, streams of sunlight seeped in through more machine-gun loopholes. Just over eighteen inches wide, they were used to allow repelling fire against enemy forces. Several rolling chairs had been pushed out from their tables, some completely knocked over, as if their occupants had left in a rush.

Seymour felt a crunch beneath his boot. He stepped back and looked down, shining a light onto the floor. A broken glass had scattered all over the concrete floor.

"Looks like someone couldn't hold their drink," Sutton remarked.

"Whatever the case is, they left here in a hurry," Seymour said, glancing at Hawk. He walked through the large room until he came to a closed door on the other side. He carefully peered inside before stepping in completely. He had entered a storage room, full of rations marked with Korean labeling. In the corner of the room were three large metal fuel barrels. "These guys really don't care about sanitation, do they?" he said to himself, before adjusting his microphone. "Ivan, Rex, this is Seymour."

"*Yeah...*" Rex's voice answered.

"I need you guys to put your muscles to use," Seymour said. "Come get these fuel barrels and take them to the generator. See if we can get some power in this place."

"*You got it,*" Rex said.

"Don't we want to secure the rest of the bunker?" Hawk asked.

"I'd rather we get the lights on, first," Seymour answered. "I don't want any surprises."

Ivan bared teeth and grunted as he wrapped his arms around the large barrel, bending his knees to lift. Rex watched and began to snicker. Ivan glared at his friend, who turned away to grab a second barrel.

"The hell you laughing at?"

"Good lord, dude...at least buy it a drink first," Rex said. He knelt to grab ahold of the next barrel.

"Oh yeah?" Ivan straightened his legs, lifting the heavy barrel over his shoulders. "*You're* the one who's bending over. Just sayin'."

"Should I just shut that door and let you two get it over with?" Terrie remarked. Both men looked at her, their faces souring with disgust. Ivan, deciding to play along, forced a smile.

"Why? You jealous?" Chuckling to himself, he carried the barrel past her, turning left to exit into the operations room. Rex lifted his fuel barrel and followed. Their eyes strained as the sunlight greeted them outside the bunker. After placing his barrel beside the generator, Ivan unscrewed the cap. Rex set his barrel down alongside Ivan's, then stretched his shoulder out.

As he did, he looked at Easley. The skinnier mercenary patrolled around the building, watchfully keeping an eye on the tree line.

"Hey, kid," Rex said. Easley stopped and looked over at him. "Be careful dude. You're a target in plain sight. There's not much to use as cover outside this building."

"Got it," Easley said, making a "peace" sign with his fingers before continuing his patrol.

The fuel cap for the generator was located along the side, as the machine itself was nearly as tall as Ivan. He unscrewed the cap and inserted the plastic funnel. Lifting with his legs, he tipped the barrel toward the funnel. Gas guzzled into the enormous fuel tank, gradually liberating the container of its immense weight. Within minutes, the entire tank had been drained.

"Damn," he said. He knew the generator was big, but did not expect it to contain such a large amount of fuel. "Whatever they were doing in there, they were using up a lot of juice."

Rex yanked on the ignition cord. The gears slowly turned and died. Rex yanked again. The gears turned and sparked. The generator roared to life.

Seymour listened to the generator start up. Lights started illuminating from the computers as they came back to life. Overhead lights in the operations room began to flicker. Dull mechanical sounds echoed through the facility as the power spread throughout the facility. As the lights in the planning room came on, Seymour and the team looked around, finally able to clearly see their surroundings. Seymour looked to Hawk.

"Alright, download your…"

Blaring audio alarms pounded their eardrums. Red strobing lights flashed from the ceiling. Seymour reactively raised his weapon, scanning the area for any threat.

A voice sounded from the speakers.

"*Security Alert! Containment breach! Security Alert! Containment Breach!*"

The bunker had gone from quiet and dark to disorienting and chaotic. The team hurried throughout the bunker. They checked along the walls, computers, and radio panels, desperately looking for any device that would silence the deafening alarm. Adrenaline shooting through her body, Terrie moved back into the operations room. The flashing lights illuminated the room, bringing to life details she didn't notice prior. One of which was another doorway. Sharing the same color as the wall, while also being covered in layers of dust, it was easily concealed in the dim light, and they had moved right past it. Grains of dust billowed into a thin cloud as Terrie opened the door.

Peering inside, she saw a spiraling stairway leading up to the upper level. "Boss!" Terrie called to Seymour. Barely hearing her call, Seymour rushed over to her. She pointed to the stairway.

Seymour hated stairways. They always made for an easy ambush site when securing a facility. He pointed his weapon upward and started up. Terrie went up next, followed by Hawk, while Sutton and Nagamine remained to locate the alarm panel.

The strobing lights nearly blinded Seymour as he moved up the spiraling staircase. It ended at a closed metal door. He grabbed the lever and pushed it downward. The door opened slowly by mechanical gears. Not having the patience to wait, Seymour thrust a kick into it. The door burst open, and Seymour stormed inside, rifle pointed.

Red and green lights flashed throughout the enormous room. The siren, like that of a tornado drill, was even louder. Terrie moved up the stairway, stopping momentarily at the upstairs doorway. Her ears felt as though they would burst from the overload of noise. Gritting her teeth, she entered the room.

Seymour turned to Hawk as she entered. "Alright, Agent, how do we turn this damn thing off?" Though standing next to her, he had to shout. Hawk scanned the room. Her eyes observed several large panels to the far end of the large room. One was indeed a circuit panel. She dashed over to it, dodging lab tables and scattered supplies like asteroids.

She tore the panel doors open and studied the switches. The flashing lights and blaring noise made reading the labels nearly impossible. Finally, she located the emergency alarm panel. She flicked the breaker switch, causing the strobing lights to vanish. The flick of another switch killed the audibles.

The command post went silent, lit now only by normal overhead florescent lights. Drawing a huge sigh of relief, Hawk turned and leaned back on the wall. Her heart was still racing, having just settled from the tense firefight. Her head pounded, as though the alarm still echoed in her brain. The chaos, however brief, had almost completely wiped whatever energy she had left.

Seymour drew a quick breath as he composed himself. He scanned his eyes throughout the room, quickly determining there was no enemy presence. The second level appeared to be one large room, stretching out nearly as wide as the bunker.

During the war, the second floor contained a layout similar to the one below. Several adobe walls created chambers for troop quarters, armory, machine gun operating chambers, offices, and a radar workshop. The inner walls had been collapsed, turning the upper level into one large laboratory. Abandoned lab equipment lay scattered about. Broken glass fragments from vials and beakers had littered the floor.

Equipment, such as lab meters, bench scales, nucleic acid sequencing kits, and so many others that Seymour had no knowledge about, lay about on the various tables. Some of the tables were neat and organized, while others were in complete disarray. Sequencing computers were powered down, connected to electronic microscopes and SPECTROLAB metal analyzers.

Geez, how'd they get all this shit up here? Seymour thought. Looking back at the stairwell entrance, he had his answer. Like everything up in this lab, the staircase was added in during the science team's reconstruction of the bunker. Originally, it contained nothing other than a ladder. Being unable to get a hydraulic lift into the command post, they built a stairway to physically haul the materials into the second floor. Practically the entire bunker had been cleaned out.

"A waste of good history, even if they were on the wrong side," he commented out loud.

"With the terrain on this island, Dr. Trevor insisted that converting this bunker would be faster than constructing a new lab," Hawk said.

Passing by several tables, Seymour gazed at a stable isotope analyzer. The machine had powered on, illuminating several chemical charts on a screen. He looked over at Hawk.

"Whatever that vaccine was, this is where your people developed it," he said. Once again, Hawk did not answer. Her silence was enough of an answer in itself.

Large machines, resembling X-ray devices and MRI's, were abandoned on the opposite side. Though similar, Seymour knew these were not medical devices. Near these machines was a sealed glass cabinet. Inside were three hazmat suits. Orange and black in color, with a hooded helmet and square glass face, they hung side-by-side on posts.

As Hawk rested, she noticed a sliver of light coming in through the nearby wall. Stepping away from the panels, she realized the light was not coming in through a window, but from a circular hole in the wall. The cavity walls were blackened, smelling like asphalt. The hole had been "burnt" nearly all the way through, exposing small cracks in the remaining inch of concrete.

Hawk walked through the lab, gazing at dried blood smeared onto the floor. Her breathing grew heavy as she walked further down. Some of the tables had been smashed through the center, as if a gigantic hammer had crashed down on top of them.

She found Seymour staring at the far wall. It was made of metal, grafted into the cement walls. It contained a single doorway. He recognized the metal wheel opening mechanism, like that on a hatch door, and the metal bars that extended from its side. It was intended to be a secure entrance, leading into a metal atrium where another seal door would lead into the chamber.

Only it wasn't secure. The exterior door had been swung wide open, and the interior was ajar.

"Oh no," she murmured. Though soft, her voice was alarmed.

"What's going on?" Terrie asked. Hawk rushed through the open doorways.

"Don't you need a suit?" Seymour asked. He watched the agent step around the interior door. Her voice growled, a combination of anger, shock, and despair.

"No....NO! Those stupid fucks! They opened it!"

Seymour and Terrie rushed in after her. After passing by the steel interior door, they found themselves inside a large, dull rectangular room with windowless grey walls. Hawk's face was animated with rage as she stared at a large metal object in the center of the room. The only way Seymour could think to describe it was a huge oval-shaped coffin. Twelve feet in length, it lay across, supported by stilts. Its exterior appeared similar to metal, though it was the smoothest, finest exterior he had ever seen. The bottom had a single triangular-shaped cavity. Over the top, twin doors had raised off the main body by small levers. Seymour and Terrie shared a glance, one as confused as the other. Seymour turned to Hawk.

"What the hell was in there?"

CHAPTER
20

With their guns strapped to their backs, the three North Korean soldiers crawled over mud and roots as they neared toward the bunker. Hearing the sound of the alarm confirmed to them the underlying purpose of the strike team's presence. The alarm had gone silent, replaced by the constant drone of the generator. Looking ahead, they could see pure sunshine breaking through the jungle. They were close.

They moved in a triangular formation, their most experienced soldier taking the lead. He crept to the perimeter line, keeping back several inches as he peered between the leaves at the bunker. They were looking at the southeast corner. To the right was the main entrance. The generator crackled and popped in the grass twenty feet in front of it.

Standing guard were two large men, built like Greek statues. The soldier saw the M60 machine guns they held; the same weapons that killed so many of his comrades. Inside that bunker were those who fought alongside him; the cowardly bunch that ambushed a platoon of unsuspecting soldiers.

Rather, the soldier justified his platoon's defeat by deeming the attackers cowardly. Moreover, they felt angered and insulted to the interference. The contents of that bunker, the findings by the scientist, by right, belonged to their homeland and Supreme General. It was not to be abused by the Western world, nor any other nation or culture.

However, deep down in his mind, he feared the truth. A team of seven-to-eight soldiers had outwitted and outgunned his superior force. They were defeated by a group with less firepower, ammo, personnel, and according to his indoctrination, inferior training and moral stance.

The soldiers knew radioing for extraction would be a useless venture. If successful, it would only lead to their deaths. Once their commanders in their homeland learned of their humiliating defeat, the soldiers would certainly be executed as an example of the punishment of failure.

Their only chance would be to eliminate the assassins.

The two other soldiers spread out, taking position six feet apart from each other. Concealed behind the plants, they observed the two men standing guard near the generator. They moved back and forth, speaking to each other in their English language. Though the soldiers didn't understand, the two brutes appeared to be mocking one another.

Two large men; two easy targets. The leader developed a plan: gun down the guards and draw the remainder of the squad out. As they exit the main door, they would gun them down.

The leader lowered his eye along the sights of his assault rifle, gesturing to his comrades to take the other.

"Shh…" he quietly signaled, removing his finger from the trigger. From around the corner of the bunker, a third individual appeared. He held his gun in hand, while conducting a standard looking patrol around the perimeter. The soldiers grinned. One target for each of them.

They slowly spread apart to take firing position. They would engage simultaneously, killing all three targets at once.

One of the soldiers moved along on his belly, pushing up dirt and grass as he positioned himself. He squeezed his hand over the grip. He moved his other arm to rest against the barrel.

His arm snagged on something. Something thin. Thin as wire.

Flames burst in his face as the trip flare ignited, shooting a ball of flame into the trees.

"Holy…" Easley shouted as the trip flare shot upward. Looking to the point of origin, he saw the motion in the plants. Human figures, wearing dark uniforms, had nearly jumped in place, reactionary to the flare. Gun barrels were pointed, both in his direction and toward his friends.

Easley lifted his gun and squeezed the trigger.

A spray of red splattered the plants as several of Easley's bullets hit their mark. The two remaining soldiers jumped back, seeing the skull of their unlucky comrade completely decimated. Realizing their plan was compromised, they fired return shots and quickly retreated into the jungle.

A flood of bullets passed by Ivan and Rex, one of them grazing Ivan's left shoulder.

"Agh! Son of a…BITCH!" Ivan yelled. Rex fired his M60 into the jungle, then rushed to Ivan's side to check the injury. The bullet had passed clean through the meat, leaving a large gash and series of burn marks.

"*Report contact!*" Seymour's voice yelled through their headphones. Easley rushed toward the tree line.

"Three shooters! One of them down. I'm in pursuit of the other two!"

Ivan quickly stood up, blood freely dripping down his arm. "I'm fine!" They watched Easley dash into the jungle after the soldiers. Ivan huffed and puffed, his face mad with anger. He felt an immediate thirst for payback. "Let's go!" He shouted. He and Rex darted into the jungle, Ivan furiously cursing each step of the way. "Oh, those FUCKS! No FUCKING way am I letting that kid hog all the action! Those bastards are MINE!"

****

Easley ducked under a low branch as he tore through the jungle to catch up with the assailants. Every few seconds he would catch a glimpse of them. Determined to get away, they managed to stay roughly a hundred feet ahead of him.

"*This is Seymour. Easley? What's your status?*"

"In pursuit. Hostiles moving southeast of your position," he said.

"*Easley, withdraw. We'll regroup and track them. Withdraw to the...*"

A series of deafening gunshots forced Easley to dive for cover. Rolling around a thick group of roots, he hugged the ground. Several bullets zipped by, shredding leaves as they ripped into the terrain. Peeking around a gap in the roots, Easley looked for the shooter. A muzzle flash gave away their position. They were aiming several yards to his left, meaning they were unaware of his exact position. Just as he aimed, the soldiers took off again, moving out from his line of sight.

"Damn it," he cursed. He sprang to his feet and darted after them. He barely moved three steps when a small circular object hurled through the air toward him. Moving through the air like a softball, it breezed past his head. It was small, dark green in color...a grenade! Easley accelerated his sprint, running clear of the blast zone. Knowing Ivan and Rex were somewhere behind him, he tapped the microphone on his headset. "Grenade!"

Just as they heard Easley's warning, the two brutes heard a dull clang as the explosive hit the ground. They couldn't see it, nor pinpoint its exact location, other than it landed somewhere ahead of them. They instantly turned and dove, as an explosive fiery flash encompassed the jungle several yards away, spouting razor sharp shrapnel into the surrounding area.

After the blast quickly faded, Ivan and Rex climbed to their feet, no harm done other than their tempers worsened.

Easley hunched slightly as he ran, feeling the force of the blast behind him. Looking ahead, he saw nothing but jungle. Having lost any visual of the hostile force, he could only hear their fleeing footsteps along with the rustling of plants several yards ahead.

He pressed on, determined to finish the mission. He came upon another thick wall of plants. He tucked his head down and sprinted through it, ignoring the pricks and splinters. He burst through, immediately encompassed by sunlight. He looked up, seeing the small clearing.

"Whoa!" he shouted, forcing himself to a sudden stop. He leaned back, nearly falling backwards as his feet skidded against the gravel, stopping precisely on the edge of a small rocky cliff. He exhaled sharply through his mouth, astonishment at his nearly self-inflicted demise worsening the adrenaline rush.

With his weapon still raised, he scanned the surrounding area for the soldiers. He couldn't hear any footsteps, gunfire, or shouting. They were probably out of his range. Or...

He leaned over the edge of the cliff. He saw the bottom, composed of a vast pile of rocks nearly eighty feet down.

From underneath the ledge it sprang.

Easley felt a flash of fright and terror, resulting in the discharge of his weapon and a brief yell.

In a heartbeat's time, he only caught the glimpse of the thing as it rose. With skin like that of an insect, and a shape almost like that of a man, it appeared as swift and silent as a trapdoor spider, thrusting its pointed appendage into his stomach. As soon as his eyes caught its glimpse, Easley's nerves flared up.

Then, as quickly as it began, he felt nothing. All control of his body left him. His muscles stiffened, his mouth gurgled involuntarily, and any balance was lost. Held upright by the strange javelin, he slumped, motionless as a corpse.

Yet, he was alive.

Ivan and Rex stopped in their tracks, hearing their friend's momentary yell and gun blast. A ghastly feeling swept over them. With no time to waste, they dashed toward the direction of the noise.

They approached a clearing. A gap in the wall of plants remained from where Easley broke through. As they ran, they could see through the opening. A tall bulky figure, with a height superior even to theirs, leaned forward.

They broke through the wall of plants, just as the figure disappeared over the edge of the cliff, with Easley's body in tow.

Both men, filled with a storm of shock and anger, rushed to the ledge.

"Mother-FUCKER!" they yelled, shooting their weapons downward. They fired several quick bursts, hoping to land a lucky shot. Down at the bottom of the cliff, was no sign of the assassin. Leaves and bushes along the plants swayed gradually, settling down from the disturbance that upset them.

"*Goddamnit, REPORT!*" Seymour was now yelling through the comm. Rex seethed, trying to get his thoughts and emotions under control. He adjusted his mic.

He spoke softly. "Man down. Easley is...K.I.A., sir."

Several moments of silence filled the comm.

"*Alright... give us your position. We'll regroup and go after them.*"

Rex breathed heavily, replaying in his mind what he saw. "It wasn't the Koreans."

CHAPTER
21

"I've flown the drone all over the place, Hatchling. There's no sign of him anywhere," Charlie said.

Seymour grimaced, standing along the ledge of the cliff. He looked to the jungle beyond the rocks, eager for Nagamine and Terrie to finish tracking down the remaining soldiers. This was his first casualty in years, the first ever for this team. In his mind, he cursed the government, especially the C.I.A. for forcing his team into this job. Ivan and Rex stood near, watching their leader intently. Like dogs begging for food, they were waiting for the go-ahead to pursue Easley's killer. Sutton taped a bandage around Ivan's injury, struggling hard not to look him in the eye. The two already had a harsh disagreement over who it was that killed Easley, and the spat nearly resulted in Ivan threatening physical harm.

Seymour kept a watchful eye on him as Sutton completed his bandage. The Doc secured his medical kit, then picked up his weapon, eagerly stepping away.

"Boss?" Charlie said.

"Sorry, Eagle Nest. Go ahead."

"How long are you guys gonna be?"

Seymour shook his head. He looked over his shoulder. Hawk was examining strange markings, like gashes, along the cliff ledge. "Unknown," he answered.

"Well, I want to warn you. You guys might want to hurry it up because..."

"Dude!" Ivan barked into his radio. "This bastard killed the nerd, and he's out there somewhere. We're not leaving him behind. However LONG that takes!"

"Ivan, calm it down," Seymour ordered. Ivan stepped forward, ready to argue. After seething for several seconds, he regained his discipline, and backed away.

"*Sir, I bring it up because there's another storm front moving our way.*"

On the outside, Seymour showed no emotion. At this point, it was extremely important for morale that the team not see him act negatively. On the inside, he was fuming.

Like we didn't have enough problems.

"How bad?" he asked.

"*Winds up to fifty miles an hour. It'll last the night,*" Charlie said. "*It looked like it was gonna pass north of us, but winds drove it south. This'll be worse than this morning. The plane can't bounce around in those kinds of waves. If you guys aren't ready in a few hours, I'm gonna have to fly out of range and pick you up when it's over.*"

"Damn," Seymour said. "You're positive there's no place for you to make landfall on this rock?"

"*Well...I mean...*" Charlie's voice sounded reluctant. "*I can try to make landing on that plain to the northeast.*"

"No!" Hawk stood up, drawing Seymour's attention.

"What?" he asked.

"He can't...he can't come here until we're finished," Hawk said. Rex scoffed, kicking a couple stones down into the cliff.

"You know, Lady, I'd ask why, but you've been telling us jack-shit from the get-go," he said. "So, I say we get moving."

"Nagamine is out there tracking the Koreans," Sutton said.

"I'm telling you, it WASN'T the fucking Koreans!" Ivan shouted. Sutton raised both hands in surrender, having no desire for a repeat argument. Hawk stepped over to the machine gunner.

"Guys, tell me what you saw," she asked.

"We only caught a glimpse of the guy," Rex said. "We came through the woods, and he had grabbed Easley off the ground. And like THAT," he clicked his fingers, "he went over the cliff."

"Give me a break," Sutton said. "He'd be splattered all over the rocks."

"Maybe you'd like to join him," Rex squared up.

"Alright, that's enough," Seymour said, pointing a finger at Rex. "Jesus, guys! You're on the same damn team! You've done, how many missions together now?" Rex said nothing, though he couldn't hide the shame from his eyes. It was all Seymour needed from him. "Get it together."

"What did it look like?" Agent Hawk asked. Ivan and Rex stared at her.

"*It?*" Ivan asked. Hawk held her breath, realizing her mistake. Even Seymour was staring at her.

What was in that metal coffin? He desperately wanted to ask.

"Answer the question!" Hawk yelled.

"Big!" Rex yelled back. "Bigger than me, bigger than HIM. We didn't get a good look at him. But he was not one of the Koreans."

"Coming around! Don't shoot us," Terrie called. She and Nagamine stepped into the clearing.

"Anything?" Seymour asked.

"We've tracked the Koreans to a small cave near a river," Terrie said. "Looks like they're setting up position there. Maybe a mile down that way." She pointed over the cliff.

"Alright," Seymour said. "Let's get moving."

"What about this guy who killed Easley?" Rex said.

"We're gonna kill these guys, find Easley, and take him home. Anyone else we encounter, we eliminate," Seymour said. He looked to Hawk. "Agent, how long do you need to download your files?"

"It shouldn't take long, but..." Her voice trailed off.

"Agent, I'd appreciate you cease with the dramatic pauses," Seymour said. His temper was beginning to show in his voice.

"Seymour, with respect and sympathy to your team, I must advise that we forget finding Easley and complete the mission. Forget killing the Koreans." Seymour shook his head.

"Not a chance," Seymour said. "They already tried a surprise attack on us. If we leave them out there, they can try again. I don't want us intercepted as we try to make our extraction. However, if there's any knowledge you'd like to add, we're all ears." The team stood silent, each of them staring at the agent.

A new idea sparked in her mind. She dwelled on it for a few seconds. Perhaps pursuit would be a good idea.

"The one who killed your man WAS, in fact, one of the Koreans," she said. "You saw the lab. Our scientists were working on advanced combat technology. That's how he made it down the cliff so quickly. These soldiers we're after must've gotten their hands on some of the tech."

"You're shitting me," Ivan said.

"If we kill them, we can secure the tech," Hawk continued.

"That tech..." Sutton said. "That wouldn't account for that stuff growing from all those bodies, would it?"

Hawk opened her mouth and stopped, making sure her lie added up with her story. In truth, she wasn't sure what that was. But revealing that info wouldn't fit well with her new agenda.

She noticed Seymour glaring at her. She avoided eye contact, while struggling to maintain her confident demeanor. She knew he suspected everything she said. He'd been suspicious ever since she and Agent Lesher arrived at his doorstep.

"In a way, yes. Think of it as a chemical spill of sorts. Probably why they abandoned the facility. Unfortunately, that's all I can tell you. However, if we can kill them and retrieve the tech, perhaps there can be a bonus for all of you." She then smiled, which quickly faded after realizing the team no longer cared about money. To them, it was about retribution.

"Trackers, lead the way," Seymour said. Terrie and Nagamine took point, leading the team into the jungle. As Hawk started following, she noticed Seymour's suspicious stare once more. So many things didn't add up.

He knew she was lying.

CHAPTER 22

Nagamine led the group to the stream of water. Though shallow, it traveled like a small river, coursing over piles of rocks between two small hills. The team stayed within cover on the hill, and traveled down its path, keeping the stream to their right. After a quarter mile, they came to the bottom of a small, but steep cliff. A tiny waterfall spilled over the side, continuously pouring fresh water into the stream. Near this cliff, an opening had naturally formed in the hill on the opposite side of the stream.

The cave's opening was a jagged shape, nearly six feet in width and no higher than an average door frame. No new tracks showed any signs that the soldiers had left.

Seymour ordered his team to spread out. Ivan and Rex took positions on opposite sides of him. Adjusting the stilts of their weapons, they lay on their stomachs in firing position. Sutton moved further up, drawing near the waterfall.

Terrie and Nagamine double-backed down the creek. After finding a place to cross over, they moved up along behind the hill, examining the terrain behind the mouth of the cave. Camouflaged in the thick plant life, they slowly moved to the back of the hill.

Seymour looked to his right. Hawk had crouched a few feet away. Rather than watching the cave, she was constantly checking her surroundings. She looked up, then back, then back to the creek.

"Quit with the head jerks, Agent, you'll give away our position," Seymour hissed. She looked at him, then turned to face the creek. He watched, Seymour could see she was constantly watching the surrounding area. Her left finger repeatedly tapped the barrel-grip of her gun. "You alright? You've been nervous this whole time, but now…"

"Are you sure they're still in there?" Hawk interrupted him.

"*Boss*," Terrie whispered into her mic. "*It doesn't appear this cave has an exit. The hill slumps down after a couple hundred feet, so the tunnel couldn't go very far.*"

"Good, then they're cornered in there," Seymour said. He looked over at Hawk. "There's your answer."

"I say we rush the inside and just blast them out," Ivan said. His energy had built up within him, as he was keen to attack. He enjoyed making fun of Easley, poking fun at his comic books, video games, and lifestyle. However, beneath that, he considered the nerd his friend.

"Relax," Seymour said. "Those guys know we're looking for them. I guarantee they're firmly watching that entrance. It'll be a shooting gallery."

"You have a plan, then?" Sutton asked. Seymour stared at the cave. In his mind, he could picture the remaining soldiers in there, huddled against the walls with their weapons pointed at the entrance. He exercised a few assault plans in his mind. Finally, he gazed up over the hill. The jungle overtop of it was thick, so he looked up to the top of the trees. Judging by the terrain, the hill was not very high. This meant the soil and rock making up the roof of the cave was not extremely thick.

"Yep," he said. "Terrie, Nagamine, plant your C-4 explosives over the top of that hill, about fifty feet past the entrance. When I give the signal, you'll detonate them. The blast will flush those bastards out. When it does...Ivan, Rex...I'll allow you two the pleasure."

"Fuckin' A," Rex said.

"Thank you, Boss," Ivan said.

****

The two trackers split up, moving toward opposite sides of the hill. They kept their movements slow and silent, to avoid being heard from below.

Terrie paused and listened. Like with the rest of the island, the jungle here was still extremely thick, making it difficult to determine distance and position. She listened to the trickling sound of the waterfall, and gradually moved toward it. She had nearly reached the top section of the hill over the cave.

Each footstep had to be placed softly in order to avoid detection from below. The splashing of water gradually grew louder. She kept track of each distance between steps, being sure she placed the explosives in the right location.

Near the base of one of the trees, Terrie located a dip in the earth. It was a naturally formed crease, both several inches wide and deep. Several cracks lined its interior. Believing it to be a hollow region, Terrie planted the C-4.

One down. She armed the explosive, and began to move. She moved back several feet, silently pushing past vines and bamboo.

As she did, she continued listening to the stream. The calm, trickling sound was peaceful and relaxing, a sharp contrast to the experience of this mission.

A dull, scraping sound drowned out that of the waterfall.

Alarmed, Terrie crouched low, aiming her machine pistol to the source of the noise. For several seconds it continued. Terrie tried to look through the plants, but could not see anything. The sound itself didn't sound at all familiar. In her mind, she could only picture sandpaper being continuously scraped along a steel brush.

Deciding to investigate, she stepped forward.

A hand swiped over her face from behind, cupping her mouth and holding her back.

"Shhh...quiet." Though he rarely spoke, Nagamine's voice was unmistakable. He removed his hand, and they knelt side-by-side. Terrie looked at her scouting partner. He never blinked as he kept his intense gaze locked in the direction of the sound.

Terrie mouthed the words, "What is that? Koreans?"

Nagamine shook his head. "Something else." The noise suddenly stopped. The sudden silence, in its own way, was more unnerving to Terrie than the unfamiliar graveling sound.

Some-*thing?*

Muffled sounds, each dull and brief, echoed from below. The scouts stood up, realizing the sound was from gunfire inside the cave. The individual shots turned into muffled rapid-fire bursts, coupled with the shouts of screams.

Seymour placed his finger on the trigger. He watched the mouth of the cave, seeing the muzzle flashes creating a flickering effect within the dark interior. He could feel the intensity and confusion from his fellow team members.

"Everybody keep still," he ordered. "Scout, what's your positions..." He ducked back and took cover. Thunderous blasts rang from the tunnel. Sparks and flames ripped from the mouth.

Vibrations shook the hill, forcing Terrie and Nagamine to spring to their feet. Turning toward the creek, they ran. Dodging the vegetation, Terrie cupped her hand over her headphone.

"Sir, something's happening! We're making our way back!" She came up on a large tree. She pivoted on her toes to move around it.

As if a battering ram were beneath it, the earth around the tree exploded upward. Layers of earth consisting of dirt, rock, and root blasted up from the earth, mixed with a fiery explosion.

"Terrie, what's going on?" Seymour said, seeing the explosions on the hill. "Did you set off the explosives?"

He watched as another explosion burst from the hill. Clouds of smoke twisted into various shapes as it lifted over the green canopy.

"Terrie? Nag?"

The second blast sent searing hot dust into Terrie's face, causing her to blindly scuttle backward. Snagging on a series of vines, she fell on her back. She looked up and gasped. With its roots completely severed in the blasts, the enormous tree leaned heavily. Branches snapped, wood crackled, and leaves flurried as eighty thousand pounds of nature came crashing down.

"Shit," Terrie said. Balancing on her elbows and heels, she continued scurrying back.

She felt herself lifted by the shoulders as Nagamine lifted her to her feet. They both turned and ran, as the forest crumbled behind them. The tree smashed down, creating a thunderous echo that soared through the jungle.

"Holy crap!" Sutton said, watching the explosion of dirt and twigs rise around the fallen tree.

"What the hell's going on here?" Rex yelled to Seymour. Seymour stood up from cover, ready to spring into action to rescue the scouts. As he did, a ball of smoke ripped from the mouth of the cave, accompanied by the sound of screams. Gunshots rang from inside the cave. Within the thick cloud, Seymour saw the silhouette of the soldier as he fled.

Covered head-to-toe in charcoal-colored dust, the soldier cleared the cloud. He raised his rifle and turned around. Yelling in Korean, he fired several shots into the cave. After emptying his mag, the soldier turned to run down the stream.

Despite the chaos and confusion, Seymour was not going to let the soldier get away. He raised his rifle and placed the soldier in his sights. His finger began squeezing the trigger.

A high-pitched whine filled the air. The cave illuminated in a blinding mixture of green-and-yellow. From its mouth, a ball of rolling light ripped through the air into the creek, inches ahead of the soldier's path. On impact it burst into a fiery explosion. Its force launched the soldier several feet into the air.

All of the mercenaries dove for cover, as smoke enveloped the surrounding jungle.

"What the freaking hell is this?!" Rex shouted.

"Everybody keep back!" Seymour called out. As he spoke, he saw Agent Hawk crawling toward the creek. "Agent! What are you doing?!" He saw the agent bring herself to a firing position, looking down the sights of her weapon.

He pushed up and moved after her. As he reached to grab her by the shoulder, his eyes went to the mouth of the cave.

As the smoke thinned, another figure stepped into the creek. Clearing several feet with a single step, it cleared the cloud of smoke.

"What the…"

For the first time in any of their careers, each member of the team did something they swore they'd never do in a combat zone.

They froze.

It stood eight feet tall, humanoid in basic form. But it was not human. Seymour gazed at the strange being as it marched from the cave. Its arms were elongated, twisting like twigs. Its right hand had three fingers, like a tripod, each of them knuckled. Smoke rose from a metallic gauntlet attached around its "wrist".

Its other arm was entirely different. Although equal in length, the hand was completely what Seymour could only describe as a metal glove. At the end of this clove were two appendages. Each was crescent shaped, with edges sharp enough to split rock. A pincer.

Its legs were double jointed, like an insect. Covering its dark grey "skin," the lifeform wore armor. A dark murky green color, it was ribbed at the torso, and extended down to its clawed boots. Though appearing solid, it seemed to bend to the creature's will, allowing for freedom of movement.

What struck a rare fear into Seymour was its face. He saw no eyes; just a dome over the top of a bald, scaly head. Its mouth was nothing other than two enormous fangs. Black and curved, they resembled a tarantula's, only twelve feet in length, pointing downward at slight, inward angles. Attached to small, fleshy pedipalps, the two fangs quivered in slow, tiny motions.

After landing several feet away, the Korean soldier rolled onto his back. Looking up, he saw the humanoid approaching. His eyes opened wide, and he tried crawling back. It pinned him down with its boot, smashing several ribs.

The soldier gurgled as he attempted to scream. The creature pointed its right arm toward him. The fingers extended completely outward like flower pedals, exposing a rounded palm. The flesh creased and folded back, as a large pointed barb protruded from the palm.

Seeing the barb dripping with a slimy substance, the Korean yelled.

The creature jabbed the barb into his stomach. A momentary cry of pain followed, and immediately ceased. The soldier's muscles contracted to the point of tearing. Foam spilled from his mouth, and blood from the wound.

Having cleared the debris and destruction, Terrie and Nagamine rushed to the edge of the hill. Looking out into the creek, they saw the creature.

A wave of terror hit the sniper. Feeling the instinctive urge to scream, she cupped her own mouth.

On the opposite side of the creek, the remaining mercenaries remained frozen from a combination of fright and astonishment. Even Ivan and Rex were perplexed, unsure of whether to retreat or engage.

The humanoid turned, feeling vibrations coming from the nearby jungle. Seymour watched as its eyeless face "gazed" at him. Somehow, though there weren't any visible eyes, it still 'stared' as though it could see him.

"Boss..? BOSS?" Ivan grunted.

"Sir, what do we do?" Sutton said. He was already backing away.

"That's no fucking Korean!" Rex yelled.

Seymour focused his mind, driving out the sensation of shock. "Everyone, fall back into the jungle."

"NO!" Hawk suddenly called out. She stood to her feet, weapon raised to her shoulder. "Kill it! Kill it!" Hawk squeezed the trigger, firing her weapon in full auto.

An ear-piercing hiss echoed from the horrific fangs, as the barrage of bullets battered its armor. One after another, each bullet burst into a thousand pieces after crushing against the alien material. The creature lifted both arms, shielding its exposed face with its gauntlets.

Hawk's firearm ran empty, and she scrambled for another one. Seymour rushed toward her, snatching the weapon from her grip.

"Are you insane, we don't know what the hell we're dealing---"

Hawk drew her Beretta and started firing. Seymour looked at the beast. Its screeches grew louder and more intense. Its hand opened up again, and the barb once again emerged. Arms lashed out, the creature sprang toward them.

There was no choice now. "ENGAGE!" Seymour yelled as he discharged his H&K. The entire team opened fire. Hitting a wall of gunfire, the beast sprang backward.

Bullets pounded its armor. Several rounds struck exposed flesh in its shoulders and neck, spewing orange bubbling fluid into the creek.

A bright yellow color illuminated from its right gauntlet. Small mechanisms unfolded from the sides. The barb retracted, and the hand clenched into a fist. The creature pointed its arm to the jungle, and the light suddenly took physical form. A loud electric whirring sound rang from the device.

Seymour instantly realized what it was.

"TAKE COVER!" he yelled, grabbing Hawk and throwing her to the ground.

The ball of green light shot into the jungle, erupting into a huge explosion. Fire and smoke encompassed the area. Seymour pulled himself to his knees. Grabbing Hawk by the vest, he pulled her backward, while the rest of the team retreated.

Several more balls of energy blasted the canvas, spewing fire in every direction. Explosions bursting in every direction, the team quickly became disoriented.

The creature fired several more shots into the canvas. It ceased, and its mechanism quickly returned to its normal shape. The barb protruded from its hand again, and it started marching toward the jungle.

Another series of gunshots rang out, striking it from behind. The creature whipped itself around. Two more enemies were perched above the cave, and were engaging with their primitive weapons.

Primitive or not, they were effective. Though most of the bullets were stopped by its armored vest, some of them found their way into exposed flesh. With several injuries detected, the beast reacted.

Nagamine and Terrie continued firing as the gauntlet began to glow. Seeing the beast aiming its device, they both sprang back into the jungle. A ball of energy zoomed in-between them, the resulting explosion throwing both of them several meters into the air.

Terrie hit the ground hard on her shoulder. Groaning in pain, she pushed herself to her feet, and pulled her rifle from its strapped position. She checked the mag, and pressed the butt of the weapon against her shoulder.

"Let's see how you like this in your face," she growled. She limped as fast as she could back to the exposed hillside, pointing her weapon down to the creek.

The creature was gone. Terrie continued looking, keeping her rifle pointed. The soldier's body was missing, and a trail of orange fluid led down the creek.

Surrounded by a huge cloud of smoke, Terrie lowered her weapon. Pain and fatigue suddenly overtook her, and she fell on her rear. Sitting up, she panted hard, looking at the blood trail. Nagamine walked up beside her. Bleeding from a gash in his forehead, his normally expressionless face now displayed astonishment and shock. Terrie looked up at him.

"What the hell was that?"

Nagamine silently shook his head. Like everyone else, he did not know.

CHAPTER
23

Like sand in the desert, small grains of dirt crumbled from the tunnel walls, forming a soft layer over the cave floor. A vast stream of sunlight poured in from above, through the gaping hole in the roof of the cave.

Stepping from the dark tunnel, Cassie Hawk entered the light. Astonished, she gazed at the burn marks throughout the tunnel. Though it had cooled, the singed area around the newly formed opening was still smoking. Looking up through the opening, Hawk could see the remaining root segments, still attached to the fallen tree, pulled up from the earth as it toppled. The severed ends of each root were black, with thinned fizzy portions broken outward like strands on a busted wire.

The tunnel smelled of burnt soil and flesh. Sediment still crumbled from the cave walls as Hawk looked deeper into the cave. Chunks of earth, the size of boulders, had collapsed from above, forming a wall of dirt and granite caving-in the tunnel.

At the bottom of the wall, she saw the lifeless body of the remaining North Korean soldier. Buried under a layer of soot, he lay motionless on his back, his jaw was wide open, as though he was in the middle of a scream when it ended. His right hand clutched a grenade, with his left index finger still wrapped around the intact pin. Hawk brushed away some of the dirt from his outfit, revealing a single puncture injury along his left ribcage.

She looked at his face. Those two eyes, wide open, seemed to stare right at her. A haunting image of someone who was dead, yet seemed alive. Seeing the open mouth, she could almost hear the scream.

Hawk closed her eyes and turned away. Collecting herself, she listened to the calm breeze entering the mouth of the cave. The gentle sound was overtaken by the chatter from the creek. Looking down the remaining tunnel, she saw the cave opening, resembling a speck of light in the distance. It was just outside where the mercenaries had regrouped.

****

Humongous strips of smoke billowed from the trees, coating the jungle in grey. The air had mostly cleared around the creek. The shallow water thrashed as Ivan and Rex walked about restlessly, their faces and shoulders scarred by burns and smoke.

Terrie sat upright in the grass along the edge of the creek, while Sutton tended to the many burns on her arms and neck. Portions of her sleeves had burnt away, exposing second degree burns on her elbows, upper arms, and shoulders.

"Ow...Bastard," she said as Sutton administered morphine.

"Quit being such a girl," he remarked. Terrie tore away the sleeves, allowing Sutton to administer ointment and bandaging. As he did, she noticed Nagamine standing down the creek where the blood trail ended. With the patience and focus of a machine, the samurai descendant continuously scanned the area, keeping watch for the strange beast.

On the hill past the cave, Seymour emerged from the trees. Beneath the scorch marks and grit on his face was a manifestation of ire. His anger was split three ways. First, he despised being manipulated into this mission, despite his error in judgement for his previous client. Second, the lack of information concerning Dr. Trevor and his team's purpose on this island, and therefore, his team's total unpreparedness. More specifically, he resented the lie he was told. And thirdly, he was angry at himself. When the creature appeared, he froze, succumbing to the dismay, and thus delaying his response.

Continuously pacing back and forth, Ivan looked up at Seymour as he approached the creek.

"Boss, what the HELL'S going on here?!" he yelled. "What the hell was that thing?"

"I'm more concerned with where the hell it's at," Sutton said, tightening a bandage around Terrie's arm. He glanced around at the trees. Every square foot of jungle concealed anything behind it, leaving him nothing to see but an endless green drape. "I mean, it could be anywhere."

"The blood trail leads that way," Rex said.

"WHATEVER it is, it's what got Easley," Ivan said.

"It was after the Koreans too," Sutton said, sealing his medical case.

"We were watching the entrance," Ivan said. "We never saw it go in. Terrie said there was no back exit. So, how the fuck did it get in there?!"

"I think I know," Seymour said. He turned and waved for everyone to follow him back up the hill.

****

"What in the name of..." Rex said, as the team gazed down at the enormous hole in the earth. Several meters past the fallen tree, the hole was just over three feet in width. The team surrounded the hole. Around the opening were piles of loose soil.

"No burn marks," Ivan said.

"I think this is what Nagamine and I heard when we were planting explosives," Terrie said. "We heard a mechanical sound, almost like a drill."

"Hang on, you mean to say this thing dug its way in here?" Rex said.

"It explains how it got in," Seymour said.

"Yeah, but why?" Sutton said. "I mean...you guys saw that laser bracelet thing, right? If it wanted them, why didn't it just vaporize them?"

"The same reason we didn't storm the entrance," Seymour said. "It knew those soldiers were watching the tunnel, ready to shoot anything that came in. So, it did what we were gonna do. Smoke them out."

"So, it's strategic?" Ivan said.

"It's also sick," Rex said. "It didn't bother vaporizing that guy. It walked right up to him and stuck him in the belly with its stinger." His voice grew soft. "I think that's how it got the nerd."

"And it took him too," Ivan said. "But...why?"

"Probably wants to eat them," Rex said. "Maybe suck their blood. You saw those big tusks, right?"

Seymour stood silently. His mind went back and forth between the creature and the metallic object he saw in the lab. He turned and began marching back to the creek.

"Terrie," he called out. "Come with me please." Terrie looked back at her team mates, each of them appearing equally perplexed. Obeying her leader's instruction, she sprinted to catch up with him.

Curious, the rest of the team followed.

Kneeling at the Korean's side, Hawk removed a syringe from her pouch. She inserted the needle in the forearm and pulled back on the plunger. Red, oxygenated blood filled the barrel. Hawk retracted the needle and snatched a vial from her kit.

"Agent Hawk!" Seymour's voice echoed throughout the tunnel, causing the agent to whip around. She quickly injected the blood into the vial and placed a cap on it. She put it in a plastic bag, and back into her pouch. She stood up and turned around to greet Seymour. He stepped into the sunlight alongside Terrie, while the rest of the team trailed behind.

"Yeah...sorry," she said. "I was just..."

"You know, I forgot to ask," he interrupted. "Are you feeling alright? You need any medical attention?" Bewildered, Hawk glared at him.

"I, uh..." she laughed nervously. "No...thank you. I'm fine." She turned to pick up her pouch.

"Good..." Seymour said, scooting the pouch away with his boot. Hawk quickly straightened her stance and squared up with him.

"What's the deal?" she yelled.

"Agent, I am giving you ONE opportunity to explain yourself," he said.

"Excuse me..."

"You have five seconds. FIVE..." Seymour continued. Hawk smirked.

"You're telling me to...Who do you think you're talking to?" she hissed.

"TWO...ONE..." He shrugged. "Terrie..." Hawk's eyes widened as Terrie rammed a closed fist into her stomach, causing the agent to double over. She followed with a right hook, plowing Hawk's left temple. The agent fell to her hands and knees, reaching for her sidearm.

Terrie pushed her hand away, while snatching her Beretta from its holster and tossing it aside. Hawk scrambled to her feet and turned, holding both hands out.

"What...agh..." She bent over from a continuing pain in her stomach. "Seymour...if the C.I.A. finds out about this, they will..."

"I think they'll have more important stuff to worry about," Seymour said, pointing to the soldier. He snapped his fingers. Hawk looked at Terrie, who had just cracked her knuckles. Hawk held a finger out.

"Don't you even think..."

Terrie kicked Hawk square in the stomach, ramming the toe of her boot under the ribcage. Hawk fell to her hands and knees, bile spitting from her mouth. Seymour stepped in front of her.

"I'm tired of you jerking me and my team around," he said. "You KNEW that thing was out here. You lied to us. Ivan explained what it was, you said it was a soldier. That, Lady, was no soldier."

Hawk looked up at him, her eyes burning with hatred and resentment. "You know I can't tell you anything."

"Don't give me this "Classified" bullshit!" he said. Hawk felt herself yanked up from behind. Placed in a chokehold by Terrie, her back arched. She gasped for breath as her airway closed off.

"You go girl," Ivan said, watching Terrie do the dirty work. Despite his aggressive nature, and sadistic thrills of slaughtering the enemy, he normally found no thrill out of seeing harm done to a woman. However, this case was an exception. A sentiment shared by the entire team.

Seymour leaned in toward Hawk, who struggled unsuccessfully to free herself from Terrie's hold.

"Ever since we got here, you've been playing us. First you were the nervous chick, then you wanted to play tough, then nervous again. When we stormed the construction site, you did your part. But then you see that thing, and suddenly you're John Wayne." Hawk struggled to speak, but couldn't get any breath. "Loosen up," Seymour said to Terrie. Hawk inhaled through her nose, then glared at Seymour.

"Fuck...you..." Terrie tightened her hold once again.

"You can be pissed all you like," he said. "That thing killed one of my men. It wiped out a whole team of soldiers before we got here. It nearly killed the rest of us...What the hell is that thing?"

Hawk bared her teeth, trying to curse further. Every struggle to free herself only resulted in a tighter grip by Terrie. It was like her neck was being crushed by an anaconda. Hawk felt herself growing lightheaded. Her movements weakened. Finally, she tapped her hand against Terrie's elbow. Terrie hesitated, looking to Seymour first, who nodded. She loosened up a tad, ready to strangle the agent further should she try anything.

"We...we weren't the first to find it..." she said. Terrie fully loosened her grip and stepped aside. Hawk rubbed a hand over her neck, still clutching her stomach. She took a breath. "August 19th, 2017, a research team discovered the *USS Indianapolis*. On July 30th, 1945, it had been sunken by a Japanese submarine after delivering uranium and parts for the atomic bomb, which later would be dropped on Hiroshima."

"Yeah, okay Lady, we've seen *Jaws*," Sutton said. "We know what the ship is."

"Since then..." Hawk spoke up, "...several research teams have sent submersibles down to explore the wreck. Using high-tech submersibles and drones, worth millions of dollars, these teams were able to get into the interior of the ship. In doing so, these teams also brought back certain relics from the wreck. One of them brought back a pair of Navy boots, another discovered a picture frame belonging to a lost sailor..."

"A moving story," Rex mocked. "Not sure what it has to do with..."

"AND...one brought up a sealed briefcase," Hawk said. The team stood silent. With the pain in her stomach subsiding, Hawk finally stood up straight. "During the Pacific Theatre, the *Indianapolis* took part in the island-hopping campaign, supporting the landing of Amchitka, intercepting Japanese cargo ships and Destroyers, the taking of Tarawa, eventually moving onto the Kwajalein Atoll Islands. In 1945, right before taking Iwo Jima, it took part in the taking of Kuretasando…this island here. Of course, that following July, it was sunken.

"The briefcase was among the assets confiscated when the U.S. eliminated the Imperial forces from this island. When they opened it, they discovered documents, written in Japanese. They turned them over to a translator, who turned them over to us. The Japanese found the capsule first…" she looked to Seymour, "Yes, that thing in the bunker. They at least had the sense not to open it. Then again, they didn't have the chance. We stormed the island, probably right after they found it, and eliminated all forces. Nobody was left alive to speak of this thing."

"You said *Capsule*," Sutton said. "You mean…"

"It's extraterrestrial," Hawk said.

"You've got to be shittin' me," Ivan said.

"That, what I saw, was a ship?" Seymour said.

"Let me guess, you guys wanted to make "first contact,"?" Rex said, making air quotes.

"We don't have a name for it. We simply called it the Pilot. Dr. Trevor was assigned by our government to set up a research facility on this island. Those construction vehicles you saw, they were originally here to construct a sturdier, high-tech facility. We wanted to keep this thing quarantined on this island. We were only interested in the technology. You saw the machinery in our lab. We developed it to scan the capsule, thus, we were able to have a three-dimensional view of our guest, perfectly contained in some sort of status."

"Did you guys already know this thing was hostile?" Seymour asked.

"We examined the capsule. It contained a strange, ion-based technology. That big supercomputer…the one you saw in the operation room…we used that to analyze the ion particle. We don't think the capsule is its main ship, but something like an escape pod. Something must have happened, hundreds, thousands, maybe even millions of years ago. That thing had to abandon its ship and drift off inside the capsule. It remained in stasis all this time, never awoken, probably because the capsule was low on power after it crashed."

"Ah, wonderful," Sutton said. "Let me guess…this Dr. Trevor guy woke it up!"

"So why are you eager to see it dead?" Seymour interrupted.

"The capsule contained some sort of 3-D display. We realized it was a digital map, using images and scans from probes sent out to that location...and..."

"And what?" Terrie said.

"Judging by the simulated trajectory, calculated by the ion particle path over the course of billions of miles, we think this thing...before whatever caused it to go into stasis...traveled from planet to planet."

"Planet to planet?" Seymour said. "Doing what?"

Hawk silently looked at him with a grave expression. Whatever it was doing, she doubted they were social calls. She then glanced down at the soldier. Sutton walked over to him, picking up Hawk's pouch. Opening it, he removed the vial of blood.

"You took this from him?" he said, pointing to the soldier. Hawk nodded. Sutton started examining the soldier, checking the eyes, mouth, and hands.

"Don't think you're his type, Doc," Ivan said.

"Shut up, you ape," Sutton said. Hawk turned back to face Seymour.

"We're not sure what this creature's fully capable of, but we suspect it might be an invasive species of sorts...Dr. Trevor, on the other hand...he wanted to attempt communication with it. We wouldn't let him, but he persisted. We were about to remove him from the project. He didn't want to, so he decided he'd get funding by another source who'd let him do what he wanted, in exchange for all the data and technology."

"Dr. Trevor turned to the North Koreans for aid?" Seymour said.

"Kidnapped his own team," Hawk said. "General Rhee saw an opportunity for power. That's why the C.I.A. wanted to go with an elite private group. As Lesher said, they were masquerading as a Chinese research team, and, well..."

"Also, you guys didn't want the inevitable coverage of sending our military after one of your own," Seymour said. "So, this thing is an alien. Obviously, it seems it's not fond of sharing this island with anybody. Is it just pissed that people shot at it, or is there something else it wants?"

"I think I have an answer," Sutton said, standing up. "This dead guy here...I don't think he's dead."

"Excuse me?"

"The blood should be coagulating by now," Sutton said. "As you can see here, his body has become completely rigid."

"Yeah, it happens to a lot of dead guys," Rex said.

"Not until three to six hours after death, dumbass," Sutton said. "I think this guy's suffering some sort of paralysis. I think that's what happened to those soldiers, and animals in that graveyard we passed by."

"It stings them, and paralyzes them?" Ivan said. "But why? To cocoon them and suck their blood later on like a spider?" He paused, suddenly remembering the wild boar, and the bodies. He pictured the strange organic material that grew from them. "That stuff...you think this thing planted it?"

"No doubt," Seymour said. Everyone looked back to Hawk, waiting for an explanation. She shook her head and shrugged her shoulders.

"I'm not completely certain what that is. We've never woken the creature. That was Trevor's doing. We haven't observed its feeding characteristics, or mannerisms," she said. "That's the truth."

"Whatever it is, it does eventually kill them," Sutton said. "We saw that those things gradually break down their host. Maybe those things break them down, and it feeds on them through a proboscis."

"But they're still alive to start with?" Terrie said. "That means..."

"Easley might still be alive!" Rex said.

"Holy shit...yeah, it's possible," Sutton said. He looked at Seymour. "Boss, it's VERY possible that Easley might still be alive. If we find him, and get him back on the plane, perhaps we can get him treated."

Hawk wanted to speak. The truth was that, if they were to locate Easley, he would have to be placed in quarantine. In fact, she wasn't even sure if the C.I.A. would even let him leave the island. However, considering the team's determination and lack of trust in her, she knew it was best to keep that to herself. She focused on the big picture. She wanted the creature put down.

"What if we run into that bastard again?" Sutton said.

"Shit, man," Ivan said, toting his machine gun. "You saw the blood trail out there. Its armor doesn't cover its whole body. We know we can hurt it. It's probably dying right now. I say, we finish it off and get our buddy back."

"I'm in favor," Terrie said.

A unanimous "Aye" echoed through the group.

"Alright," Seymour said. "We need to move quickly then. There's another storm moving our way." He looked toward the cave entrance, where Nagamine was standing guard. "Nag! You know what to do!"

"Hai!" The tracker led the way. The team exited the cave and followed him into the jungle, as a distant rumble of thunder groaned in the distant sky.

CHAPTER 24

Like a moving mountain range, a wall of storm clouds rolled toward the island. Their thunderous echoes grew stronger as they approached. The breeze transformed into a steady wind. The sunlight was growing steadily dim along the canopy.

Hawk resisted the urge to hold her hand over her bruised face. Marching through the jungle, her mind zigzagged between her anxiety and her humiliation. Each glance toward Terrie brought a temptation for a skirmish. Hawk's pride was diminished, having been bested so easily. Of course, Terrie was a much more seasoned, battle-hardened veteran, while Hawk by her own admission, spent much of her service in the lab.

Each time her humiliation surfaced, it was quickly drowned out by the current situation. The jungle grew darker as the sunlight gradually diminished. She slowly began to regret this decision to pursue the creature. It clearly knew how to move within the jungle. While conscious of life and death, it didn't seem to have fear. Each movement in the trees drew her attention. She felt as though it could be anywhere.

Yet, they were following its blood trail. Nagamine took the lead, accompanied closely by Seymour. Every few feet, they found another trace, puddled in the ground or smeared in the leaves.

The dark orange color contrasted heavily with the plants, making it easy to spot. They followed the trail for a half mile, by then the traces grew faint. Each smear on the leaves was no more than a few drips, and with more distance in-between.

Nagamine held up a fist. The team held position, and he stepped further ahead. He kneeled at the ground, examining the brush. Seymour cautiously watched the surrounding jungle. His eyes memorized each twisted shape in the canvas, looking for anything resembling their new target.

He looked back at Nagamine. The tracker glanced back at him, and waved him over.

Seymour closed the distance and kneeled beside him. "What's wrong?"

Nagamine looked at him. "Trail's gone."

"You think it's dead?" Seymour asked. Nagamine shook his head. He stood up and led through a nearby bamboo bush. Seymour instinctively raised his weapon, pointing it down at the body laying behind the bush. Eight feet in length, the creature lay, covered in tiny maggots and worms.

Black in color, its body was shriveled, as if there was nothing on the inside. The neck was completely ravaged where it had been shot. The fangs were completely missing from its face, leaving a gaping hole. Nagamine drew his Ninjato and reared his arm. He thrust the blade into the creature's torso.

The chest broke open effortlessly, revealing a hollow interior. Looking at the body, Seymour saw none of its armor or weaponry. He stepped behind the bush and waved to Hawk.

She hurried over and observed the body. "Oh, Lord," she muttered.

"Agent, you know more about this than me," Seymour said. "Is this what I think it is?"

Hawk nodded. "It molted." She stood up. "It might be a healing factor. Whenever it receives damage, it'll shed its exterior exoskeleton. The process might help accelerate cell regeneration, and therefore repair any internal damage."

"Great, so is it back to full health?" he asked.

"I don't know," Hawk said. "I didn't sit and have a one-on-one with it. I was only here to oversee the transfer of equipment, and left before Dr. Trevor turned."

"Well, what we do know is that it could be anywhere," Seymour said, looking all around at the surrounding jungle.

"Shit," Rex muttered.

"Shh," Terrie hissed at him. The team waited, keeping low in the bushes. Ivan glanced at his buddy, noticing him slightly bouncing on his toes.

"Tee," he whispered. "What's the problem?"

"I have to take a leak," Rex said. Growing antsy, he continued watching Seymour converse with Hawk. The current level of threat seemed reasonably low, and the team wasn't moving. He definitely did not want to be caught in a firefight, especially with this alien creature, with a full bladder. "Screw it," he said. He moved over to the side. Sutton shook his head, silently criticizing the machine gunner as he walked into the jungle.

"Oh, you've gotta be kidding," Ivan muttered to himself. He stood up and started following Rex.

Rex started to unzip when he glanced back and saw Ivan approach.

"What? You want a peek?" he joked.

"Believe me when I say...I'd rather fucking die," Ivan said. "Unfortunately, somebody's gotta keep watch, otherwise your big ass will get picked off by that thing out there."

"What a hero," Rex said. He proceeded to relieve himself, while Ivan scanned the jungle with his machine gun. His mind was a constant conversation, like a radio show in his head. They were hunting an honest-to-God alien. His mind frequently switched from amazement at the realization of the Pilot's existence, to fear. They knew little about the creature itself other than what they'd seen so far. Then his mind centered on the prospect of killing it, to which his ego exploded. Being able to claim to be the only one to kill an extraterrestrial was an almost impossible feat.

The drizzle coming from his friend seemed relentless. *He really did have to go.*

Watching the plants, Ivan started feeling antsy. Only now did the lack of visibility really start bothering him. His mind replayed the Pilot's emergence from the cave, how it snuck in and surprised the enemy.

The wind blew, bringing the surrounding wilderness to life. Sensing all kinds of movement around him, Ivan tensed.

Only one thing didn't move. To the right, something was perfectly still. Perfectly round. Taller than a man. A face, looking at him through the trees. Ivan nearly shrieked as he pointed his gun.

"No! No! Don't!" Seymour shouted. Ivan whipped his head back, seeing his leader approaching. Rex had just zipped up, grinning at Ivan.

Ivan looked back. The object was still there, nearly ten feet high. As the brush moved, he realized it was not upright, but held at a slant. It was non-alive and inanimate. Possibly a tree trunk. Whatever it was, it wasn't the creature. He gave a strong exhale, then glanced back at his boss. Seymour walked past him toward the object.

"Thank God I was about to chew your asses out for breaking formation," Seymour said. "You almost blew us all up."

"Beggin' your pardon, Boss?" Ivan said. He joined Seymour, followed by the rest of the team. They approached the object. Cigar shaped, its red tip was propped up on a tree branch, covered in moss. Twenty-two feet in length, it laid at a slant, with its propellers embedded in the ground.

"Oh shit...is that a torpedo?" Rex said.

"Yeah," Seymour said. He looked at Ivan. "Anti-ship torpedo left over from World War 2."

"All over Asia are unexploded ordinances such as these, leftover from the war," Hawk said. "Europe too."

"Yeah, well, this one almost became un-unexploded," Seymour glared at Ivan.

"A torpedo, eh," Ivan said, "...from World War Two. I don't recall seeing any submarines." Seymour snickered and pointed up with his finger.

Everyone gazed upward. Perched high in the two-hundred-foot tree, the plane rested in the branches, entangled in the canopy directly above them. Nearly fifty feet in length, with a wingspan of sixty-five feet, it had remained there for seventy-three years.

"Yokosuka P1Y. It's a heavy bomber," Seymour said. "As you already figured out for yourself, it was shot down during the war, probably by our lovely *USS Indianapolis*, and ended up here. The torpedo had to have come loose when it crashed." Seymour looked at the torpedo, then back up at the plane. "Since it didn't get the chance to deliver the torpedo, it likely didn't deliver its other payload."

"Two-thousand pounds of bombs," Hawk said. Ivan cleared his throat, realizing he almost ignited a blast that would've nearly consumed the whole side of the island.

"Now that the history lesson's over, let's carry on," Seymour said. He faced the team. "There's no more trail. Nag's only found a couple more tracks, then the trail just disappears after."

"No problem," Rex said. "Let's just go in a sweep pattern and finish the job. Thing's gotta be close to dead by now."

"Negative," Seymour said. "It molted its skin, or what we thought was skin. It has like an exoskeleton, similar to bugs. Agent Hawk here thinks it might be part of a healing process."

"Alright, so lets un-heal it," Terrie said. Seymour would've normally expected that answer from Ivan. The mercenaries were eager to save their brother.

Another thunderous burst echoed from the sky. If they waited too much longer, they would have to hold up on the island until morning while Charlie flew out of range to avoid the storm.

"Agent, Dr. Sutton, what is the estimated likelihood of survival for Craig Easley?"

"At this point, slim," Hawk said. "It's been, what, a couple of hours now. Whatever it's doing to the bodies, it's probably well in effect on him now."

"Oh yeah, right," Rex scoffed. "Coming from the lady who manipulated us into going after this thing. She's probably lying to get out of dodge."

"No, she's right," Sutton said. His voice was somber. "I don't think there's any hope for him. Whatever it does to its victims, it begins straight away. Maybe it's making food out of them...I don't know."

"I know one thing, guys," Seymour said. "We're gonna double back to the bunker, let Hawk finish what she needs, then we'll get out of here. Then we'll come back, better equipped, and blow this bastard to hell."

The team stood silent for several seconds. It was a struggle to conceive leaving a man behind. However, each of them realized Seymour was right. The odds were not in their favor. With the creature at full strength, with superior firepower and stealth, it had the advantage.

The wind kicked up harder.

"Believe me, we'll be coming back," Terrie said.

The team turned and moved in a single file formation.

CHAPTER
25

The ShinMaywa rose and fell with each wave as the storm neared. Rock 'n Roll blared over the speakers, keeping Charlie lively as he battened down the unsecured cargo. As he moved about the plane, his eyes watched the massive wall of clouds move in. The sky turned into an ugly black, and the increasing scream of the wind gradually became more audible.

Charlie turned up the volume, blasting AC/DC's *Thunderstruck.* He secured the drone, having just returned it from its island reconnaissance. He attached a charger to its battery, tapping his foot to the beat of the song. He sealed the device into the cargo hold near the armory. He stood up and looked out the window, just in time to see the large wave rolling toward the plane.

The plane leaned hard as the water lifted it. Charlie hugged one of the bunks to keep himself from falling over as the plane fishtailed. Like a roller coaster, the plane fell several feet down as the wave passed by. Charlie rushed toward his computers.

The screen displayed a vast blue layer, representative of the ocean. Overtop it was a green windmill shape, slowly rotating as it moved southwest. The storm had upgraded into a tropical storm, and was continuing to strengthen.

"Oh, shit," he said. He wouldn't be able to wait much longer, and he hadn't heard anything from the team. He reached for his radio headset, switching off the music.

The speakers went silent, replaced by a deafening blast of thunder. The wind clawed at the hull and passed over the wings, generating a loud screeching whine. The sunlight had now been completely overtaken by the enormous clouds.

As Charlie sat at the cockpit, several raindrops began splattering on the windshield. Heavy rain was soon to follow. It would not be long before the weather struck the island.

"Eagle Nest to Hatchling. What's your status?"

****

The team quickened their pace, feeling the weight of the approaching storm. The jungle came alive around them. Plants of different shapes and sizes danced in the wind. The sunny glow along the upper forest darkened. With visibility decreasing, the team shortened their distance between one another.

"We're doubling back to the bunker," Seymour said. He cupped his hands around his radio to block out the wind. "We won't be long. The agent will download her data, and we'll be ready for extraction."

"Glad to hear that, because the storm's moving in fast. I can't wait here any longer."

"Move the plane toward the harbor," Seymour said. "We'll double-time it there, once we have the package."

"No," Hawk yelled, swiftly turning toward Seymour.

"Agent, we don't have a lot of time," Seymour yelled over the wind. "If we don't leave soon, he'll have to fly the plane out into clearer conditions and wait out the storm. We'll be stuck here all night!"

The team quickly ganged up on the two.

"Don't know what your deal is, Agent, but I'm not fond of staying here," Rex said.

"I know what this is," Sutton said. "We're loose ends. We've seen the creature and the lab. They don't want us getting out of here."

"Stop!" Hawk shouted. "You remember those choppers, back at the harbor?!"

"Yeah, they were shot down," Seymour said. He remembered how they were shot down. The impact craters from fifty cal. Machine guns, as well as the other damage. "They were shot down by the soldiers..."

"You realize why? The thing was trying to get off the island! If Charlie flies to the harbor early, and that thing gets to him before we do..."

A loud electrical buzzing sound reverberated, as a blinding flash of light lit the surrounding jungle. A ball of energy, the size of a beachball, zipped from the darkness, striking a nearby tree. It erupted into a fiery explosion, as another ball of energy shot out the jungle, hitting the ground several feet away from the group.

The team scattered as the second explosion roared. Seymour raised his weapon to provide cover fire. He discharged several shots in the direction of the blasts.

Two more balls of energy exploded, zipping from the left. The explosion threw Seymour to the ground, and forced the team to disperse.

"Where the hell is it?!" Ivan yelled. Rex stood up and blasted his M60 wildly into the jungle.

Several more blasts exploded around them. Huge balls of fire spurted into the trees, the force of the blasts driving the mercenaries further apart. Ivan and Rex jumped as one of the blasts exploded nearby, followed immediately by a second blast.

The world spun as Terrie struggled to her feet. Thrown by one of the explosions, she had been slammed into a tree, nearly knocked unconscious. Through her blurry vision, she saw blurry streaks of light from the raging fire and oncoming energy bursts.

She pushed herself upright, slumping back against the tree. Her head throbbed as she fought to stay awake. Looking forward, she saw the huge fire. Shouts of her team members echoed throughout the area as they scattered. A series of thumping sounds reverberated off the ground. Like soft drum beats, they quickly grew louder.

Looking up, she saw a tall figure rapidly approaching. She gasped, and reached for her rifle. It had fallen from her grip, landing several feet to her right. With no time, she reached for her machine pistol.

"Whoa! WHOA!" Ivan said, grabbing her hand before it clutched the weapon. "Girl! It's me!" He picked her up off the ground, putting her arm around his shoulders, while Rex picked up her weapon.

A blast of energy surged towards them, exploding on the tree. The trunk burst open, forcing the mercenaries to scurry away. The tree leaned, slowly tilting on the unsupported trunk.

Sutton saw the flash as he struggled to his feet. Completely disoriented, he was unsure which direction was which. Pointing his rifle, he turned to-and-fro, looking for any of his teammates.

Shouts rang from the nearest explosion. "Doc! We need ya!" It was Ivan's voice. He sprinted toward the recent explosion and stopped for a better look. Through the plants, he could see Ivan and Rex carrying Terrie from the burning tree. His radio headset had nearly come off when he hit the ground. He adjusted it, brushing the dirt from the headphones.

"Stay where you are, I'm coming!" he shouted into his microphone. Sutton dashed toward them, running as hard as he could. He brushed past a bamboo plant, then hooked around a large tree.

He just made his way to the other side when it sprang in front of him. He saw the fangs protruding as the creature hissed. He instantly shrieked and raised his weapon, as its jutting barb pierced his chest plate. A world of pain hit his whole body like a bolt of lightning. He tried to squeeze the trigger, but his muscles would not respond. He wheezed as he fought for control. He felt a combination of saliva and other fluid building in his mouth, spilling over his gums. His jaw clenched, and all sense of balance and control left him. He toppled over backward, completely frozen.

The creature felt the vibration of running footsteps. It turned its head toward the sound. Two muzzle flares flashed as Seymour and Nagamine opened fire on the creatures. It hissed and dove into the jungle, disappearing into the darkness. Seymour continued firing, sending several bullets along the creature's path.

Hearing the sound of running footsteps, Seymour quickly turned, ready to fire. Agent Hawk emerged from the darkness.

"Hey-hey! It's me," she said. Her eyes went down to the fallen medic.

"Get him up!" Seymour yelled. Nagamine and Hawk knelt down and grabbed the Doc. There was nearly no mobility as they pulled on his arms. His body was nearly stiff as concrete as they brought him to his feet.

"Ivan, hold position. We're regrouping," Seymour said. He placed his night vision goggles over his eyes, constantly looking around for the creature. A sudden crack, like that of thunder, burst from the fire. Seymour turned, seeing the tree succumbing to its own weight.

"Shit!" Ivan said, looking high up at the towering tree as it leaned heavily. Bits of wood crackled as branches snapped. A flood of adrenaline dulled Terrie's pain, and brought her mind to focus. She planted her feet on the ground, pulling away from Ivan.

"GO! Let's go!" she yelled. She snatched her rifle from Rex and sprinted. The two gunners followed. Ivan pointed ahead toward where he had seen the muzzle flashes.

"That way!" he yelled. The tree crashed, tearing up much of the terrain on its way down. Gusts of wind caused the fire to flare, instantly getting pushed backward by the colliding storm winds.

Through his night vision, Seymour watched the tree collapse. The fire generated bursts of light in his goggles, forcing him to squint. Three human figures were running in their direction.

"Come this way," he said. He lifted a flare and broke the top, releasing a flash of sizzling sparks.

The three mercenaries ran toward the burst of light.

"Don't shoot, it's us!" Rex called as they neared. They arrived, and instantly saw their comrade paralyzed on the ground.

"Oh, my God...DOC!" Terrie yelled.

"Everybody form a perimeter!" Seymour shouted, his commanding voice getting control of the group. The team created a five-star perimeter, each of the five remaining mercenaries acting as a point on the star, with Hawk and Sutton in the middle. "Nagamine, you know which way we're headed."

"Follow my lead," Nagamine said, his voice calm and relaxed. Seymour glanced back to the agent.

"Alright, Hawk, can you carry..."

Another series of energy blasts exploded near the group, driving them back. Hawk fell to the ground with Sutton, while the mercenaries rushed into a firing formation. All at once, they fired their weapons toward the direction of the blast. Bullets shredded trees and brush, nearly creating a hole in the jungle. All at once, they ceased fire.

"You think we got it?" Rex asked.

Seymour shook his head. "No." The team backed away, forming a human shield around Sutton. Several empty magazines hit the ground as the team reloaded.

"How the hell are we gonna get out of here?" Terrie said. "I can't see a damned thing."

Ivan strung another chain of ammo into his M60. "Let's just go for it. Have you seen the way it shoots?!" He pointed toward all the fire. "This thing can't hit squat!"

"I don't know, dude," Rex said. "It almost looks like it's missing on purpose." Consistently looking down his sights, watching the jungle, Seymour planned a course of action.

A realization came to mind. He looked down at the paralyzed medic.

"Rex...you're right. It ambushed us...forced us to disperse," he said. "It wants to take us alive, and it can only get close enough when we're scattered."

"Alright...so we stay together," Ivan said. "Let's keep moving, not allow ourselves to be separated."

"No..." Seymour said. "It's not gonna work that way. It's not going to let up." He lowered his weapon and knelt down to Sutton. Hawk moved out of the way as Seymour opened the medic's vest. Seymour removed his four blocks of C-4 and Sutton's remote trigger.

"What are you doing?" Terrie said, watching Seymour strap the explosives to his vest.

"When I go, you guys hightail it toward the bunker," he said. "Hold position there, then get your asses to the harbor. Whatever you do, don't separate."

"Wait...what?" Rex said.

"Victor!" Terrie protested, realizing what Seymour's plan was.

"That's an order, Terrie!" Seymour said. "Now GO!" He turned and dashed into the jungle.

Through the blinding forest, Seymour ran. After distancing himself from the team, he fired off several rounds from his rifle into the forest to put the creature's attention on him, wherever it was.

"Come on! Come get me, you son of a bitch," he growled. Looking around, he saw nothing but writhing jungle. He continued running, brushing past an endless barrage of plants and vines. He stopped again, scanning the area with his rifle. Pointing the barrel up, he fired off another couple of rounds.

Clutching the detonator, he waited for the creature to emerge. He carefully watched all the movement around him, waiting for the humanoid shape to emerge.

A streak of lightning flashed throughout the sky. For a brief instant, the jungle was lit in a bright bluish luminosity. A loud crack of thunder followed, and the ground reverberated.

Following the thunder, another sound filled Seymour's eardrums. A sound he wasn't familiar with. A wet, sticky sound like that of a peeling onion. Another flash of lightning lit the jungle as Seymour turned toward the sound. Through the waving plants, he noticed something. A vast opening with no plants, in the same direction in which the sound emerged.

He made another mad dash, tearing through leaves. Bursting through a final wall of plants, the terrain suddenly disappeared. Now, he was in an open area. Even in the darkness, he knew the area was black and dead. The ground was squishy, but not from rain, as the precipitation hadn't yet begun. It was rotten.

The smell was the next thing he noticed. As a SEAL, he had been exposed to so many bitter odors and tastes, as he was trained to eat anything to maintain survival. Even the worst of smells hardly bothered him. But this was different. The stench—such a horrible smell, it was a struggle not to gag.

Yet, it seemed familiar. A repugnant, rotten stench…like what he had experienced that morning.

Letting his rifle hang from its strap, Seymour snatched another flare from his vest. It ignited with a large flash, casting a bright red glow onto the surrounding area. Seymour looked around, seeing the many corpses that surrounded him.

As he suspected, he had wandered into another gravesite. The human bodies were extremely shriveled, their identities completely erased, reduced to a mass of rotten flesh inside dark uniforms. Like a miniature forest, several pods grew from each corpse. Seymour stepped further into the gravesite, observing the bodies, wondering if Easley was among them.

The pods were like fungus, growing from the bodies they fed off. Many of them were as tall as Seymour. In their surface, he saw veiny lines moving up the structure.

Is this like terraforming, or something? Seymour thought to himself.

In his peripheral vision, he caught movement from the tree line. Just then, the flare burnt out, covering him in complete darkness. He snatched his last remaining flare and quickly broke the seal. Red sparks flashed as the flare ignited. Red light reflected off the body armor, maximizing the glow over its face. Though it had no eyes, it appeared able to see, and it was gazing directly at Seymour.

With its fangs protruding with a threatening hiss, the beast advanced into the light. Its hand opened up, and its stinger protruded from the folded flesh.

Seymour dropped the flare and snatched the detonator. He moved his thumb over the trigger.

The creature came to a sudden halt. It hissed again, this time at a lower pitch. Seymour kept his thumb over the button. Seymour silently cursed.

"Just a little closer," he whispered. Considering the creature's armor and ability to regenerate, he wanted it as close as possible to absorb the entire force of the blast. "Come on, you coward," he said louder.

The creature watched him, remaining in a forward posture. The tips of the metal pincer rapidly clicked together, as though the creature was determined to move on him.

It straightened its stance. Its stinger retracted into its palm, and the beast slowly took a step back. Every movement contained caution. Its gauntlet illuminated with a dim pulsing light.

Seymour raised the detonator again, putting minor pressure on the trigger. "I dare you. Go ahead, blast me. See if you can do it before I blow you, and your precious garden away. I have nothing to lose."

Taunting the creature, he stepped toward it. The creature leaned forward, releasing a loud threatening hiss. Seymour briefly halted, then continued. He held the detonator outward, taunting the alien.

A loud bang echoed through the jungle. The creature screeched as orange blood burst from its neck. It turned and fled into the jungle, while several more bursts rang out. Bullets struck its back plate of armor as it disappeared into the darkness.

Seymour crouched in a ready position, switching glances between the direction of the gunshots and the creature's path. Running footsteps drew his attention behind him.

Terrie stepped out of the jungle.

"What the hell are you doing?" Seymour said.

"Nice try, but no way am I letting you blow yourself up," she said. Seymour looked back to the woods, angered by the missed opportunity to kill the creature. "Boss, we don't have time. We need to get out of here."

Seymour exhaled sharply, realizing she was correct. The storm was worsening. The wind grew stronger, and rain had started pouring down. They would never track the creature down in this darkness and weather.

Seymour switched off the trigger, and tucked it away. He turned and ran, brushing against one of the large fungus pods as he followed Terrie into the jungle.

The pod slowly rocked to-and-fro before settling.

Its exterior layer pulsed gently, as though it was breathing. It continued this motion for several seconds. From the top, a strand of its shell peeled back. An inch wide, it curled downward, generating a wet sticky noise.

CHAPTER
26

The ocean churned around the island as the typhoon twisted in the sky. Sixty mile-per-hour winds howled as they gusted through the trees. A torrential downpour splattered into the jungle. Leaves and branches rained down from the trees, torn from their bases from the unrelenting winds.

Rex cursed as he tilted the fuel drum into the generator's gas tank. Rain pelted him relentlessly, while debris from the trees fell around him.

Ivan stood at the bunker entrance, standing watch as Rex fueled the generator. He stood firm with his back pressed against the open door, fighting it from being blown shut by the wind. It wasn't the storm that made him nervous. His eyes watched the jungle, knowing somewhere, the creature lurked.

Bolts of lightning slashed the sky, as though a war was taking place in the atmosphere. Rex dropped the drum and checked the gauge. The tank was at eighty percent capacity.

"Good enough," he said. He grabbed his weapon and sprinted back to the bunker, with the wind at his back. Rain dripped from his face and vest as he marched through the small tunnel. Ivan slammed the door shut, and lowered the locking mechanism into place. He pushed against the door to ensure it was secure, then followed Rex into the operations room.

Rex shook like a wet canine, splattering water all over the room. The lights were dimly lit in order to minimize visibility from the outside.

"That'll last us through the storm," he said. He looked to Ivan, who was now peering out the machine gun hole. Wind hissed as it blew through the opening, stinging his eyes. "You're not gonna see anything out there."

"Can't help it, man," Ivan said. He slammed a fist into the wall. He hated leaving Easley behind. He watched the plants flailing in the wind, looking for the beast to step out. "I almost hope this fucker comes here." He rubbed the barrel of his M60. "God…give me a shot at him…"

"Not if I get him first," Rex smirked. Ivan turned to look at him. His face was serious at first, but a small grin soon broke through.

"Keep in mind, I'm still three ahead of you. Bitch," he said. He tapped Rex on the shoulder and walked to the planning room.

Nagamine stood, staring out of one of the machine gun loopholes. Water rained in through the open segment, constantly spraying his face. Unfazed, he stood like a machine, expressionless, watching the outside perimeter.

You know, you've been doing that for a couple of hours now, was what Rex wanted to say. He knew his words would fall flat, like talking to a statue. He walked past the tracker. "I wish I had your patience," he said instead as he walked by. As usual, he wasn't sure whether Nag ignored him.

His face dripping wet, the tracker moved to another loophole carved out of the wall of the nearby office, peering out to the south side of the bunker.

Rex checked the storage room. Several boxes were piled into the corner, marked with Asian lettering. He tore one of them open and looked inside. The box had ten smaller boxes in it. He pulled one out and examined it. It was a Chinese MRE, with instructions on the back for use. He tore the box open, revealing the heating pouch full of rice, a sauce packet, spoon, and a small clear plastic pouch. He looked at the pile of boxes. There couldn't have been more than twenty. He did the math in his head, then thought of the estimated number of soldiers on the island.

"Damn," he said. "The North really does have a problem feeding their troops." He turned toward Ivan. He was peering through one of the openings. "Hey!" Rex called out. Ivan turned just in time to catch the MRE tossed to him. Ivan looked at it, then shook his head.

"I'm good," he said.

Rex shrugged. "If you're eating, you're living," he said.

"Eating that shit, not so sure," Ivan said. He gazed outside once more, then followed Rex back to the operations room. Rex took a seat in one of the radio chairs and started sorting out the MRE contents.

Ivan checked the other office. He peered through the loophole, seeing nothing but darkness. He turned and glanced down at the several weapons left behind. They were mostly assault rifles, and a couple of pistols on the desk.

Beside the door, he noticed two canisters. He walked around the desk, and pushed the door shut for a better look. Each canister was attached to a harness, with a hose protruding from the top. They were flamethrowers.

He checked the gauges. Both tanks were on empty. He checked the gun, making sure the triggers worked properly. Determining the mechanisms were fine, he lifted both tanks and opened the door.

"Tee, get the other fuel drum," Ivan said. Rex's face lit up with glee when he saw Ivan with the flamethrowers. He quickly stood up and started for the storage room.

He turned the corner, passing the stairway entrance as Terrie stepped out. She was visibly fatigued, slumping into a wheeling chair.

"How's the doc?" Ivan asked. Terrie wiped a hand over her face, then shook her head.

"Not good," she said. "He's..." She stopped, realizing they'd probably rather not hear the gruesome details of his condition. "I don't think he's gonna make it."

****

"I'm keeping – on the radar---I'll keep—posted," Charlie's voice crackled over the long-range radio. Seymour stood at the end of the lab, where he would have the best reception.

"Alright, we'll be on the move as soon as the storm lets up," he said. "Do NOT attempt to come here until you've heard from us."

"Roger," Charlie said.

"Hatchling out," Seymour said. He placed the radio down and silently cursed the storm. His mind was in constant motion, planning for any scenario in which they would encounter the creature.

He turned, watching Agent Hawk tending to Sutton. They placed blankets over a lab table for cushioning, and laid him across. They managed to straighten his arms and legs so he could lay flat.

His appearance had grown sicklier. His skin seemed to be a shade darker, his eyes bloodshot. Seymour noticed that he seemed a few pounds skinnier. His frightened expression remained frozen on his face.

However, nothing troubled Seymour more than the growth on Sutton's chest. They opened his vest and tore his shirt open. Embedded in his skin, the dark grey substance grew. Nearly eight inches in width and dome-shaped, its ends appeared embedded into Sutton's flesh. Red veins pulsed near the edges, changing into a dark green as they moved over the top of the cap.

Hawk prodded the object with a utensil. It appeared to have the same firmness and texture as a mushroom.

"Agent, what in the hell is that?" Seymour said. Hawk turned and pulled away her facemask.

"I can't say for sure," she said. "The spore is organic; it appears to acquire a living host to grow. It grows like a fungus. In the initial stages, it requires living organic tissue. Later on, after the host is deceased, the spore seems to reach a maturity to where it feeds off the dead tissue. Whenever the Pilot stings a victim, it injects a poison rendering paralysis. At the same time, it injects this strange spore."

"Alright, why?" Seymour said. "Why does it inject it into them?" Hawk replaced her mask and examined the cap. She gently brushed a scalpel over the surface in a brushing motion. Dark slimy fluid collected over the blade, dripping away as she lifted it.

"It secretes this thick black liquid, which seems to have an effect on the surrounding environment."

"Like how?" Seymour asked. "I mean, what's its purpose?"

"I'm not sure," Hawk said.

"Listen, Agent..." Seymour ran his hands through his hair. He walked across the lab to Sutton's table. "Agent...Doctor...as you know; I'm no scientist. I'm nothing more than a soldier. In fact, I'm not even that anymore. I'm a hired gun, paid to handle a client's dirty work. But, I can tell you this, that Pilot out there is not planting these things for decoration."

"No, it's not," Hawk said.

"You said it yourself, that fluid stuff affects the surrounding environment. We saw it at the gravesites. Could it be a way of altering the environment to suit its needs?"

"That's highly possible," Hawk said. Seymour stared at Sutton's face. He wondered if he was awake. The thought of which brought the devastating fear that Sutton was in considerable pain. This was no way for any decent person to die.

"I want it off of him," Seymour said. Hawk's eyes widened.

"I...I don't know if I can," she said. "I'm not a surgeon. I don't have a team. He'd have to be in a quarantined environment."

"You have one right there!" Seymour pointed toward the sealed containment, where the capsule was held. "You have scanning equipment right there, best there ever is. Scan him through it, figure out how deeply this thing is rooted inside him, then cut it out."

Hawk felt herself growing increasingly nervous.

"Seymour...those are designed for analyzing metallic material. They're not medical devices. And cutting the spore...that's extremely risky," Hawk said. "Considering his current state, the growth of the spore, lack of proper surgical equipment...he probably wouldn't survive the operation."

"We're stuck here all night," Seymour said. "Charlie had to fly out of the storm. There's no way we're getting him to a hospital in time. He's dead either way." Seymour looked at Sutton again, now really hoping he wasn't conscious. He took a breath and looked down for a moment. "He should have morphine in his pack. Could you please give it to him?" His voice was gentler.

Hawk nodded and walked to the next table where they had placed Sutton's medical kit. She pulled out a morphine auto injector and inserted the needle into Sutton's forearm.

After injecting the morphine, she disposed of the needle and walked over to the large x-ray scanner. A circular power-save button was glowing in a bright green color. She pressed it, and it changed to clear white. Electronic sounds hummed from the machine as it powered on.

"Give it a couple of minutes," she said. "I'm not sure how accurate the images will be. This thing wasn't designed for organic material."

Seymour nodded. Biding time, he started walking along the lab, observing the equipment. He looked at the concrete walls. There were remnants of engravings, mostly Japanese lettering. Likely, the soldiers had gotten bored, and searched for things to do. Much of the engravings were worn, and others destroyed when the interior walls were torn down for construction of the lab. He thought of Hawk's story about the USS Indianapolis, and the documents it secretly contained.

"You said that capsule was originally discovered in World War Two," he said. "That means it's been on this island AT LEAST since then."

"At least," Hawk said. "God only knows when it arrived on Earth, or how long that capsule has been floating out there." The machine buzzed as it finished starting up. The screen came to life, with touchscreen buttons glowing, ready for operation.

Hawk looked at it, and then peered inside the containment room at the capsule.

"You're already aware of the story," she said. "Back in the seventh century, there were stories of large streaks of light that came down from the sky, touching down on this island. Of course, we know today they were describing a series of meteorites. The stories say that the lights struck down, and silver dust burst from the impact and covered the island. Of course, we have no scientific explanation for that. For all we know, it's just a story passed on through the centuries. Whatever it means, it's why the island's called Kuretasando." She looked at Seymour, knowing he understood the translation.

Seymour turned away, staring at the impact cavity in the far wall.

"Crater Sands."

CHAPTER
27

The internal door closed with a loud fizzling sound. The overhead lights lit up inside the containment chamber. Cassie Hawk breathed slowly through her ventilator, struggling to calm her nerves. The orange and black hazmat suit was heavy, yet very flexible. The facemask was clear, with a tiny airflow built in to eliminate fogging.

In front of her, Sutton lay over a table which she and Seymour moved inside. The IV dripped fluid into his arm. She inserted a sedative into his drip, in case he was conscious. To her right was another table. On it were surgical instruments from Sutton's med kit spread out over a sterile piece of cloth. Next to them was a microscope, with several glass slides.

I'm not a surgeon, she repeatedly thought. She took another deep breath and pinched her gloved fingers around the scalpel. She looked up. A camera, installed in the upper right corner, was pointed directly at her.

Outside in the lab, Seymour hunched over a computer monitor. Watching Hawk preparing to cut into the strange spore, he felt his stomach begin to ache. It was a rare occasion in which he felt helpless. To him, helplessness was the worst feeling. He initially felt that way when diagnosed with cancer. However, his fighting spirit took over. He would not let himself succumb to anything. Not even the wrath of nature.

Only this time, it was not him, but Sutton on the surgical bed. And even cancer paled in comparison to what was killing him.

"*Okay, let's begin,*" he heard Hawk say through the speaker.

It was more for herself than anything. For Hawk to get in the right mindset, she had to think of this as a dissection, rather than a surgery. Her plan was to remove the spore piece-by-piece. She held the scalpel over the cap and paused, while deciding whether it was a good idea to start at the center or near the edges.

"Eenie-meenie-miney—screw it," she said. She pressed the blade into the center of the cap. Dark fluid squirted from the incision, while red blood from the host leaked from the broken veins. After cutting the blade across the cap, she used the blade to peel back one of the sides. The upper layer was about a half-centimeter thick. Soaking up some of the fluid with gauze, Hawk saw that the inside of the skin was white, appearing rubbery in texture. It reminded her of a ring layer of a mushroom. She cut another incision over the cap, creating four equal sized flaps. Using forceps, she peeled all four flaps back, exposing the next layer.

"Just like that frog in basic biology," she said to herself.

The next layer was composed of thin, light-colored tissue. Hawk brushed the blade over them. They were leaflike plates, like gills, rooted to another layer. Hawk took a breath as she figured out what to do next. Unable to see past the gills, she knew she would have to remove them before cutting deeper.

She took clamps from the surgical setup. With them, she pinched several of the plates and pulled. They came loose fairly easily, tearing from the interior of the spore. Spurts of fluid and blood sprayed outward as the plates detached.

Hawk used suction to drain the fluid, and gazed at the inside of the spore.

"Whatever this thing is, it's definitely alive," she said, knowing Seymour was listening.

"*Alive? Can you elaborate?*"

"Obviously not an animal, at least so it seems," Hawk said. "I hate to keep going back to the fungus comparison, but that's what it seems like."

"*So, this alien likes to infect people with a bad fungal infection?*" Seymour said. "*It doesn't make sense. Why?*"

"I'm working on that," Hawk said. She listened to the growling thunder outside as she picked the scalpel up. The heavy rain resulted in a constant battering sound above. Usually that sound was soothing to Hawk's ears. Now, it was only distracting.

She looked at the inner layer. "This looks like a tunica. In biology, that's what we call a layer that covers an organ."

"*Do fungi have those?*"

"Some do," she said. "It's more common in zoology and plants."

"*If that's an organ, perhaps that's how you kill it.*"

"Maybe," Hawk said.

She looked at the x-ray photo, then back into the spore's cavity. She estimated it was rooted at least two inches into Sutton's chest. The very thought induced a wave of nausea. Hawk closed her eyes and took a breath. After several seconds, she regained control.

She gently pressed the blade into the layer. The tissue was thin and wet. She held the suction tube over it, draining the spilled fluid. With a tiny pair of straight scissors, she cut away the two flaps, creating a circular opening.

Inside was a huge mixture of cords and veins stretching over a blubbery, flesh ball. It was completely different from the outer layers. This tissue was something similar to what she would expect to find in an animal.

She made a small incision over the top.

"What the…"

A long pause followed as she gazed at the insides.

Seymour watched the monitor as Hawk cut into the spore. The agent grabbed a magnifying glass and leaned in for a closer look. For several minutes, she said nothing. Every so often, she moved the scalpel or forceps, but it didn't appear she was doing much cutting.

Shouldn't you be removing the thing? he thought.

He watched as Hawk straightened her posture. She looked at the equipment, then at the camera. He couldn't see her face, but her bodily movements suggested she was nervous.

"Agent, you alright?" he spoke into the microphone. He watched Hawk look up at the camera. She placed the tools down and walked toward the door. With a key, she opened the touchscreen pad, and typed in the exit code.

Seymour could hear the loud hiss as the interior door opened.

"Agent, what's going on?" he said. Hawk didn't answer as she stepped into the foyer. The door electronically sealed, hissing until adequate pressure was obtained. From the walls, decontamination gas sprayed from small openings. The gas stopped, and clear liquid rained down from the ceiling, washing the uniform of the alien's fluid.

Once the water drained, Hawk quickly started removing the suit. Keeping the gloves on, she worked on small little notches in the shoulders. The helmet loosened, and she let it drop to the floor. She removed the suit bit by bit, ending with the gloved portions.

The exterior door opened. Dressed only in a t-shirt and underwear, she stepped out. She snatched a towel and started patting herself down.

"What the hell's going on?" Seymour said. "Why'd you stop?" Hawk stepped back into her tactical pants.

"I'm so sorry," she said. "But I can't save him." Seymour's initial instinct was to yell, and bombard her with insults for quitting. He tensed, tempted to give into the anger. He reminded himself that they were dealing with something unprecedented, and that he already knew Sutton's chances were slim.

"What did you see?" he asked. His voice was calm, his demeanor collected. Hawk got her military gear back on. She clipped her vest together. Her mind replayed the images she saw, and she debated whether to tell the truth.

"As the scan had suggested, the spore is rooted in too deeply," she said. "If I were to remove all of it, it would just leave a giant hole in his chest, exposing his heart and lungs, and a portion of his stomach. Infection would set in, and he'd die. It'd be as much torture as what he's currently going through."

She jumped as Seymour turned and kicked one of the lab tables. The table toppled over, spilling electronic equipment onto the floor. Hawk tensed, watching a million dollars-worth of supplies crash down. Seymour walked a few steps away, taking a moment to cool off.

"So, what the hell is it?" he said.

Hawk started to sweat. She wiped her face once more with the towel. "When the Pilot stings its victim, it instantly injects a venom which immediately induces paralysis. At the same time, it inserts one of these spores, which are probably microscopic in the beginning. It sprouts inside the host's body like a weed, first feeding off the living blood. Once the host's blood is drained, and therefore deceased, the spore begins a different level of feeding, where it gradually breaks down the dead tissue. From what I can see, the process begins immediately." She tossed the towel to the floor. "Once you're stung, you're dead."

"Christ," Seymour said. "I still don't get it. Why does this thing do this to the victims? What's its purpose?" Hawk said nothing and looked away. Seymour stared at her. He could tell she felt an obligation to keep the information classified. "Don't keep anything from me. I watched you dig at that thing. You said something about an inner layer. You dug at it further, then you left in a hurry." He marched up to her, moving around to stand face-to-face.

He enunciated each word. "What. Did. You. See?"

Hawk knew the C.I.A. didn't want her giving any more information. She was sure to be in hot water for the info. she already released to them. It wasn't as though she could simply lie, and claim that she told the mercenaries nothing. The debriefing process for Top Secret operations such as this was a process involving many steps. More than one of those steps would involve lie detection.

On the flip-side, she was stuck here with these mercenaries. Already, they proved they could beat the info. out of her; an experience which still left her humiliated with herself. What clawed at her mentality further, was the knowledge that they would be able to do it again, should they choose.

And there was no doubt in her mind that they would.

"I cut away the tunica. Underneath, was organic tissue. Not Sutton's. The spore appears to be containing some type of sac…"

"What do you mean, a sac?" Seymour said.

"Upon dissecting it, and examining the samples in the microscope, I believe it contains three layers. If my theory is right, the sac contains an endoderm layer, a mesoderm layer, and an ectoderm. These layers contain…" she stopped, realizing Seymour didn't care about the scientific details. "It's an embryo."

His eyes widened, and he took a step back.

"An embryo?" he said. He looked down at the monitor, focusing on the spore growing from Sutton's chest. He thought of the two vast graveyards he encountered. The enormous spores growing from the humans and animals. "You mean to tell me it's making more of itself?"

"It must be how the species procreates,' Hawk said. "It goes from planet to planet, forming new nests on each one. Eventually the indigenous population is wiped out, and the Pilot moves on to another planet. I think it's all instinctive, a natural instinct to preserve its species."

"And we're next," Seymour said. He listened to the howling of the wind and the crackling of thunder. The chaos and destructive nature of the storm seemed symbolic. "We need to get the hell off this island."

CHAPTER
28

Ivan tweaked the valve slightly to allow a modest amount of gas flow from the tanks to the shaft. The firing mechanism was shaped like an AR-15, with two handles. The first handle was located at the back of the shaft, containing the valve lever. The second handle, shaped more like a pistol grip, was behind the nozzle. It contained the firing trigger.

The piezo igniter sparked a flame. Pointing the nozzle into an empty space in the planning room, Ivan twitched the trigger slightly. A ball of flame burst from the nozzle, quickly disappearing into a ball of smoke.

It works, he thought to himself. He sealed the valve, and unclipped the harness. Holding the flamethrower by the strap, he carried it back into the operations room.

Rex's voice grew loud and audible as Ivan turned the corner.

"What happened? We know what happened. That traitor doctor guy, whom we were supposed to rescue, felt so righteous that he had to open that capsule. The thing woke up, pissed off, and it turned on them."

"I know that," Terrie said. "What I meant was, how did it take them all on by itself?"

"Did you not SEE its firepower?" Rex said. "The thing packs a punch. Then there's that crab-claw glove it has. I think that thing can change form, and can be used for many purposes. That's how it dug in behind those soldiers in the cave. The bastard's sneaky and cunning, fearless, ugly as hell—I might add."

"And has superior weaponry," Ivan chimed in.

"I know, but against a whole platoon?" Terrie said. "I'm just astonished it managed to do it singlehandedly."

"It heals," Ivan said. "We saw it ourselves. It molts when it's injured. It takes time to regenerate, and then it comes back for more."

"If that's the case, if the bastard takes enough damage, it can die," she said. Ivan held up the flamethrower.

"Wait 'til it gets a load of this," he said. "I'd like to see it regenerate after I toast it."

"Hell yes," Rex said. "Is the other one good to go?"

"In the other room," Ivan said. Rex quickly got up and exited through the doorway. Ivan took a seat in one of the chairs, then pulled another one up to rest his feet on. Terrie had disassembled her sniper rifle for cleaning, and was finishing putting it back together. She shivered with each crack of thunder, glancing toward the porthole each time lightning flashed. She was nervous. As was he. Even for hardened combat veterans, it wasn't unnatural.

Ivan noticed Nagamine conducting another patrol check of the operation room. Since they arrived, he moved from loophole to loophole, looking out into the jungle. Even he appeared to have angst.

"If you want, I can take watch?" Ivan said. Nagamine quietly looked back at him and shook his head, declining his offer. He gazed out the loophole, and eventually moved back into the planning room, passing Rex along the way. Holding his flamethrower by the strap, Rex watched him stand to the next loophole and gaze outside.

It was a sight like no other. Nagamine, the fearless assassin, was nervous. The fear he felt quickly passed on to Rex, who looked away and quietly moved back into the operations room. He slumped in a seat, putting his feet up on the radio panel. He listened to the generator, using it as a white noise to help him drift to sleep.

****

The lights were out, and the mercenaries all asleep as Seymour came down the stairwell. He debated waking them, wanting to inform them of the new information he acquired. However, he knew they needed the sleep, and the information would only provide further angst. In five hours, he would be waking them up to begin the journey to the harbor; an appropriate time to inform them.

Seymour closed the door to the Planning Room office. He moved the chair around the desk and positioned it to face the loophole. He sank into the seat, rifle in lap as he stared out at the stormy night.

His mind fought him as he tried to drift off. Images of the beast flashed in his mind as rapidly as the lightning. He pictured its fangs, clicking together as though keen on impaling him. And of course, there were those horrific graveyards.

Or should he call them nests? He wasn't sure. During his many missions, he'd seen his share of mass graves. Villages full of people wiped out by insurgents, or so he was led to believe. Many would be buried in shallow graves, others not buried at all. Until today, he thought he'd seen the worst of it all. Yet, what was occurring on this island was certainly worse. This creature, and what it had done, truly haunted him.

He thought of Sutton upstairs, and what was happening to him. He was not looking forward to letting the team know Sutton couldn't be saved. Worse, he worried about the upcoming patrol through the jungle. He thought of the creature stalking them, invisible in the terrain.

He found himself staring at the loophole. The lightning flickered, casting a bluish light on the two-foot long missing section of cement. Too small for the creature to slip through. Yet, he hated leaving it wide open for it to come around and look in. The darkness in the room didn't help. All it did was make him feel more vulnerable.

With each flash of lightning, Seymour envisioned the creature's face, peering at him through the loophole. As if through unconscious motion, Seymour tilted the rifle until its barrel was pointed toward the opening. Though it wasn't good arms practice, he rested his finger on the trigger. Never looking away, he kept his gaze on that hole, knowing the beast was somewhere out there, waiting for them.

He leaned back in the chair, his eyes and gun pointed at that loophole.

Please take a peek in here. I dare ya, you ugly son of a bitch.

****

Cassie Hawk placed her pack onto a lab table. She unzipped it and sorted through her equipment. Amongst her supplies was her data storage device, shaped like a common flash drive, but far more technologically advanced. She plugged it into a hard drive, linked to the supercomputer below.

Moving the mouse, she opened the main file, linking her to all of the storage information. She clicked a button, opening another window. A bar appeared on the screen. The words *ACCESS CODE* flashed in red letters.

Hawk clicked the buttons on the keyboard. *K-3-M-A-9-D-C-L-0-F. Enter.* The letters flashed for several more seconds as the computer loaded. The screen went black for a brief moment, before opening to another window. Red letters flashed again. *ACCESS CODE 2.*

Hawk quickly typed. *H-1-#-Q- L-6-F-X-N-O-8.* As before, the computer took a moment to verify the code. It flashed black, then took her to the next screen. It gave her a list of files to download. At the bottom corner of the screen, she clicked the button reading *Download All Files.*

Another access code bar emerged on screen. *A-B-W-J-D-5-M-O-9-5-F*. The computer verified the code, and began the downloading process.

Hawk stood up from the monitor and returned to her pack. She pulled it open, revealing an internal pouch. She unzipped it, pulling out her issued satellite phone.

There was only one contact number installed. She opened the stairwell door and peeked down. Nobody appeared to be nearby. She shut the door, and pressed *send*.

A voice answered. *"Operative code?"*

"Delta-Five-Charlie-One-November-Eight-One," she said.

"Give me your status update."

"Situation critical," Hawk said. "Situation is a Code Phoenix. I repeat, Code Phoenix." There was a small pause.

"A Code Phoenix? Are you sure?"

"Damned sure," she said.

"Do you have the data files?"

"Affirmative," Hawk said. "Downloading now."

"Can you extract during the storm?"

"Negative," Hawk said. "Not until morning. What is the estimated time of cleanup?"

"I can postpone it until noon. Be off the island by then."

"Copy that."

CHAPTER
29

For four hours, Nagamine continued his routine of checking each loophole. After he declined all of their offers to take watch, the team had drifted asleep. The winds outside still gusted, though they seemed to have decreased speed. The torrential downpour had decreased to steady rain. The thunder continued grumbling in the night sky, joined by the constant lightning.

He remained single-minded in his watch. He did not grow bored or restless. Trained from a young age, he knew to maintain constant awareness of his surroundings. He learned to persevere for days without sleep. He could feel the threat lurking beyond those trees. Something in him knew that it was aware of their presence.

Nagamine walked by the offices and gazed into the operations room. The lights were still dim, and the three mercenaries inside appeared conked out. Ivan's snoring filled the room. As silent as ever, Nagamine silently moved to the nearest porthole, nearest to Rex. For the hundredth time, he gazed out into the stormy darkness. As usual, even when looking with his night vision, he saw nothing. Nagamine turned his eyes down toward Rex. He was slumped in his chair, perfectly still.

"I know you're awake," he said. Rex opened one eye, and grinned.

"I'm like you," he whispered. "I can't fucking sleep." He looked at Ivan, who let out another snore. "I envy him." Nagamine didn't say anything, and continued gazing out the porthole. Rex rubbed his hand over his eyes. He stood up and looked out the porthole. He nearly offered to take over from Nag, but decided not to, knowing he would be declined.

Nagamine stared out for several minutes, then finally stepped away, intending to check out the nearby office.

He stopped and listened. Within the sounds of crackling thunder and the generator's droning, there was something else. A sound so slight, yet so near. Nagamine closed his eyes and held his breath, focusing solely on the sense of hearing. A series of tapping sounds, with no particular pattern, were coming from the planning room. Nagamine hurried back into the planning room, raising his weapon as he approached the wall.

The sound stopped as he arrived. He stood off to the side, carefully peeking to inspect the nearest porthole. Gazing through his night vision goggles, he saw nothing moving but thrashing forest. He removed the goggles and looked at the cement opening.

On the outside corner were chips and scratches, as though someone had taken a hammer and chisel to the frame. He saw bits of gravel on the bottom of the frame, and additional scratches on the top. It appeared as though something tried squeezing through, but couldn't.

The sound appeared again, this time outside the storage chamber. Nagamine swiftly moved in to investigate. Standing beside the boxes of MREs, he listened carefully. He touched the walls, feeling the extremely slight vibration. The scraping sound moved upward.

Another chiseling sound came from the other wall. It was ground level, beneath the nearest portholes. Nagamine moved away from the storage, taking each step as silently as possible. He pressed his back to the wall and took position just out of view of the porthole.

There was another chiseling sound, barely audible, as though someone was twisting a screwdriver against the cement. Such faint scraping of consistent volume, as though whatever was conducting the noises was being deliberate to keep from being heard.

Nagamine silently drew his sword, keeping just out of view. He clutched the handle with both hands, pointing the blade down with a reverse grip. A streak of lightning flashed, sending a brief stream of light through the loophole. He heard the chiseling again, this time further up the wall.

Lightning creased the sky once more. Nagamine looked into the room, seeing the large shadow flash against the opposite wall.

He rotated to the right, plunging the blade through the loophole.

A stream of fluid erupted, and a screeching hiss pierced the air. Nagamine withdrew the sword, its blade coated in an orangish blood.

The screech echoed throughout the lower level, waking Seymour up from a light sleep. He jumped to his feet and burst from the office. With his rifle pressed against his shoulder, he hurried near Nagamine.

The other mercenaries quickly followed.

"Cover the front entrance!" Seymour quickly ordered. Rex and Ivan immediately backtracked, while Terrie remained in the planning room. Seymour stayed close to the wall, carefully peeking through the opening. He noticed the blood on Nagamine's sword.

"It climbed," the tracker said. He shook the blood from the blade and sheathed it.

"You think it's dead?" Terrie asked. Seymour shook his head. He noticed Nagamine looking up toward the ceiling.

"What's wrong?"

"Shh!" Nagamine held a finger to his mouth. He then pointed up high along the wall. Seymour listened, and heard the chiseling sound.

"It's climbing the wall," he said.

Rex and Ivan took position in the operations room. Ivan strapped his flamethrower harness over his shoulders, while Rex carefully watched the front entrance. He listened for any unusual sounds, though it was difficult to hear anything over the wind, thunder, and generator.

Ivan clipped the harness and clutched both handles of the shaft.

"Wait 'til that bastard gets a load of this," he said. Rex said nothing as he continued listening. The generator droned on and on, and another burst of thunder roared.

The generator spit and moaned. A few popping sounds filled the air, and the droning came to a dead stop.

The lights went black, coating the mercenaries in a blanket of darkness.

"The fuck..."

"Damn it," Seymour whispered as the planning room went dark. "Everyone switch to night vision. Nag, you watch these openings. Terrie, with me!" He hurried around to the front. Ivan and Rex were placing their night vision goggles over their faces as he arrived.

"Did it kill the generator?" Terrie asked.

"Most likely," he said. He hurried to the front door. "Terrie and Ivan with me. Rex provide cover."

"You sure you want to go outside?" Rex said. "I think it's trying to drive us out."

"It's gonna continue to engage unless we kill it," Seymour said. He looked at Ivan and his flamethrower. "You ready with that thing?" Ivan smiled and nodded. They hurried down the hallway and gathered at the door.

Seymour lifted the latch and kicked the door open. They burst from the opening, and swept the area. The wind tore at them as they moved toward the generator. Looking all around, they saw nothing nearby.

Hawk woke up in a daze. She was covered in complete darkness, as though she was trapped underground. An immediate sense of claustrophobia struck. Adrenaline hit her and she shot out of her seat. She immediately bumped into the desk, nearly falling overtop of it.

She steadied herself, then held a hand in front of her face. She couldn't see it. She was in a complete absence of light, left entirely blind to her surroundings. Arms extended out, she worked her way around the table.

"Seymour!" she called out. "Hello? Anyone?"

A knocking sound filled the air, causing Hawk to freeze. She listened intently, realizing the sound was coming high along the far wall. It sounded as though someone was taking an ice pick to the blast cavity. Bits of broken cement pebbles fell to the floor. The chiseling intensified. Large chunks of debris crashed down to the floor.

Blind, confused, and alarmed, Hawk tried to feel her way to the door. She stopped and turned around. *The data!*

She looked back toward the sound. Something was prying its way through the hollow area in the wall. Hawk moved around the table, knowing her bag was on the next one over. Feeling along the corners, she blindly stepped away, reaching for the other table.

"Come on, where are you?" she said. She felt the corners with her fingertips. She brushed her hands over the surface, feeling for her pack. Loud cracks popped from the cement, followed by the sound of a large chunk breaking away. She didn't have time. She swept her arm over the table. Her wrist hit the nylon side. She grabbed it, finding nothing but air as she accidently pushed it away. She heard it fall over the side and hit the floor.

"Shit!" She knelt down and fumbled for it.

Seymour knelt by the generator. The entire side had been ravaged, as though someone unloaded a machine gun to it. Several puncture marks riddled the side, and the pumps had been shredded, leaking oil and gas all over the ground.

He lowered his eyes to the ground. Several strange holes were in the dirt. With no specific order or arrangement, most of the strange holes only went an inch deep, no wider than that from a tent post.

He thought of the southside outpost, where he had seen the same mark.

"SHIT! BOSS," Ivan yelled out. Seymour sprung up and turned. Ivan and Terrie were both looking high up to the bunker wall.

Dozens of creatures scattered all over the building. Several had insect-like appearances, with long protruding spider-like legs attached to oval shaped bodies. Additional appendages curled over their abdomens like tentacles on a squid. Many others were humanoid in appearance, with narrower bodies containing two legs and arms. However, there was nothing human about them at all.

They covered the wall like termites on a tree, gathering toward a specific point in the corner. Several others moved down the wall, toward the mercenaries. Their appendages bent at the joints, as though ready to spring from the walls.

Seymour opened fire, tearing bullets into the nearest group of creatures. A deathly screech filled the air as the torsos of two beasts erupted into bubbling orange fluid. They fell to the ground, while several others leapt from the walls. The humanoids landed on their feet, with both arms extended out. Large pointed barbs protruded from each hand, dripping with venomous fluid. Each beast had a set of mandibles containing jagged teeth or fangs. Saliva dripped from each mouth as the creatures approached.

"Come get some," Ivan said. He pointed his flamethrower and squeezed the trigger. A tsunami of fire ripped from the nozzle, engulfing the creatures. Seymour aimed upward and sprayed a series of bullets into the large gathering above. Orange blood rained down, and several creatures dropped from the wall.

Terrie aimed her sniper rifle. With so many creatures covering the wall, it was effortless to place a target in the crosshairs. She squeezed the trigger, placing a bullet into the abdomen of one of the arachnid creatures. Its rounded body burst into a pool of goo, and the creature dropped from the wall.

"BEHIND YOU, BOSS!" Rex yelled. He stepped from the bunker entrance, aiming his M60 to the north tree line. Seymour ceased fire and looked, seeing a river of the arachnid beasts rapidly approaching.

"Son of a bitch!" he said. The horde was thirty yards away and closing fast. He turned and opened fire into the horde, as Rex fired the M60. Several creatures exploded into a mixture of guts and exoskeleton fragments.

Ivan aimed his nozzle and fired a burst of flame into the horde. The stream hit the middle of the group, causing several of them to split off into different directions. Seymour ejected his empty mag, and slammed a new one home. He fired several more bursts into the horde, then turned his sights back to the bunker. Focusing in on the large group gathered on the far corner, he noticed the arachnid beasts digging their scythe-like appendages into the wall.

The hollow area.

Several chunks of cement crashed down behind her as Hawk searched on her hands and knees for the pack. Crawling beside the table in the pitch black, her hand grazed the nylon strap. Moving her hand back, her fingers found it again. Grabbing it tightly, she stood up and unzipped it. Reaching inside, she found her night vision goggles.

The chiseling stopped, followed by a dreadful series of hissing. Hawk pulled the goggles over her face and turned around. The crater in the wall had been opened up entirely. Underneath it, she saw several large bodies climbing down the wall like ants. One was on the floor, moving toward her. With a body length of four feet and a leg-span of six, the creature resembled a spider. Its face contained no eyes, though it possessed several fanged mandibles.

She shrieked and drew her Beretta. The creature sprang toward her, rearing its front legs like pickaxes. Its two tentacles unwrapped from their coiled position, and rose over the creature's head. A barb protruded from the ends, drooling a sappy fluid.

Hawk pointed the gun and squeezed the trigger. Her ears rang as the gun went off, splintering the invader's facial features. The beast reeled backwards, flailing its tentacles as though it were in agony. Behind it, several other creatures worked their way through the hole in the wall. Hawk shot several rounds toward the nearest one.

The slide locked back. She ejected the bag and fumbled for a fresh one.

"Shit...shit..." she cursed as she struggled to grab the mag from its pouch. The beasts crawled over their dead comrades toward her. The nearest one, a humanoid beast with stinger exposed from each hand, sprang toward her.

Hawk screamed and dove to the right, narrowly dodging the two stingers. Hawk got on her elbows and knees and tried to crawl away. Hitting her head on the leg of a lab table, she stopped and turned. Straightening her goggles, she looked up, seeing the beast quickly moving toward her. Its mandibles folded over two pincer-like appendages that was its mouth.

Trapped and helpless, Hawk yelled.

The creature's torso tore open as several gunshots rang out. The creature fell away from her into a pool of its own blood.

Several more gunshots rang out, generating several screeches from the beasts. Hawk rolled over and grabbed her pack, as Seymour stepped around the lab tables toward her. He fired several rounds into the horde then grabbed her by the vest.

"We can't hold them off forever!" he yelled as he pulled her to her feet. Nagamine and Terrie covered the stairway entrance. Shell casings riddled the floor as they emptied their submachine guns into the invading horde. Hawk checked her pack, making sure her flash drive was intact.

She gave a thumbs-up, and followed Seymour out the door. Nagamine and Terrie were first to rush down the stairs. Seymour fired several more rounds to keep the creatures back while Hawk went next.

The H&K's ran empty. Seymour let the weapon sling, and he drew his revolver. One of the humanoids rapidly approached. Seymour pointed the gun and fired. The .357 bullet ruptured the creature's head, spreading orange blood and brain matter all over the lab.

Several more of the creatures gathered upon him. Crawling over one another, and over their dead comrades, the beasts completely filled the room. A series of screeches drowned out the wind and thunder as they moved in on their prey.

Seymour backed down the stairs, shooting the remaining seven rounds into the crowd. With the cylinder empty, he turned and jumped the remaining stairs, landing in front of the open doorway. He moved out of the way as Nag and Terrie took firing positions.

Alien creatures tore through the doorway, chipping the frames as they filled the stairway. Like locusts, they filled the entire stairwell. Numerous arachnid creatures climbed the walls, rapidly moving toward the door. In seconds, the entire stairwell was alive. Nagamine and Terrie fired several bursts up at the horde, causing several eruptions of guts. Terrie's machine pistol emptied, and she quickly grabbed a fresh mag. Looking back up, the creatures were near the door.

"There's too many!" she yelled. "They're coming down faster than we can shoot them!"

"There's more coming from the front!" Ivan yelled from the bunker entrance. "They're all over the place."

"Shut the goddamned door," Seymour yelled. Hawk and Nag pushed the heavy steel door inward. It was like pushing against a wall. The door's hinges were rusted, slowing the rotation of the joints. The door squealed as it slowly moved. Hawk shook her head.

"This isn't gonna work! It won't shut!" she yelled. Nag gave up and fired another burst into the stairwell. Two beasts dropped, only for the remaining horde to scurry overtop them. Nag's weapon emptied. Seymour took his place, firing several rounds into the mass.

Rex rushed toward the doorway, wearing his flamethrower harness.

"Might wanna move," he said, pointing the shaft into the stairwell. Seymour was already out of the way as Rex prodded the nozzle into the stairwell. Rex squeezed the trigger, and a river of fire sprayed from the nozzle.

Flames consumed the entire stairwell. Screams filled the air as alien creatures scurried in all directions. Bodies encased in flame rampaged all over the stairwell. Dead creatures rained from the walls, as smoke billowed from the doorway. A wall of heat hit the mercenaries, driving them back from the stairway.

The fire and smoke rapidly spread to the top of the stairway, forcing the herd back into the lab. Like a raging river, the fire continued into the lab.

Several creatures covered in flames scuttled throughout, smashing into tables and lab equipment. Like termites being smoked out of woodwork, the aliens began working their way out through the hole in the wall.

They worked their way down the outside exterior. They climbed on all sides, gathering near the loopholes. In a collaborative effort, the arachnid beasts used their rigid forelegs to chisel away at the edges. They viciously clawed at the cement, widening the opening as they broke away large chunks of debris.

The operations room filled with black smoke, causing the mercenaries to gag. The air smelled of charred flesh and fuel. In moments, the room turned black. Holding his breath, Ivan picked up his M60. He let the flamethrower shaft hang from its hose, and he stuck the machine gun through the loophole, firing at the creatures that chiseled at the walls.

"Boss?" he yelled. Seymour looked outside, seeing the army of creatures moving about. "You still think running's a good plan?"

"We can't stay here. We're gonna have to run for it," Seymour said.

"Where the hell are we gonna go?!" Hawk shouted.

"Anywhere but here!" Seymour said.

A loud, fiery hiss rang from the planning room office. Realizing his trip-flare had been triggered, Seymour moved to the hallway.Bits of gravel rained from the loopholes as the creatures clawed their way in. Terrie and Hawk followed him.

"Oh, not good," Terrie muttered.

"Everyone to the entrance!" Seymour yelled. "Head to the…"

An ear-piercing screech rang out. Seymour rushed back into the operations room. The partially shut stairwell door burst open, and several flaming creatures scurried out.

"Holy mother!" Ivan shouted, seeing several bodies of fire tear into the room. Blinded by smoke and flame, he fired blindly into the horde. He felt Rex's hand grabbing him by the shoulder harness.

"Go! Go!" Rex yelled, dragging Ivan into the hallway corridor. Seymour, Hawk, and Terrie retreated back to the planning room.

Nagamine fired several shots into the nearest beast. It dropped dead in a pool of boiling blood. Two other creatures, both completely encased in fire, sprang toward him. They climbed over their dead comrade, and onto the nearby fuel tank.

Nagamine turned and dashed into the operations office. He slammed the door shut behind him, and dove under the desk.

The fuel barrel exploded like a bomb. The entire wall shattered like glass, leaving enormous hunks of cement everywhere. Typhoon winds rushed into the new opening, twirling the fire into twisting funnel shapes.

With its supports completely ravaged, the second floor collapsed onto the operations room. Thousands of pounds of concrete smashed into the flooring, creating a concussion which rippled through the remaining portion of the bunker. A wave of dust and smoke followed, completely filling the planning room.

Alien creatures fell around as the side of the building crumbled. High pitched hisses echoed as the army of beasts started digging through the rubble.

CHAPTER
30

Ivan and Rex burst from the entrance just as the entire front side crumbled. Fire ripped throughout the open space, forcing the creatures to scatter. Flames whipped about, stirred by the intense wind.

Ivan put a hand over his eyes to block the rain. He looked at the circling horde of aliens, then back to the bunker. He saw several creatures, humanoid and insect-like, quickly beginning to move in on them. Barbs protruded from limbs, and terrifying screeches resounded. Ivan pointed his M60 and fired.

"Come get some, you ugly pricks!" he shouted. Rex turned, seeing several other creatures moving in from behind them. Standing back-to-back with Ivan, he fired a stream of fire from his flamethrower. An orange flash illuminated the jungle as a wall of flame consumed the three nearest aliens.

"We need to get the others," Rex said. He turned to run toward the rubble. He stopped after only a few steps. Several creatures squeezed their way out of the debris.

"God! Where are they coming from?!" he yelled, overwhelmed and frustrated.

"They came from those pods! That damn alien infected everything on this damned island!" Ivan yelled. "All the wildlife...everything became hosts for those spores! And now they've hatched!"

Several more creatures emerged from the rubble, while others climbed over the top of what remained of the structure.

"Son of a bitch, they're all over us! We can't wait," Rex said. Ivan continued firing, sweeping the barrel of his gun at the various hordes. Rex grabbed him by the shoulder. "Dude, we gotta go!" Ivan gritted his teeth, firing off several more rounds before darting to the woods. They jumped through the tree line, fighting jungle and weather as they fled.

Rex looked back. The plants rustled behind them. The creatures were pursuing by the dozen.

"They just don't quit!" he yelled. He turned around and fired a stream of fire. The fire coursed through the jungle, instantly withering the smaller plants. Alien screams echoed, and they could see the plants rustling around them as their pursuers circled.

Ivan sprayed dozens of bullets into the jungle. Finally, his M60 ran empty.

"Shit!" he cursed. He dropped the machine gun and snatched the dangling flamethrower shaft. After sending a stream of fire toward the sound, the two men continued fleeing into the jungle.

****

Hawk gagged as she struggled for breath. Smoke and dust accumulated throughout the planning room, making the air thick and toxic. Seymour fired through the loopholes, fighting to keep the creatures from digging their way in. Terrie shot her machine-pistol into the planning office, as one of the humanoids pried itself through. Its face imploded as the 9mm bullets pierced through it, causing its corpse to hang from the opening.

"I'm running low," she said. Seymour drove another creature back with his weapon, then glanced out the loophole. He looked at the trench in the ground that led from the bunker.

"There should be a back exit somewhere through here!" he shouted.

Terrie glanced out, seeing the beasts scurrying about. "Are we sure we want to go out there?"

"Not much choice. We don't want to stay here! If those things don't get us, we suffocate. Either we take our chances out there or die for sure in here." Seymour said. He glanced over at Hawk, who was struggling to reload her pistol. "Agent, are you aware of any back exit?"

Hawk coughed and wheezed. Her eyes were bloodshot, and her mouth was dry. Squinting hard, she looked over at the storage room.

"The boxes!" she said, spitting black saliva as she spoke. "There's a hatch under the MRE boxes!" Still gagging for breath, she rushed into the storage room. She pulled the pile of boxes away from the wall, scattering them onto the floor. Terrie ran over and assisted. They pulled several boxes from the corner, revealing a large steel hatch door.

Hawk turned a lever on its top, and pulled up tightly. The door would not budge. Hawk pulled harder, pushing up with her feet as she held on to the handle. Terrie pushed her aside and pulled up on the hatch.

"Damn it!" she yelled, unable to open it.

"It's been closed for over seventy years. It's rusted shut," Hawk said. Seymour fired several more rounds through the loophole, Seymour ran to the hatch.

"Move!" he shouted. Hawk and Terrie stepped out of the way as Seymour slammed the butt of his weapon down hard on the frame. He struck the hatch several times, breaking off tiny bits of rust from the edges and hinge. He grabbed the lever and pulled up with all of his strength. The hatch squeaked as it slowly opened. The lever snapped free, causing Seymour to fall backward against the wall. The hatch door was stuck open at a forty-five-degree angle. Terrie ignited a flare stick and dropped it down the shaft. It hit the floor only ten feet down, illuminating a small weapons closet.

Large chunks of cement burst into the planning room as the creatures widened the loopholes. A humanoid creature started crawling through the nearest one. Seymour pushed himself off from the wall, and raised his weapon. Numerous cavities exploded as he pumped several rounds into the invader. He looked over his shoulder to Terrie and Hawk.

"Go! Go! Go!" he yelled. Hawk lowered herself onto her stomach and slipped through the hatch. The ladder bars were completely covered in rust and soot. Red light flickered from the flare as Hawk lowered herself down the ladder. Clear of the smoke, she drew a deep breath. The air smelled of rot and a foul taste, but it was cleaner than the fumes above.

Terrie quickly followed her down into the small storage area. Terrie removed a flashlight from her vest and shined it on the door.

A loud slamming noise drew their attention back upward, as Seymour kicked the hatch door to widen it. Laying on his stomach, he squeezed his muscular bulk through the partially open hatch, pulling it shut as soon as he was completely through.

Hawk yanked the lever to the tunnel door.

"Wait!" Seymour shouted, stopping her before she could open it. She stopped and listened, hearing the screeches coming from outside. Seymour removed two grenades from his vest and pulled the pins, keeping the handles intact. He looked at Terrie, who stood ready by the door. "Get ready to run for the trees. These bastards will be on us like flies on shit." Hawk and Terrie gave a thumbs-up, signaling they were ready.

Terrie turned the lever and pressed against the door. It opened outward, leading to a narrow trench. Five or six creatures were in the tunnel, looking toward the door as it opened. Seymour launched the grenades, their handles springing free and igniting the charge. Terrie slammed the door shut.

The grenades exploded, sending shrapnel and concussive force into the tunnel. Terrie opened the door again, and Seymour took point. Three of the creatures were blown apart by the blasts, while two others writhed on the ground, severely wounded. He aimed his rifle to the edge of the trench, as two arachnid creatures approached the edge. He fired two bursts, landing headshots on each one.

Terrie and Hawk followed him out. Seymour knelt down, giving each of them a boost to climb out of the trench. Terrie went first, followed by Hawk. Several creatures were rapidly approaching on both sides of the trench. Seymour jumped and clutched the edge with both hands, pulling himself up in a chin-up manner.

"Where the hell are the others?!" Terrie asked.

"No time! Get going!" Seymour said, pushing himself up from the edge. "Run for the trees."

The three sprinted, firing several rounds into the swarm. Numerous creatures swarmed over the bunker as though claiming territory, while several others pursued the fresh meat.

****

Nagamine rose from behind the desk, seeing the office door completely blown off its hinges. Fire and smoke had already filled the room. Looking through the smoke, Nagamine saw the rubble that blocked his way. He was trapped in the office, the only intact segment of the bunker's front side.

Several sharp appendages stabbed in-between the rubble segments. The creatures were trying desperately to get to him. He turned around and looked through the loophole. Multiple creatures were digging at the wall, breaking fragments from the opening. He was absolutely trapped.

With enemies digging their way in from both sides, and the air nearly unbreathable, Nag knew he only had minutes. He checked his ammunition. His current mag was nearly spent, and he only had one full one remaining. He switched them out, then let the weapon hang from its strap. He pulled two grenades from his vest. He approached the entrance, as two jagged forelegs protruded through the rubble. The arms wiggled to pry apart the debris. The alien withdrew its arms, leaving a six-inch hole in the "wall".

Nagamine drew the pins and slipped both grenades through the hole. He turned and jumped behind the desk. The aliens screeched, and the grenades exploded. A concussion wave swept into the office, pushing the desk back nearly against the wall.

Nagamine pushed it back to make space as he stood up. The wall of debris had collapsed, and the aliens behind it blown to pieces. It would be seconds before more gathered in. He jumped over the desk, and tore out of the office.

He looked up, seeing several beasts perched up on the second floor. Legs bent in a crouching position, they looked down at him. He then glanced behind him. The rain had dampened the fire, and several creatures were once again moving in onto the bunker. Outnumbered and low on ammo, Nagamine sprinted toward the trees. The creatures sprang like grasshoppers, pursuing him into the jungle.

****

"Twenty-six! Twenty-seven!" Rex shouted as he cast a flame over two creatures.

"Still ahead of you!" Ivan said. He blazed the forest with his flamethrower. The dark forest lit in a hellish flicker, giving the mercenaries a view into the depths of the forest. Fire raged about, climbing the trees. Between the trees, bodies of fire ran about as burning aliens fled. The rain continued pummeling the forest, gradually putting out the flame.

Ivan led the retreat into the jungle, while Rex maintained a constant blaze behind them. Clawing sounds and rustling leaves gave away the presence of a humanoid creature flanking at him from the left. He turned, stopping the beast's assault with a stream of fire. The creature screamed and backed away, blazing in the forest. The intense heat and fire quickly overwhelmed it, and its body slumped in the dirt.

"Twenty-eight!" Rex said.

"Still behind," Ivan shouted. Looking ahead, he saw two large bushes in his way. Leaning in with his shoulder, he plowed through. When looking back up, they had come into a small open area, on the edge of a steep hill. "Whoa!" He halted himself, and gazed at the hill. In the black of night, it was impossible to see how far down it led.

"Crap, if you think we're lost now—just wait 'til we go down there," Rex said.

"We can't stay *here!*" Ivan said. The scraping sound of sharp talons grinding against the dirt drew their attention backwards. Ivan turned and pointed his nozzle. He squeezed the trigger. A tiny burst of flame, the size of a soccer-ball, ripped from the nozzle and evaporated. "Shit!" Ivan cursed. Air had gotten into the pipe. Two arachnid-shaped creatures ripped through the plants and crawled toward them. Ivan jumped out of the way.

Rex fired a burst of flame from his flamethrower. The creatures darted in opposite directions, avoiding the stream. Rex yelled, still triggering the flamethrower. He swept the nozzle to the right, its stream of fire following the creature.

Ivan backed away from the approaching alien. Its tentacles uncoiled, and looped over its body. Ivan fell backward, narrowly avoiding the duel strike as the tentacles lunged toward him. On his back, Ivan pulled his Desert Eagle from his leg holster. The creature scurried toward him to strike. He fired several rounds into its head, causing blood and saliva to burst like a volcano. The creature flailed its tentacles and legs, rolling frantically along the ground. Ivan sprung back to his feet, and shot several rounds into the dying alien's body. After the flailing stopped, Ivan ripped the harness from his shoulders. He reloaded his pistol and knelt down to inspect the valves.

Rainwater gradually put out the surrounding fire as Rex waited for the creatures to re-emerge. He taunted them in his mind, daring them to attack once more. His finger trembled on the nozzle trigger.

"Come on, you fuckers," he muttered out loud. "Come get some." As if in direct response, several humanoids sprang from the darkness. Abandoning his flamethrower, Ivan retreated backwards while firing several rounds from his pistol.

Rex's stream of fire barely missed him as he engulfed the two creatures. They retreated backwards, writhing to put the flames out. Rex ran forward, coating them in even more flame.

"Ah-ha!" he yelled victoriously. "Whatcha runnin' for! You not like that?!"

It listened to the screams of its children as the prey inflicted its fury. It watched their bodies blaze in extreme heat, unable to reach the target.

Its goal of flushing its enemies out was successful, though at greater cost than it desired. The flamethrowers provided a substantial defense against its tactics, destroying much of its spawn.

The Pilot did not experience grief, nor anger. It contained only a basic instinct: expansion of the species. This instinct drove its logic, and therefore its strategic planning.

This target was not worth the cost.

The gauntlet illuminated in bright colors, and the Pilot extended its arm.

"Burn, motherfucker, burn!" Rex yelled in glory as he blazed the forest. A large yellow-green flash drew his attention.

It came at the speed of light. The ball of energy shot through the jungle, hitting him square in the stomach. In the briefest of instances, Rex felt a combination of intense heat and pressure, as the energy ball punched through him like a battering ram. The energy ball burst into a huge explosion, triggering an immediate second explosion as the canisters ruptured.

A huge ball of fire ripped upward into the trees, throwing Ivan completely off his feet. He landed square on his back, splashing into a pool of mud.

****

A thunderous boom echoed through the jungle, bringing Seymour to a stop. He had been leading Terrie and Hawk toward the dim flashes caused by the flamethrowers, intending to regroup with the rest of the team. The radios and headpieces had been lost during the chaos, and he had no way of communicating.

Through the jungle, they could see dim flickering of orange and red. He felt that dreaded sixth sense. Something horrific had just happened. He looked behind them. The creatures were not in sight, but their movements and hisses could be heard within the depths of the jungle.

There was no time to plan. The best likeliness of reuniting with the team was to follow the flashes. He continued running, waving for the others to follow.

****

Fire crackled everywhere as fuel from the canisters burned. The world seemed blurry as Ivan leaned up. He had hit the ground hard, knocking the wind out of him. Worst, water and mud had splattered over his eyes, further limiting his vision.

He wiped his fingertips over his eyes, brushing the mud away. He rolled to his right.

Two feet beside him, Rex's arm lay in the muck, completely blown away near the bicep area. Several feet past it was a leg, severed below the knee. Ivan gasped and pushed back. He leaned up and looked around. Scattered everywhere were scorched bits of his friend. The fire blazed all around him, nearly forming a circle.

From straight ahead, a shape broke through the wall of fire. Horror and helplessness consumed Ivan as he saw the towering Pilot approach him. Those massive black fangs jittered, and the three fingers opened up, exposing the stinger.

"No! NO!" Ivan yelled, kicking with his legs. The creature stood over him, and lunged with its stinger. Ivan screamed. He threw his arms out, wrapping both hands around the creature's wrist. The barb stopped, less than an inch from his chest.

Muscles bulged, and teeth grinded as Ivan fought against the Pilot's superior strength. He sneered, feeling the stinger closing in slowly.

Torturously slow. A slimy substance dripped from its tip, spilling onto his chest.

Ivan's eyes went to the creature's face. Its eyeless dome of a head gazed at him, those fangs jittering as though making a taunting expression. Ivan wheezed through his teeth, desperately trying to keep it off.

"No! NO!" he screamed. An ear-piercing hiss rang out, and the fangs yawned upward until they were protruding out from its face. In a hammer-like motion, the Pilot rammed its head down on Ivan's face, spearing its fangs through both of his eyes.

Ivan screamed and writhed, the pain and terror eliminating the strength from his arms. The beast's arm slipped through his fingers, the barb puncturing his stomach.

CHAPTER
31

The echo from Ivan's screams drove Seymour to quicken his pace. Twigs and leaves slapped his face as he ran. Terrie and Hawk sprinted to keep up with him.

The air was still hot, though the fires were steadily dying down from the rain. The glow from the flame brightened as Seymour drew nearer. The screams had stopped, spurring a deep sense of dread. The air grew hotter, and the smoke thicker.

The flames were waist high when Seymour arrived. The air smelled of burnt flesh and fuel, and the ground was littered with various human remains. Terrie arrived moments after Seymour. She immediately cupped a hand over her mouth. Entrails, curled like rope, were strung about all over. She saw the severed arm and leg, with no trace of the torso. Metal fragments of the flamethrower were embedded into the ground and trees like shrapnel.

Hawk arrived, gasping for breath. She looked down at the carnage. "Oh, Lord..."

Seymour looked down at the arm. Recognizing the glove, he knew it was Rex's. A couple of feet to the right, the mud had been kicked up as though a struggle took place. Several feet off to the side, the other flamethrower lay intact. Fire had scorched the canisters, and several dents marked the sides, but did not ignite the fuel. Looking around, there was no trace of Ivan.

"You think they got him?" Terrie asked. Seymour didn't answer, as he wasn't sure. "What the hell are all these things?"

"They grew out of those spores," Seymour said. "Those friggin graveyards are nest sites for these things. If I knew what they held..." he glared at Hawk, "we'd have blown those nests up when we came across them. But of course, we weren't given certain information."

Hawk faced him, her face livid. "Seymour, we've been through this. We suspected that this creature was dangerous. Until tonight, I didn't know what that thing was capable of. As I said, our computers estimated that this thing had visited many planets, maybe several galaxies, and NEVER went to the same place twice. It gave me cause for concern. Seeing the aftermath of what took place confirmed the threat for me!"

A bloodcurdling scream echoed through the jungle, drawing the attention of all three. A second scream immediately followed.

"Help!" the voice cried out. Seymour felt a chill. It was Ivan's voice. All three of them quickly darted toward the sound. Ivan called out again, in a loud gurgling voice. "Heelllp!"

Terrie followed Seymour closely as they ran along the edge of the hill. Despite the adrenaline she was experiencing, her mind was still sharp. Something about this didn't seem right.

Lightning sparked above, casting a glow over the jungle. Seymour saw a wall of blue, where the light shone down into a clearing several yards ahead of them.

"I see him!" Seymour said, pointing toward a gap in the plants.

"Wait!" Terrie shouted, grabbing Seymour by the shoulder. He stopped and looked at her.

"What?"

She unslung her sniper rifle, and raised the weapon eye level. She peered through the night-vision scope. Ivan was slumped against a tree. His head was slung, his body was motionless...

His eyes gone! Reduced to black blots in the night-vision.

Movement near his head drew her attention. She focused in.

"Oh, God!" she said. The creature was the size of a squirrel, with long legs resembling a cricket's. Two front appendages, almost as thin as wire, were embedded into Ivan's throat. They wiggled like fishing line. As they did, Ivan's slack jaw jittered ever-so-slightly. "Help...me..."

Terrie placed the critter center in her crosshairs. She pulled the trigger, exploding it into several different pieces. She lowered the gun, her face tense with horror.

"The damn thing was manipulating his vocal cords," she said.

"Are you serious?" Hawk said. "Why?"

"Sons-of-bitches have a bunch of tricks up their sleeves," Seymour said. "It was setting a friggin trap. It was luring us in to..." he paused, looking up into the trees. With his night-vision goggles lost in the firefight, he struggled to see anything. "Terrie, point that thing up into the trees."

Terrie shouldered her weapon and pointed it upward. Perched in the trees above, were several of the offspring creatures. They were already scurrying down the branches, moving in on their position.

"Oh shit...they're onto us!" Terrie yelled.

Seymour raised his weapon. "How many?"

"A whole damn circus!" Terrie said.

She immediately placed one of the creatures in her crosshairs and fired. The creature exploded into a cloud of blood, its body falling from the tree. The other creatures screeched, while quickening their pace.

****

Nagamine backed away, firing several bursts from his MP5. Arachnid creatures hissed as bullets tore into their exoskeletons, exploding fragments and blood from their bodies.

He turned to the right, dropping to a kneeling position as a humanoid ran at him from the side. He fired two bursts, shredding the creature's abdomen. It fell forward, blood spraying from its wounds. Its mandibles flailed over its mouth, and its pointed arms reached forward. Desperate to get to its prey, it crawled forward.

Nagamine pointed the MP5. Like a hitman executing an assignment, he pressed it to the creature's head point blank and fired. The head burst into several shell fragments and blood, the severed mandibles twitching in the mixture of brain matter and mud.

It was his last shot, running his last remaining magazine dry. With no more ammo, he discarded the weapon and drew his Sig-SaurP226.

He ducked under vines and branches as he struggled to run through the terrain. He had heard the explosion and could barely see the orange glow of the fire. Gunfire echoed throughout the jungle, though he couldn't precisely pinpoint where it was coming from. Nagamine followed his best instinct, which told him to go for the light. He didn't have much time, as the rain was quickly killing the fire.

He ran through the terrain, watching the orange glow become evermore dim. He found himself surrounded by smoke, indicating he was near. The glow nearly disappeared, almost down to simmering embers. Nag snatched a flare from his pocket and ignited it. The tip broke into a flame, lighting the way as he stepped into the clearing.

The flare flashed a red glow onto the clearing, bringing to view the carnage and devastation. Nagamine saw the ravaged remains, immediately realizing they belonged to Rex.

Two creatures reared up from the mud. Both were humanoid in appearance, charred entrails dangling from their mandibles. Nagamine tossed the flare at them, causing both creatures to spring to their feet.

Nagamine grasped his pistol with both hands, firing multiple shots into the nearest alien. It took six rounds in the chest, before it fell to the ground. Nagamine pivoted to aim for the second one as it sprang. Despite taking three rounds in the abdomen, the creature closed in.

Nagamine fell into a somersault, rolling out of the creature's path. It swiftly turned to pursue.

As Nagamine rolled to his feet, he drew his ninjato from its sheath. He turned, swinging the blade in a horizontal line. Bubbling blood burst as the blade passed through the creature's neck. The mandibles continued to flail as the head fell from the body. The headless figure twitched on its legs before finally dropping into the mud.

Cast in a red glow from the flare, Nagamine drew a quick breath. A new smell entered his nose. He glanced to the flare, seeing a shadow emerge from the tree line. He turned to the left and fired his pistol.

Bullets crushed against its armor as the Pilot launched itself at him. It swung its pincer glove, knocking the pistol clear from Nagamine's grasp. The stinger protruded, and the alien shoved its right arm toward its prey.

Nagamine swiped his blade up and across, in a windshield wiper movement. The Pilot screeched, withdrawing its arm. The severed stinger dangled from a tiny strand of tissue. Venom and blood spilled from the stump. The creature hissed violently, stepping back. The stinger broke away as the stump sank back into the palm.

Seizing the opportunity, Nagamine lunged forward. Clutching the handle with both hands, he struck down vertically. The Pilot raised its left arm, deflecting the blade with the strange metal glove. Nagamine immediately struck again, the blade generating sparks as it was again deflected by the glove.

The Pilot hissed as it retaliated. The pincer opened, and the beast lunged back at its enemy. Nagamine shuffled back. The tips struck together as the pincer closed inches from his face. He yelled as he slashed the sword in a low, horizontal strike. The blade clanged against the body armor, and the Pilot moved in.

Its claw opened and thrust forward. Nagamine thrust the blade out, clanging it into the center of the glove. The pincer closed, locking in on the blade. The two stood mano-a-mano, locked in a deadly embrace.

Nagamine sneered, trying to pull his sword free from the claw. The creature, by far superior in strength, slowly pulled back. Nagamine kept his grasp, looking into the face of his enemy, which seemed to stare back. Though there were no eyes, it clearly was looking at him.

The pincers tightened, resulting in a loud crashing sound. Nagamine stumbled back. The blade of his sword broke just above the hilt. He dropped the handle and reached for his knife.

The three fingers on the Pilot's right hand clenched into a fist. The beast snarled and swung its arm downward, catching Nagamine in the temple. He fell several feet backward. Blood spat from his mouth as he lay on his back.

The creature clicked its pincers as it marched toward him.

****

Terrie ignited a flare, sparking a red glow into the trees. Seymour blasted his rifle at the incoming creatures. Bodies fell from the canopy, only for others to arrive in their place. Shooting upward, his magazine emptied.

"I'm on my last mag!" he shouted.

Hawk fired several rounds from her Beretta. The slide locked back. She ejected the mag, grabbing the last one from her pouch. She too, was on her last.

"We're not gonna last," she said. She slammed the mag in, and pulled the slide to chamber the first round.

Seymour struggled to think of a plan. With his weapon set on Semi-auto, he picked and chose his shots carefully. Soon he'd be out, leaving him only with his revolver. And that wouldn't last long either.

A thought then stuck in his mind. The flamethrower. Not his first choice for jungle warfare, but it certainly beat having no ammo at all.

"Withdraw!" he shouted, leading the team through the path back toward the hill.

The team retreated, with Terrie providing cover support. Creatures rained onto the ground, pursuing the team through the jungle. Terrie held her rifle from the waist. A humanoid creature closed in from a yard away, barbs protruding from each hand. She tilted the barrel up, sending a round into its chest. The beast fell backward, only for several arachnid creatures to crawl over it.

Snatching a grenade from her vest, Terrie pulled the pin and dropped it at her feet. She turned around and sprinted to catch up. A blast ignited behind her, shooting shrapnel throughout the surrounding jungle.

Seymour glanced back, making sure Terrie was still with him. He saw the cloud of smoke behind her. The explosion had driven the horde back, though he could still hear them scurrying through the woods.

He turned his eyes forward, keeping track of the path before him. They were almost there.

****

Nagamine reached again for his knife. He yanked it from its sheath as the creature stepped over him. It raised its clawed boot and stomped it down onto his wrist, pinning it into the ground. Bones in his forearms and wrist snapped, drawing a yell from Nagamine.

Its pincer clicked, then opened. The Pilot thrusted the apparatus downward, clamping the pincers around Nagamine's neck. He felt the sharp edges close in beneath his jawline, sinking into his skin.

The Pilot stepped back, lifting its prize. Nagamine's feet kicked nearly a yard off the ground as the Pilot lifted its arm high. Slicing and choking sensations tormented the tracker as he dangled from the claw. Grabbing the claw with his one functional hand, he tried in vain to pull the pincers apart.

Blood gushed from his neck as the pincers began to tighten. The constriction was slow and torturous, as though the Pilot was punishing him for the severing of its stinger. The edges sliced through muscle and vocal tissue, and clamped down hard on the spinal column. Applying extra pressure, the neckbone snapped, and the two pincers met.

****

The red flare still blazed as Seymour arrived in the clearing. He stopped dead in his tracks, seeing Nagamine held up in the creature's grasp. A moment later, the metal clang of the pincers rang out, and Nagamine's head and body fell separately to the ground.

The Pilot turned its gaze, spotting him as he raised his rifle. It raised its glove, shielding its face from the bombardment Seymour rapidly fired at the creature's head.

Terrie and Hawk arrived behind him, and immediately started firing at the beast. The Pilot turned and retreated into the jungle. Yelling in anger, Seymour ran after it, firing his last burst of ammo in the creature's trajectory. He drew his revolver, ready to run after it.

"No, stop!" Terrie yelled. Seymour kept his gaze on the dark canvas, desperate to kill the creature and avenge his men. He stepped back, allowing reason to overtake his emotion.

CHAPTER
32

The team quickly checked behind them. The creatures appeared to have given up their pursuit. However, with the thick terrain, and howling of the wind, they could be anywhere. Hawk and Terrie watched the perimeter as Seymour inspected the flamethrower. He pressed the trigger, determining the root of the problem.

He bled the pipe, clearing it of the air that jammed the flow, pointing the nozzle into the jungle to test it. At the press of the trigger, a stream of fire shot into the trees.

After strapping the harness over his shoulders, he looked down at Nagamine's beheaded corpse. A few feet away from it was the severed stinger, and the broken sword. *At least the bastard didn't get away unscathed.* However, considering the creature's healing process, he knew the injury was likely not permanent.

Seymour lifted the shaft and sprayed a stream of fire into the woods. The flames did not trigger any motion nor screeches, indicating the creatures were not in the immediate proximity. He looked to the ground, seeing Nagamine's pistol. He picked it up, then walked over to the body. He gave a brief moment of silence, then dug for any remaining contents in Nag's vest. He had one grenade left over, and two extra mags for the pistol. He held them out to Hawk. "Here, take these."

A wave of guilt swept over the agent. She reluctantly accepted the gun and magazines, replacing her empty Beretta.

"Why aren't they making another run at us?" Terrie whispered.

"They're probably regrouping," Seymour said. "That alien, the Pilot, it's like a tactician. It ordered its soldiers in and flushed us out. Even just a few minutes ago; it diverted us. Its spawn...how it made Ivan call out to us...they knew they were setting a trap. They seem to understand our language."

"They're an invasive species," Hawk said. "The Pilot goes planet to planet, infecting the indigenous life with its spore. It spawns its own little army, and they wipe out the population, propagating the species.

When they do, they probably face resistance, and have to learn tactics to overcome any defenses."

"We're probably not the first intelligent species it's come across," Seymour said.

"No...God only knows how many worlds this thing has wiped out," Hawk said. She put a hand on her head, stunned by the realization. "We're lucky to have made it this far."

"It probably didn't expect us to have these." He tapped the flamethrower.

"They definitely don't like fire," Terrie said.

"The younger ones...They're smaller. They can be killed much more easily than the Pilot," Seymour said.

"It might be due to maturity," Hawk said. "Or it could just be different characteristics. As you saw, some looked much different than others. Hell, some are as small as a cat. The insect-looking ones seem to take more damage than the humanoids. Plus, none of them have the technology the Pilot possesses."

"Maturity?" Seymour said. "You think, the longer these things live, the more they evolve?"

"I'm learning just as you are," Hawk said. "Like I said, I only suspected a threat. I wasn't aware of HOW this thing would bring disaster."

"Speaking of *how*... HOW are we getting out of here? Do we have a plan?" Terrie asked.

"We can't stay here," Seymour said. "We need to find a place to hole-up until morning."

"I say we make our way to the harbor," Hawk said.

"In this storm?" Seymour said. "Not a good idea. We'll make our way to the construction site. There's weapons, and ammo, and we can hole up inside the remaining bulldozers..."

"We don't have that kind of time," Hawk said. Seymour glared at her.

"You're *learning as we are*, eh?" he said. "Seems like there's something you're already aware of that we're not purvey to."

Hawk lamented, looking up to the sky. "There's an air-strike scheduled to begin tomorrow."

"Ohhh...an airstrike! Well, that's just LOVELY," Seymour said. "And just when were you gonna tell us about that?"

"I didn't know we were gonna be attacked," Hawk said. "I called after we discovered the embryo. I figured we'd last the night in the bunker, then leave a little before dawn when the storm let up. As long as we made a straight shot to the harbor, we'd be gone in time."

"Obviously we weren't supposed to know about it," Terrie said.

"Another part of the coverup," Seymour said. "Let me guess; they're going to coat this island in napalm, aren't they?"

"We don't have a choice," Hawk said. "Look how fast they've spread! Even the North Koreans understood this. You saw that those helicopters had been shot down by their own people and torched, by the looks of it. If these things get off the island...if they got into a major city...just imagine!"

"I think the C.I.A. is more concerned with the coverup aspect," Seymour said. "But luckily, it does solve that issue."

"When does the strike begin?" Terrie asked.

"Noon," Hawk said.

"I guess we're going to the harbor," Seymour said.

"Are you able to contact Charlie?" Terrie asked. "I know he doesn't want to fly in this storm, but..."

"I lost the radio in the bunker," Seymour said. "Ivan had the other one, AND the transponder." He looked at Hawk. "You still have that satellite phone?" She shook her head, as it too was lost during the chaos. "Alright, let's get moving. We can contact him from the Zodiac...assuming we make it there alive." He turned and led the way through the jungle.

Every few meters, he would spark a flame, hoping to deter the creatures from another attack.

CHAPTER 33

"Eagle Nest to Hatchling, report status, over," Charlie said into the transmitter. It was his tenth attempt to make contact. He had flown seventy miles south, keeping out of range of the typhoon. His plane bounced along the waters, as the edge of the storm still battered the Philippine Sea. The worst of the storm was now passing through. The winds had decreased to forty miles per hour. By the time he would arrive at the island, the storm would have passed almost entirely.

Seymour was thirty minutes overdue for his zero-five-hundred check-in. It was unlike his leader to miss such a deadline. These were *his* rules, and he above everyone else followed them to the letter. The radio silence made Charlie increasingly uneasy.

Charlie started pondering the possibilities. He hoped for equipment malfunction. Considering the weather and terrain, it was a possibility. He debated in his mind what to do. Each time he felt the urge to fly to the island, he would recall Seymour's instruction; "Do NOT attempt to come here unless you've heard from us." Charlie leaned over the console again and pressed the transmitter.

"Hatchling, this is Eagle Nest, acknowledge transmission," he said. No answer came through. "Hatchling...Seymour...Anybody, please respond." He depressed the transmitter. Nothing. "Shit!" he said to himself. He stepped away to pace along the first compartment. He stopped to look at his various monitors. He had managed to get a satellite image of the island. He glared at the center, knowing that's where the bunker was located. His eyes trailed down to the peninsula, where he would dock the plane at the harbor.

Seymour's instruction replayed in his mind again. At the present, there was nothing he could do. He took a seat in the cockpit, watching the waves roll about in the seemingly infinite ocean.

A low-pitched beep sounded from one of the computers. Charlie stood up and walked into the compartment. One of the monitors switched on, displaying a digital global map sheet. A red dot appeared on the western Pacific, seventy miles north of his position.

The emergency transponder had been activated.

A fuzzy static crackled over the radio, causing Charlie to run back into the cockpit. He quickly pressed the transmitter.

"This is Eagle Nest. Did not receive your transmission," he said. "I repeat...did NOT receive. Please repeat." Static came through once again. Charlie could recognize the sound of howling wind. Wherever it was coming from, it was not within the bunker. "Seymour?"

"...me..." a voice spoke through the static and wind.

"Please repeat," Charlie said.

The voice came through again, spoken extremely slowly. "Re...quesssst...piiccckuup..."

"The fuck?" Charlie muttered. He clicked the transmitter. "Ivan?"

"Y-Y-Y-Yes." His voice was very slow. The brief levity Charlie felt dissipated, replaced by increased nervousness. Even when drunk, he'd never heard the brute speak so slobbery.

"Where's Seymour? Where's the others?" he asked. Static crackled over the radio, but no answer. "Ivan? Please respond." He waited, but there was no response. Something was wrong. He feared the team was in trouble. The fact that Seymour himself was not answering was already a bad sign.

Charlie moved back to the map. He manipulated the touch screen to zoom in on the island. The blip was flashing near the north side. He then compared the location to the satellite image on the island, and the images he saved from his drone. It was the flat plain near the northern cliffs. It would be a bumpy landing, but he felt he could pull it off. He hurried back to the cockpit.

"This is Charlie," he said, dropping the formal etiquette. "I'm on route. Stand by."

The engines roared to life, and the propellers twirled. The plane skidded forward along the surface, until finally the nose tilted upward. In seconds, the plane was airborne, moving north toward Kuretasando.

CHAPTER
34

The clouds thinned as the storm finally passed over the island, allowing the morning sun to pierce the atmosphere. The canopy was a luminous gold as the trees took in the sunlight. The winds died down to a gentle breeze, reducing the squirming jungle back to its normal tranquility.

Mud squished under Seymour's boots as he led the team southwest. A thick, misty fog covered the forest floor, inhibiting his vision. It was like walking through the clouds, only these clouds were nearer to Hell than Heaven. Rain water dripped from the trees in a steady drizzle, as though the rainfall hadn't ceased.

The journey through the island had been long and tense. Fighting against the elements, while consistently being on the lookout for creatures all-in-all was a mental and physical strain. Mud, grit, and slime had completely covered their gear and uniforms, adding over twenty pounds to each person. The fog and humidity thickened the air, making the simple act of breathing a task in itself.

It was nothing Seymour wasn't trained for. He not only had trained to survive the elements, but to embrace them. Terrie had similar training, though she wasn't as conditioned to them as Seymour. She was more used to desert conditions as opposed to tropical.

Hawk lagged the most. Her soaked uniform felt as though it weighed a hundred pounds, and her breathing almost felt like waterboarding. Years of lab work and pencil pushing had greatly diminished her training and conditioning from her military experience. Though she didn't complain, she couldn't mask her fatigue. Breathing in and out her mouth, she was slouching with each step, momentarily leaning on each tree she passed. Her face was as drenched as her uniform from both sweat and rain.

Seymour led them through the thick fog, hacking vines and leaves out of his way. All night long he kept the flamethrower pointed, ready to singe any creature they might come across. The mist began to take on a golden sparkle, as the morning sun's rays were breaking through jungle exterior. They were nearing the coast.

Seymour moved around a large bamboo bush, then observed the path. There was a clearing ahead. Seeing the black, murky area, Seymour knew that it was not a natural gap. The vile smell confirmed it for him. They had arrived at a nest site.

It was the first nest that they discovered. It was an indication they were near the harbor. For Seymour, it was also an indication for danger. He quickly debated the options in his mind. He thought of moving around the nest and continuing to the harbor. Doing so, they would risk ambush, not just in moving toward the harbor, but in waiting for Charlie. Another option would be to attack first, and flush out the enemy.

Having grown sick of surprises, attacking first was the more appealing plan. With the nozzle pointed, he slowly approached the gravesite. Hawk looked toward the decay.

"What are you doing?" she whispered.

"Shh," Seymour hissed. He placed his finger on the trigger, then rushed in. It only took seven or eight running steps to close the distance. He yelled as he stopped at the edge, trigger halfway depressed.

The area was dark and silent. No creatures moved about in the area. Seymour looked at the forest of pods. The hosts from which they grew had been reduced to black piles of mush. Hawk and Terrie stepped alongside Seymour and gazed at the dead-zone.

Like onion peels, the sides of several of the pods had curled downward in over a dozen separate strands. They were empty, except for a pool of the black, slimy substance that leaked into the surrounding forest.

"Good lord," Terrie muttered. It was clear that the creatures they stored had hatched free.

"Where are they?" Hawk said.

"I wouldn't be surprised if these were among those that attacked us last night," Seymour said. He stepped further into the nest, passing numerous pods. There were over thirty, all of which were hatched. He finally stopped. "If they wanted to ambush us, they'd do it here."

"Why haven't we seen any?" Terrie asked. She looked to Hawk, who shrugged her shoulders.

"I don't know," she said. "One thing's for sure, we haven't killed them all."

"Not by a long shot," Seymour said. "For all we know, they're all over this damned island. It's like they're deliberately..." he trailed off, slightly tilting his head to listen. Terrie and Hawk remained quiet, listening carefully. At first, all they could hear was the tide splashing in. Hawk shook her head.

"I don't hear...wait..." she stopped. A slight droning sound took over. It was mechanical, coming from above. Plane engines!

In unison, they turned east and ran, brushing through the terrain for the nearby coast. The sunlight grew brighter with each step, and the droning grew louder. The shore was a small ledge, lined with trees and various other plants. Stepping between two large trees, they looked out into the Pacific.

"There!" Seymour pointed. Up in the sky, the ShinMaywa was gliding northbound, a half mile from the coast. It was gradually lowering its altitude, in the initial stages of preparing for a landing run. "What the hell is he doing?"

"He's flying north," Terrie said. "Why would he...wait..." She turned to Seymour. "Didn't he mention there was a flat plain to the north?" Seymour nodded, keeping his eyes on the ShinMaywa. "He might be landing there."

"But why there?" Hawk asked. "Why not just make landing at the harbor?"

"Why is he coming here *at all?*" Seymour said. "I told him not to come here until we've contacted him."

"We're over an hour overdue for a check-in," Terrie said.

"Doesn't matter," Seymour said. "He understood the situation. He wouldn't have come in unless he was called. Only Ivan and I had the radios, and there's no way..." he stopped and thought for a moment. "Ivan has the radio..." he muttered to himself. His mind flashed back to the firefight, how the creature manipulated Ivan's vocals to lure them. *He has the radio...and the transponder!* He looked to the south, seeing the sunken ships near the peninsula. "Oh no," he muttered.

Looking at the ships, Hawk suddenly understood the danger. The creatures were luring the aircraft toward the island.

"There's a radio in the Zodiac!" Seymour shouted.

They immediately took off running, quickly disappearing into the wilderness. Seymour was running fast, dodging obstacles as he hurried toward the peninsula, determined to get to the Zodiac before Charlie made his landing.

****

As he came around to the north, Charlie steered the plane nearer to the island. He watched the jungle seemingly "move" underneath him like a film as he flew over it. He turned west, following the northern coast.

He watched as the coastline changed from a vast tree line to a large rocky hill.

Finally, he located a hole in the vast roof of trees. The plain was atop a large hill that overlooked the Pacific. It was made mainly of grass, which was a brighter green than the rest of the island. In the middle of it, he noticed a string of small buildings. Though he only saw them for an instant, it was clear they were very old and broken down. Charlie snickered to himself, realizing this plain was used to launch aircraft in WW2, and the buildings were maintenance shacks. The grass was surprisingly short, as though it had been recently trimmed. *What, did they mow for me or something?*

Though Charlie preferred a water landing, the plain appeared flat enough. He flew over it, looking for any signs of the team.

"This is Eagle Nest," he said. "I'm preparing to make my landing." There was no response. He glanced back to the computer. The transponder signal was still coming from somewhere in the plain.

Maybe they're in one of those old shacks? he thought to himself. He steered the plane to the north to circle back, preparing for his landing run.

****

Seymour tucked his chin as he crashed through several thick bushes. The terrain acted as a never-ending blockade as he raced over several rolling hills. Every square foot of jungle was covered in roots and vines, which would easily snag on their feet as they ran.

Needing to lose the dead weight, Seymour tore his harness off and dropped the flamethrower in the muck. He continued running, followed closely by Hawk and Terrie. They moved over level ground for barely ten meters before the path slanted into a downward hill. The jungle thinned as they worked their way down.

They reached the bottom of the hill and came up on the ravaged remains of the outpost and harbor. Seymour stopped to look out to the horizon. The ShinMaywa was no longer in view.

"Hawk! Where's the boat?" he shouted. Exhausted and out of breath, Hawk stumbled to catch up. Her lungs felt as though they were on the verge of exploding, resulting in Hawk clutching her side.

"Come on," she said. Pushing through the pain, she took the lead. Running past the choppers and building, she led the group into the next cluster of trees.

****

175

The ShinMaywa began its approach. Charlie lowered the landing gear, and he lowered the plane's altitude, carefully watching the meters. He pulled the throttle to reduce RPM, and lowered the nose.

He crossed the threshold and pulled the throttle out completely. He pulled back on the control to keep the nose from dropping. The wheels made contact with the plain, resulting in a heavy bounce.

Charlie looked ahead. He only had another three hundred yards to bring the plane to a stop.

"Hold it steady," he whispered to himself. As the aircraft leveled out on the ground, he pressed his feet to the pedals. The plane gradually slowed, jittering as it moved along the slightly uneven terrain. As it came to a stop, Charlie pulled the mixture knob, killing the engine.

He stepped out and looked toward the old shacks, waiting for the team to step out. The doors were shut, and the windows were busted. So far, nobody was in sight. He lifted his portable radio to his mouth.

"This is Eagle Nest, I've landed. Repeat, I've landed. Please embark." He waited, and yet nobody arrived. "Fuck," he muttered. He strapped his radio to his vest and held his rifle close.

He started for the shacks.

****

"It's there!" Hawk shouted, leading the group into a small cove. Seymour dashed past her, seeing the Zodiac tucked underneath the reach of branches. He ducked underneath the low branches and climbed over the gunwale.

He stepped up to the helm, and snatched the microphone extender.

"Eagle Nest! Eagle Nest, come in!"

****

"What the…" Charlie had just stepped out of the ShinMaywa when his portable radio started blaring. "Boss? I'm here where the hell are you guys?"

"*Where are you?*"

"The north plain," he said. "You guys activated the transmitter."

"*No, that wasn't us! Take off! Take off immediately!*"

Charlie knew better than to question him. He turned and ran toward the plane. He hopped inside, shutting the door behind him. Taking his seat in the cockpit, he observed his surroundings to gauge his distances.

He pushed the knobs in and started the engine. Moving the plane forward, he slowly circled to starboard to ready the plane into takeoff position.

He was halfway through his circle when he glanced back toward the shacks. The doors were open.

A loud thud hit the portside hull.

What the hell? Charlie hit the brakes, stopping the plane. He stood up from his seat, and looked through the window. Another thud hit the hull directly beneath him.

A loud slam caused him to look back into the cabin. He could see sunlight streaming in near the back. He stood up from his seat and approached. The cabin door had been opened.

A loud hiss pierced his eardrums, prompting Charlie to snatch his H&K from the co-pilot seat. By the time he shouldered it, a greenish-grey figure climbed its way into the plane. The creature stood upright on two legs like a man. Mandibles flailed from its face, and each digit on both three-fingered hands bent back, exposing rounded palms. Flesh folded back like flaps as pointed barbs protruded from the palms.

The creature screeched and rushed through the cabin toward him.

"Holy Christ!" Charlie yelled, squeezing the trigger. The gun blasted at full-auto, sending over a dozen rounds into the creature's torso. Chunks of exoskeleton burst from its chest and abdomen, spilling gallons of orange blood. The creature screamed and fell back. It twitched as it lay in the pool of bubbling fluid.

Charlie's eyes were wide open, his breath nearly driven from his lungs. He kept the gun pointed at the corpse as he recovered from the sudden burst of adrenaline and shock.

A shadow overtook the cabin entry. Another hiss filled the air, as another creature climbed its way in. Charlie yelled as he pointed the gun and fired. Several rounds ripped through the creature's head. Its body slumped to the floor, partially hanging out the cabin entrance. Charlie ran through the cabin to shut the door. He stepped over the first dead creature, splattering its blood over his boots. With a hand on the door, he pressed his boot against the second creature to push it clear from the doorway.

His eyes turned to the landscape. The plain had come alive, with over two dozen creatures scurrying toward the plane like ants. Some were humanoid, while others had an insect-like appearance. Charlie shrieked and pulled the door shut.

A beast leapt into the frame, blocking the door. Charlie fell backward, hitting a nearby gunrack. Laying against the wall, he pointed his rifle toward the creature. The beast jolted with the repeated blasts, as though it were having a seizure. Its body slumped against the floor, only to be pulled backward by more creatures.

"Holy...." Charlie yelled as he scrambled to his feet. He reached for a fresh weapon on the gun rack, only to jump away as an arachnid creature scurried toward him. Its pointed limbs clanged against the metal floor. Tentacle appendages unfolded, wet barbs protruding from the tips. Charlie scampered backward, throwing anything he could at the creature. He grabbed a metal box from the shelf and launched it. It broke against the creature's head and fell to the floor, scattering its contents.

Charlie backed into the cockpit, finally pulling his pistol from its holster, immediately shooting a round off which skimmed the creature's back. Clasping the gun with both hands, Charlie focused his aim. Several rounds burst into its head, splattering innards onto the cabin floor.

Still holding his pistol, Charlie sat at the controls, immediately throttling the plane forward for a fast takeoff. The ShinMaywa continued its semicircle as it turned to face outward.

Thumps rattled throughout as the creatures climbed onto the hull. Humanoids leapt onto the nose, and onto the windshield. Several creatures mounted onto the starboard wing, causing the plane to slightly tilt. Charlie was now blind, steering with uneven weight distribution.

Metal clanging from the cabin caused him to look behind him. Several creatures had boarded the vessel and were now storming the cabin. In an automatic reaction, Charlie sprung from his seat, letting go of the steering as he pointed his gun toward the horde. He fired several rounds and closed the cabin door.

The plane straightened its path from a semicircle, still rolling forward at increasing speed. Charlie emptied his pistol into the nearest creature. As he slammed a fresh mag in, a heavy jolt launched him back against the console.

The wing had smashed into the shack, stopping the plane's momentum. Charlie killed the throttle, then kicked the door shut. He looked around, seeing creatures climbing all over the plane. He pressed the radio transmitter.

"BOSS! I've crashed! I'm trapped! They're all over me! I've..."

The door flung open, and creatures flooded the cockpit. Charlie turned, screaming as he fired several rounds into the crowding horde. The nearest arachnid beast rammed its bulk into him like a rhinoceros. Charlie fell back hard against the controls, the impact shaking the gun from his hand.

Charlie looked up, seeing the tentacles unfold. He screamed. The tentacles lashed down, driving both barbs into his stomach. The scream turned to a brief gurgle as all control was taken from Charlie. Fluid spilled from his lips, and every muscle became rigid, immobilizing him completely.

He slid from the console, and slumped to the floor, as the embedded tentacles pulsed.

The Pilot walked amongst its army, approaching the plane. The starboard wing had crashed into the guard shacks, severely damaging the rudders. It would require repair before departure. It was nothing the Pilot couldn't handle.

It entered the cabin entryway. The spawn vacated the cockpit, making way for their leader. The Pilot walked the length of the aircraft to the cockpit, intending to inspect the primitive design. As it walked, its foot knocked over the fallen metal container. Its flap opened, exposing the flare gun it contained.

CHAPTER
35

"Son-of-a-bitch! Goddamnit!" Seymour yelled, repeatedly slamming the mic down onto the Zodiac's console. He could hear Charlie's scream over the radio as he was overwhelmed. Like a man possessed, he struck the helm and the dashboard.

"Seymour!" Hawk called out in an attempt to calm him down. Seymour ripped his H&K from its strap and threw it to the floor, and kicked the seat before finally stopping. He looked to Terrie, who had turned away to hide her distress. Like Seymour, she was overcome with grief and anger. "Seymour!" Hawk called to him again.

"WHAT?" he shouted. Hawk hesitated a moment. Seymour stormed off the zodiac. In a whirlwind of anger, he lost all patience. "Spit it out!"

"W-We have to stop it," Hawk's voice croaked. "It's going to use your plane to escape. It's gonna get off the island." Seymour stared at her. He shook his head in disgust and walked past her. Hawk followed him with her eyes. "We have to stop it."

Seymour swiftly turned around. "WE?" He marched toward her. "It was YOUR man who let that thing out. Not us! We were here to eliminate the Koreans. We were not hired to go to war with an alien! You're the one who's been lying to us this whole time. YOU got my men killed. You and that goddamned agency!"

"I know..." Hawk muttered. She turned away, unable to look him in the eyes. "I'm sorry. Believe me, I'm sorry. We wanted to contain the situation, but not risk the scientific operation itself. We have the data on this drive, but there's so much more. We wanted to preserve the site." She turned again to face him. "But the situation is grave. If even one of those things gets off this island, we could be looking at the end of the human race!"

"That's on YOU!" he said. "Besides, isn't your airstrike supposed to take care of that?"

"Yes...but if they use your plane, they can escape before the Air Force gets here."

"Charlie said he crashed," Seymour interrupted her.

"Would that thing even know how to fly it?" Terrie asked.

"That thing has operated technology beyond our limits!" Hawk said. "It's flown a ship over lightyears of space, across GALAXIES! Yes, I think it can figure out how a plane works." Seymour stared at the ocean, saying nothing. Hawk watched him. It appeared as though he had given up. His expression blank, he started walking inland.

Hawk started walking after him. "We have to do something!"

"How?" Seymour yelled at her. "You saw what happened last night. God knows how many of those things there are. And there's only three of us. On top of that, we don't have much to fight with!"

Seymour continued to walk off. Hawk began to follow, only for Terrie to step in her way. Flashing back to yesterday's brutal encounter, Hawk held out both hands in defense.

"Listen, I know you're pissed at me. But there's no time for…"

"Let me handle him," Terrie interrupted. Hawk exhaled, relieved. "If Charlie crashed the plane, you think the Pilot can patch it up?"

"Assuming the damage is minor enough, it's likely the Pilot is capable of repairing it," she said. Terrie nodded, then turned to follow Seymour.

****

Brush crunched under his boots as Seymour marched through the jungle. There was no worry about anything ambushing him. At this point, he didn't care. He approached the harbor, feeling the freshness of the breeze as he looked out into the ocean.

"I can hear you," he called out.

"I wasn't trying to hide," Terrie said, stepping from the tree line. She walked up to him, glancing at the horizon. The ocean had calmed from the storm. The waves reduced to gentle ripples, and the clouds had scattered, exposing a blue sky. "You know, if not for the destruction…and all the dead people, I'd say this actually looked like paradise."

Seymour said nothing, though Terrie did notice the small grin that briefly showed. "So, what?" she said. "You're just giving up now?"

"We've lost the whole team," he said. "I'm not gonna sacrifice you as well."

"Today, tomorrow, maybe Thursday…who knows when," Terrie said. "But if those things escape, I'll be dead. Me, and everyone else on the planet. Besides, we're probably gonna be detained for life by the C.I.A. anyway." She laughed at her own joke, though Seymour didn't. "Listen…you think you're the only one who's lost their way? The two of us, plus all the others…we're all the same. At one time, we were all good soldiers, fighting for freedom, liberty, what have you. Whether we were manipulated by the government is irrelevant. We were good people with good intentions. Now look at us. We travel around the world, doing soldier-stuff, but we're not soldiers. We just shoot bad guys, take the paycheck, and hope the guy paying us isn't worse than who we just took down."

"Is there a point to this monologue?" Seymour said.

"Though we're the same, you're different," she said. "We got in this business because we had the skills, and figured we'd use it to make a shiny paycheck. You, though…you didn't just up and leave the Navy. You got cancer. They thought you were a goner, and they let you go. But like everything else in your life, you beat it. And you wanted to keep fighting the good fight, and settled for this, figuring it was the closest thing."

"I'm still waiting on the point…"

"You're not one to lose," Terrie said. "You're certainly not one to give up. I mean…you're a SEAL for heaven sake!"

"Was," Seymour said.

"I guess we'll find out," Terrie said. "You above anyone else knows it's not the stripes that make you a SEAL. It's the attitude…the PERSEVERANCE!" She paused and took a breath, looking out at the ocean once more. "Listen, our guys dying, it was not your fault. We were dealt a shitty deal. But you know as well as I do, that Pilot is gonna get off this island. And when it does, all this…" she pointed to the beautiful horizon, "…will be gone. It'll be black, from those friggin nests. And we're the only ones able to stop it. A SEAL wouldn't stand by and let it happen. Not even out of concern for his teammate. A SEAL would trust his teammate to back him up."

Seymour inhaled a deep, soulful breath, taking in every word as he gazed out at the Pacific. He finally looked over at Terrie.

"We're probably not gonna survive this," he said. Terrie nodded. "But if we do…I might just have to take you salsa dancing."

Terrie smiled. "If we make it out of here, I'll take you up on that."

Seymour removed his revolver from its holster and checked the cylinder. All eight slots were loaded. He holstered it back and looked at Terrie.

"Never thought I'd actually use this cliché for real, but…let's go save the world."

CHAPTER 36

Seymour opened the spare munitions compartment in the Zodiac and shoved a fresh magazine into his H&K. He tossed a fresh MP5 to Hawk, who promptly caught it and loaded it. Terrie rushed a cleaning of her rifle barrel, brushing some dirt from the inside. She collected some fresh magazines for the sniper rifle and her machine-pistol, while also collecting one of the spare MP5s. All three of them were boarded in the Zodiac, readying for their upcoming assault.

"Do you have a plan in mind?" Hawk asked.

"We'll have to take the boat up along the north side of the island. Like yesterday, we'll have to climb up, although it won't be as steep. Then we'll hike our way to the plain, and analyze the situation from there."

"There'll be an army of those things waiting for us," Terrie said. "We won't last long in a firefight. I say we focus on sabotaging the plane, then get the hell out of dodge with the Zodiac. I'm sure the Agency will find us."

"How will we sabotage the ShinMaywa?" Hawk asked. "Shoot the hell out of it?"

"That's one way," Terrie said.

"That'll be hard to do if we're fighting off a horde of those things," Seymour pointed out.

"And we don't have enough ammo to do that for very long," Terrie said. "Unfortunately, it's not as simple as blowing them all up."

She noticed Seymour perking up, as though an idea came to mind.

"Maybe it is," he said. He started the Zodiac's engine and drove the vessel out of the cove. Terrie and Hawk both waited as he steered the boat toward the harbor. He passed the sunken ship and pulled up to one of the vacant docks. Terrie stepped out first and secured the line to a cleat.

"What's your idea?" she asked. Seymour climbed onto the dock, then knelt to help Hawk up.

"The soldier boys left behind some toys," he said. He led them up to the outpost. They entered the building and passed through the observation room. Seymour opened a back door, leading into a large storage room.

"Hot damn," Terrie said as she looked at all the leftover munitions. Even Hawk was surprised by the amount of firepower.

"They really were geared up for retaliation," she said.

"Load up!" Seymour said. Seymour moved to the back of the room, where the North Koreans had stored their C-4.

Terrie quickly opened a case, revealing an RPG. "Now we're talking."

She grabbed two empty duffle bags and brought them to Seymour, who started loading them up with C-4 blocks.

"How much are we bringing?"

"All of it," he answered.

"You have an idea in mind?" Terrie asked.

"Sort of," he said. "Hopefully we can set these explosives and somehow lure those aliens into a trap. I'm still working on the luring part." He lifted the duffle bag over his shoulder. "Let's go!"

The group loaded the munitions and supplies and boarded the zodiac. Seymour put the engine in reverse, backing the boat out from the dock. He pointed the bow to the north, and placed the boat in full throttle. It took off like a rocket, spraying water from the stern.

****

Traveling at fifty knots, it took eleven minutes to reach the north side of the island. Seymour reduced speed as he curved the boat to follow the shore. Terrie took advantage of the travel, eyeing the now-peaceful ocean and sky. It brought her a much-needed relaxation, which would soon dissipate. The wind and sun helped to dry them off, lessening the damp heaviness in their gear. The shoreline had mostly been an abundance of green, with hardly any space for docking. As they moved along the northside, they came upon a large rocky hillside.

Seymour looked up at the landscape. The hill grew larger further west, though the abundance seemed less as the hill rose.

"The landing site's over there," he said. "That's where the horde will probably be."

"You sure on that?" Hawk said.

"Judging by the militaristic tactfulness your alien has displayed, he'll likely be setting up a defense while he gets the plane ready. He's been stalking us since we've eliminated the Koreans, which is probably how he learned of the ShinMaywa. The objective of that attack last night wasn't just to capture us and use us as hosts. The main goal was to get our radio in order to contact Charlie and manipulate him to bring the ShinMaywa. Its objective is to get off this island, so I guarantee he'll have his little soldiers guarding the perimeter. Probably the reason why we haven't seen any all night. He didn't want his forces scattered all over the island."

"So, what's our next move?" Hawk asked.

"We'll climb up here, and then work our way over by foot," Seymour answered.

He steered the boat into the shallow waters, careful not to crash the rigid hull against any of the rocks. Pulling up to the foot of the hill, he killed the engine. Terrie stepped out and secured the spring line between a couple of rocks. Seymour stepped off the boat and looked up at the hill. While it wasn't as steep, it would still require climbing gear to scale.

He broke out the harnesses, then snapped his fingers at Hawk. She walked up to him, carefully watching her step as the ocean splashed the rocks. Seymour extended a harness over to her.

"You get to climb this time," he said. "You up to it?"

Hawk nodded and accepted the harness. Seymour tossed one to Terrie, and then grabbed one for himself. He fastened it around his shoulders and waist, then strapped the duffle bag over his back. Normally he'd attach a line to it and haul it up separately, but time was short.

Seymour initiated his climb. He felt the hill with his hands, finding his first hold. The rocky edges of the hill made for easier climbing compared to the cliff. He ascended twenty feet before commencing the first drilling. After inserting the bolt, he continued upward, drilling every twenty feet.

After a hundred and twenty feet, he came up at the ledge. After climbing his way over, he instantly kneeled to a firing position and scanned the immediate area. Seeing no creatures, he looked down at Terrie and Hawk and signaled for them to initiate their climb.

Terrie went first, clipping her harness to the cable. She found a hold, and lifted herself against the rocks. As she ascended several yards, Hawk began her climb. Using the cable as support, they were able to climb at an accelerated rate. Seymour provided cover as they climbed. The jungle was not as thick on this side of the island, allowing for greater visibility.

Terrie and Hawk both emerged over the ledge. They removed their harnesses and checked their weapons.

"All set," Terrie said.

"Alright, keep low and stay quiet. Follow my lead, and be ready to move fast," Seymour said. "Be ready for anything."

With their weapons raised, they entered the jungle, pushing west toward the plains. As they started their patrol, Terrie took one final glance at the horizon. It was majestic: so peaceful.

A beautiful calm before the horror she knew awaited them.

CHAPTER 37

The humanoid clicked its mandibles as it moved through the nest. It walked by two other humanoid spawns as it approached one of the large pods. It was full, soon to give birth. Streams of black secretion ran down its sides, spilling from pores. Its host had been almost completely decomposed, leaving nothing other than a lump of soggy residue.

The humanoid leaned its head against the pod. Its mandibles curled outward, making way as the proboscis protruded from its throat. The soft, fleshy appendage acted like a hose, sucking the black stream into the creature's body. It ingested a gallon of the secretion before retracting the proboscis. Its mandibles uncurled into their normal position, and the creature resumed its patrol.

It stuck close to the perimeter to enact its purpose in guarding the nest. Its two humanoid comrades moved about separately. One slowly roamed the nest's interior, while the other stood firm at the tree line. A forth companion, an arachnid spawn, had moved toward a tree in the center of the nest. Clawed digits protruded from tiny apertures in its pointed forelegs and dug into the trunk of the tree. Like a spider, it slowly climbed.

The humanoid watched the nest, monitoring any signs of threat. Like the rest of its species, it did not experience emotion. It did not grow bored. It did not seek thrill. It only contained purpose: propagate and preserve the species. Its life only had value as a member of that species. Like its fellow spawn, it was a drone. It contained no regard for itself outside of sustaining its body in order to conduct its purpose.

Sensory nerves based along its neck and forearms detected faint signals from deep within the jungle. The creature stopped its motion, allowing its brain to analyze and determine the source. Since its birth, the creature had learned the various natural vibrations and sounds from the jungle. They each had a basic repetition to them, a slight symptom indicative of the environment.

These new vibrations were extremely faint, however without the common repetition of the natural vibrations from the wind and trees. The creature postured itself, preparing to signal the others with a high-pitched screech.

A new vibration lit its nerves. It was brief and precise. A single movement, zipping through the trees, generating a faint whistling sound. A new vibration appeared, like a tiny explosion. This one was much closer. Within the nest!

The drone turned toward the vibration, just in time to see the humanoid comrade fall backward. Its upper torso was ripped open just below the neck. Blood gushed into the ground, mixing in with the black secretion.

Another whistle zipped through the air. As the drone picked up on the vibration, the other humanoid fell to the ground. Its head was completely ravaged, with a gaping hole penetrating above the mandibles.

Blood suddenly rained from the tree. The arachnid spawn fell from its perched position. Several gaping impact craters lined its torso. They were smaller than the wounds from the other drones, though greater in number. It picked up new vibrations. Thuds against the forest floor, rapidly growing nearer.

The drone protruded its barbs, as the indigenous intruder leapt from the tree line. And as quickly as it appeared, the drone felt the multiple penetrating impacts, as the intruder unleashed its weapon. It attempted to screech, to alarm the horde, only for blood to bubble from its throat.

The silencer muffled the sound as Seymour fired several rounds from his H&K. Gunshot wounds exploded from the humanoid's chest, the impact force knocking it down on its back. The creature twitched as bubbling orange fluid gushed from its wounds. It tried lifting its arm upward, determined to place its barb into the intruder and potential host.

Seymour kicked his boot down on the creature's arm, pinning it to the ground. He pressed the silencer against the humanoid's forehead and pulled the trigger. Exoskeleton, blood, mud, and black secretion splattered behind its head as the bullet passed through.

Seymour took a step back, feeling a small satisfaction from the execution. He checked the other bodies, confirming the kills. Terrie stepped out from the jungle, a silencer inserted into her rifle barrel.

"Whew," Seymour said. "That was a little too close. Nice shooting." Terrie silently thanked him with a nod, then looked back to the perimeter as Hawk stepped out from the jungle into the nest. She looked pale gazing at the numerous pods growing from the various hosts.

"Thank God Terrie has a good eye," she muttered.

Nearly a quarter mile into the jungle, Terrie decided to scout ahead. First, she detected the foul odor. Following the smell for several hundred yards, she slowed her movements. With the use of stealth, and distance on her side with her sniper scope, she spotted a dark, swampy region. Immediately recognizing it as a nesting site, she double-backed to inform Seymour and Hawk.

"It's not easy to sneak up on these things," Hawk continued. "We're gonna have to be extra careful when we approach the plain."

"Well, we need to start moving," Terrie said. She started moving west. She stopped as she looked back at Seymour. He was studying one of the bodies, from which a juvenile pod was growing. She recognized the host. "Oh, God," she said, covering her mouth.

Seymour leaned over Ivan's body, looking at his comrade's shrunken appearance. All of the color had left his face, which was barely recognizable. The pod had grown to nearly two feet in height. Its veins took on a greenish color. Seymour ran his hand near Ivan's neck, removing his U.S.M.C. dog tags which he always kept.

Terrie watched as Seymour examined his body for a moment. He then stood up and took a step back. He shouldered his rifle, aiming at the pod. With the silencer still attached, he put several rounds through the center of the pod. Black secretion spilled, along with a mixture of white and orange fluid.

No way was Seymour going to allow that thing to continue feeding off Ivan. He nodded at Terrie, who led the way up the hill.

****

With her weapon strapped over her back, Terrie grabbed hold of the next branch as she scaled the tree. She hauled herself up, placing her knees over the top of the branch. She was thirty feet in the air, hidden in the canopy as she looked out into the vast plain.

Even without the use of binoculars, she could see the various movement. The plain was alive with alien creatures. She slowly positioned her sniper scope for a closer view. Alien spawn, both humanoid and insect-like, scurried all over the plain. They varied in sizes. Most of the humanoids stood between four-and-six feet in height, with the arachnids being a similar variety in length. Then there were other creatures, smaller ones, as small as squirrels moving about. Looking further out, she could see the ShinMaywa. Creatures climbed all over it, completely covering the engines and tail.

A glimmer of light bounced from the wing. Terrie panned the scope over, seeing the Pilot standing under the wing. Its arms were raised, and a sizzling light radiated from one of its gauntlets.

Seymour and Hawk waited below, looking out at the plain with their binoculars. They could see the horde of creatures, and could barely see the ShinMaywa from their position on the ground. Seymour gauged that it was at least a thousand yards out, well out of range of the RPG. Getting closer would be impossible.

Terrie climbed down from the tree, making sure to be slow and quiet. Once on the ground, she gathered with Seymour and Hawk.

"I can't make the shot," she said. "They're all over it. Damn bugs."

"What's its condition?" Seymour asked.

"Hard to tell, but it appears one of the stabilizers broke loose in the crash," Terrie said.

"Did you see the Pilot?" Hawk asked.

"Yeah. By the looks of it, it's using its metal bracelet thing to weld the wing back together," Terrie said.

"Damn, I was right," Hawk said.

"I'd say it's almost done," Terrie said. "We don't have much time."

"Can you shoot the engines?" Seymour said.

"With those things crawling all over it?" Terrie shook her head.

"We need to draw them away," Seymour said.

"We could plant explosives further into the jungle and set them off," Hawk said. "They might go investigate."

"All of them?" Seymour said, expressing doubt. "No, at best, only a handful of them would be drawn off. Something that'll really piss them off."

"Put on MSNBC," Terrie joked.

"There is that," Seymour said. "Maybe I should've just blown that bastard up last night when I had the...chance..." He trailed off, as his mind replayed his encounter with the Pilot.

He remembered standing in the middle of that nest, with two blocks of C-4 strapped to his vest. He remembered the Pilot rushing out from the jungle, rapidly approaching. It marched toward him, its barb ready to sting and paralyze him. As Seymour was about to sacrifice himself and detonate the C-4, it stopped. He assumed it kept distance due to self-preservation, not realizing those pods contained its spawn.

"Holy shit," he said out loud. *It wasn't protecting itself...*

"Victor," Terrie said, ready to talk him out of blaming himself.

"I know what to do," Seymour interrupted. "We're gonna put that C-4 to use."

CHAPTER
38

Mud and secretion splashed as the team rushed throughout the nest. Seymour placed the open duffle bag down just outside the border. All three of them grabbed several blocks of C-4. They hurried about the nest, planting explosives near the center and perimeter.

"This'll sure piss them off," Terrie said, planting a block near one of the center pods.

"That's the point," Seymour said. He placed several blocks on the north side. He turned and whistled toward Hawk, signaling for her to toss him a couple more blocks. She reached into the duffle bag and tossed two more his way. After catching them like softballs, he moved a little further beyond the perimeter. He dug at the ground with his boot and inserted the C-4 into the hole.

Terrie and Hawk continued placing charges, making sure the triggering device was inserted into each one. Seymour hurried to the duffle bag and grabbed a couple more. Per Seymour's instruction, Terrie made sure to dig some holes into the ground, burying some of the charges beneath the mud.

Hawk placed an explosive at the center of the nest, near a mature pod. After activating the trigger, she looked at the six-foot-tall vessel. Its sides were beginning to pulsate. She immediately realized it was close to giving birth.

"We're running short on time," Hawk said. Seymour looked her way, seeing the pulsating pod.

"Alright," he said. "Let's get moving. We're just about done." Terrie and Hawk placed their last explosives and then regrouped at the bag of explosives. After brushing dirt over the explosives, Seymour started moving across the nest to meet up with them. As he did, he passed by another mature pod. Its sides were beginning to pulsate. He took a block of C-4 from his vest. After inserting the triggering device into the side, he tossed the block near the pod.

"Happy birthday," he said. He rejoined Terrie and Hawk at the bag.
"Are we all set?" Hawk said.
"Almost," Seymour said. "There's one more step." They each
grabbed several more explosives and moved into the surrounding jungle.

****

The air sizzled as the Pilot ignited the fusion laser from its gauntlet.
The tool, often used as a weapon capable of generating vast destruction,
served multiple functions necessary for the species' survival. The
concentrated stream of energy fused the stabilizer back to the frame of
the starboard wing. As it finished, the glove on its left appendage altered
its form. The pincers folded back, disappearing into slots inside the
glove, as other needle-shaped devices protruded from the rounded tip.
The Pilot moved under the damaged turbine engine, using the tools to
remove the debris from the fan, and reposition the stator vanes. Its spawn
scurried throughout the plain, patiently guarding their leader as it
prepared its departure. The Pilot clicked its fangs as it deactivated the
laser.

It observed the primitive vehicle, composed of technology inferior
to anything the Pilot was accustomed to. The Pilot, however, was not
critical of the indigenous species' technological expertise. It experienced
no such emotion. It was nothing other than data, which the Pilot would
use to develop tactics to enact its purpose. Each encounter with the local
creatures, particularly the intelligent alpha species, gave it knowledge on
how to impose its function onto the remainder of this planet.

Sensory nerves along its neck lit up, generating a shuddering
sensation along its exoskeleton. The horde screeched and hissed, as each
spawn detected a massive vibration from within the jungle. A downward
shockwave swept the ground, accompanied by a thunderous echo.

An explosion.

In unison, they turned their attention to the terrain. Through tiny
particles along their forehead, invisible to the human eye, the Pilot and
its army witnessed the huge funnel of smoke burst from the trees, trailing
high into the air.

Climbing atop the ShinMaywa, the Pilot saw the burning of the
trees where the smoke originated. Its brain analyzed the distance and
position. The nest! Signals ignited like sparks within its nervous system,
serving as an adrenaline boost. Protective instincts took over.

The Pilot leapt like an insect from the ShinMaywa, and led a
forward charge into the jungle. Like a hive mentality, the horde
followed. Only a few stayed to protect the launch site.

A river of charcoal colored creatures, humanoid, and arachnid in appearance, flooded the jungle, following their leader in a mad rush to protect the unborn young. There was no fear or sadness felt amongst them. Only urgency, fueled by a drive to fulfill their purpose. Protect and preserve the species.

The pincers reemerged from its claw, and the gauntlet initiated its glow. The smell of smoke and charred remains permeated the air as the horde drew near the nest. The jungle began to turn black, but not from the natural emission from the pods. The plants and trees were scorched. The orange glow of fire flickered along several of the trees.

The horde swarmed the nest. The whole environment was desolated, with burnt fragments of the pods scattered about. The secretion fluid was tainted with the blood and remains of the plundered offspring.

The creatures roamed about, snarling aggressively as they searched for any perpetrators. The Pilot stepped through the devastation. There was nothing to salvage, as none of the pods survived the explosion.

It watched a river of blood and secretion travel down into an indentation in the ground. Scorched earth, husk, and spawn surrounded these strange craters, pushed outward as though launched. Smoke rose from this hole, and scattered like volcanic ash. Gazing over the nest, the Pilot noticed several of these craters. The earth around them had exploded outward.

Something else caught the Pilot's attention. Something was in the muck, scorched, but still intact. A rectangular cube, black in color. It was covered in mud, as though it had been buried, then uprooted in the explosion. A metallic device protruded from the side. A red light flashed from the end.

Information flooded its brain like a computer. It recalled its encounter with the indigenous warrior. That explosive weapon it used to threaten its nest.

It was a trap.

The creature flared its fangs and screeched as it darted into the trees.

"Hit it!" Seymour yelled, watching through Terrie's sniper scope as the horde gathered.

Terrie pressed the button on the activation device. C-4 blocks, buried in the muck within the nest, and scattered throughout the surrounding jungle, detonated. The three of them ducked for cover as the secondary explosions consumed the horde.

Balls of flame erupted at once, filling the jungle with fire and debris. Fragments of exoskeleton launched through the air like tiny meteorites. The jungle became a volcanic zone, with balls of fire stretching into the atmosphere.

Momentary shrieks of distress were quickly silenced as the army of spawn was blown to oblivion, reduced to a layer of smoldering innards that covered the smoking landscape. A breeze kicked up, spinning the smoke into a large funnel, and pushed the vile smell of cooking entrails through the terrain.

Seymour stepped out from behind the tree where he hid, using himself as bait to lure any surviving creatures. Terrie emerged from a depression in the ground and took her rifle back from Seymour. She used her scope and aimed it toward the nest. She saw nothing but burning carcasses and smoke. Hawk stepped out from behind another tree and looked out at the devastation, astonished that the plan actually worked.

"Holy shit!" Hawk said, while waving her hand around the air to brush the smoke away.

"Let's make sure they're all dead," Seymour said. He ran to the nest as though staging a forward assault. In seconds, he was consumed within the black twisting smoke. The air began to clear as he searched the nest. He stood in a mushy mud substance, made of a mixture of soil, secretion, and alien remains. The blasts had ravaged an enormous section of jungle, creating a large clearing. No living spawn crawled within the ruins.

Hawk walked several yards outside the nest perimeter, pointing her firearm in every direction she faced. Smoldering plants surrounded her. Burnt limbs, blown completely off the bodies of spawn, crushed under her feet like walnuts. Nothing moved within the jungle other than flickering fire.

"Here," Terrie called out. Seymour stepped out from the nest and joined Hawk as they regrouped with Terrie. They found her standing in the middle of what almost appeared to be crater, where several blocks of C-4 had been planted outside the nest. Ravaged jungle surrounded the crater, with branches of a nearby tree completely scorched, and the smaller plants reduced to scattered fragments.

Terrie pointed to the ground, toward a small glimmer of light. Several feet from the crater, a three-inch metal fragment lay in the ground. Triangular in shape, the fragment was blackened, and jagged around the edges.

"Part of its armor," Hawk said. "Damn, we got the bastard."

"We can only hope," Seymour said. His eyes swept the surrounding jungle, looking for a body.

"Hope?" Hawk said. "We blew it to freaking pieces!" Her voice was animated, full of victory.

"We're not done yet," Seymour said.

****

The creatures felt the heavy shockwave ripple through the island as the blast consumed their comrades. Various screeches and cries left the remaining group, who had remained to defend their leader's newly obtained vehicle. The creatures grew confused and bewildered. They could not investigate, as their assigned role was defense. Limited to their drone mentality, they knew nothing other than what the hive required of them. Every hive required a leader, an evolved ruler who commanded the species. Their leader was nowhere to be seen, and none of them would evolve into a liege.

The creatures scurried around the plain, keeping close enough to their territory to ward off intruders. They chirped and hissed, attempting to communicate with the horde.

"I count twelve," Seymour whispered, peeking between the vines of a thick bush as he observed the spawn.

"We've taken more than that," Terrie said. She tapped her hand over her RPG. "I'm dying to use this bad boy."

"I'll take the left," Seymour said. "Let me draw them closer, and you'll get your wish. You only have one round, so don't miss. Then use your rifle to pick off the ones that are left, while Hawk and I advance." Seymour leaned back to look at Hawk. "Agent, wait until Terrie fires the rocket. If any survive, they'll move in on her. Understood?"

"Yes sir," Hawk said.

"Alright then," Seymour said.

He jumped to his feet and dashed out from the jungle. He stepped into the clear, sunny plain and dashed up the small nearby hill. A humanoid creature turned, seeing Seymour running straight at it. Spurred from its defensive function, it snarled and projected its stingers.

"That's *my* ride," Seymour remarked. He squeezed the trigger, igniting an automatic burst from his rifle barrel. The humanoid's neck disappeared into splatters of bubbling orange, and the head peeled off. Echoing gunshots, combined with the spawn's dying screeches drew the attention of the scattered aliens.

Four of them, two humanoid, two insect-like, scurried in unison straight for the target. Several meters behind them, four more creatures followed, as though preparing a second wave of assault. Seymour turned his rifle to the left, as a single arachnid quickly advanced. He backed away, moving slightly to the left to keep out of Terrie's line of fire. He pointed his rifle towards the first group. He focused on the leader and aimed low, squeezing off several rounds.

The humanoid advanced at the head of the pack, determined to embed its stingers into the intruder. Loud bursts of sound crackled in the air, and nerves lit up in the creature's lower extremities. Bullets had ravaged its legs at the knee joints. Still trying to advance, the creature fell forward. The pack bunched up, trying to move over and around their fallen comrade. For a brief moment, they bunched up.

A sparkling projectile tore from the tree line. Zipping through the clear plain, it struck square in the middle of the small pack of creatures.

Bang!

The rocket detonated on impact, blasting a mixture of guts and dirt forty feet around it.

"Nice!" Seymour yelled out. The second wave of creatures scattered. Two of them stayed behind the smoldering remains of their siblings, while the other two, a humanoid and an arachnid, rushed the jungle.

Seymour aimed his rifle, ready to lay down suppressing fire.

Hawk burst from the tree line, MP5 pointed at the incoming hostiles. Bullets peppered the arachnid's back, ripping up its exoskeleton and internal organs. As its freshly dead carcass rolled onto its side, Hawk put several rounds into the humanoid. With its abdomen and upper torso shredded, the creature fell back. Hawk quickly moved forward.

Several yards behind the impact crater, one of the humanoids snarled at her. It leaned forward, mandibles and arms sprawled in an aggressive stance. Barbs protruded, and the creature initiated a run. Hawk snatched a grenade from her vest, removing the pin with her teeth. After calculating its speed and path, she threw the grenade with all her might. It curved in the air, landing down at the creature's feet. The resulting explosion tore its legs out from under it, sending its torso hurling several feet off the ground.

Seymour pivoted to the left, ready to open fire on the individual creature. Thirty feet away, the creature stopped its advance. It raised its tentacles over its back, pointing the barbed tips toward Seymour. Thick fluid spat from the tentacles, resulting in a brief, wet noise. Seymour felt a sudden jolt, as his rifle, pointed down, suddenly thrust back into him with a force that knocked him on his back.

"What in the name of..." Seymour said, kicking against the ground to back up. He held his rifle away from him. The arachnid's barb was embedded in his rifle, pierced completely through the lower receiver. Looking toward the alien, it had resumed its advance, now twenty-feet away.

Its head erupted, as a crack of sound echoed from the trees. Dead from Terrie's sniper bullet, the creature slumped down on its belly. Seymour tossed the weapon to the side and scrambled to his feet.

"Watch out!" he called. "They have projectiles!" He yanked his revolver from its holster, as the remaining creatures moved in on the team. They were spread out, each of them arachnid in appearance. Clutching the grip of his revolver, he put six rounds into the nearest bug.

Hawk took the one on the right, spraying several rounds into its abdomen. Its body broke like a shell, releasing its entrails onto the grass. The final creature scurried toward her, tearing the ground under its appendages. Hawk aimed to shoot.

Only a small burst left her gun before the mag ran dry. In a moment, the creature was nearly on her. Unable to reload, she threw the weapon at its head, and reached for her side arm.

Seymour ran to help. He aimed his revolver and fired the last two rounds. One struck its abdomen, another on its back leg. The creature lurched, detecting its injuries. Its jaws clicked, and it let out a horrific cry. It was only injured. It turned its attention back onto Hawk.

She pulled her pistol free from its holster. Before she could aim, she saw the tentacles pointing at her, barbs completely emerged.

"Look out!" Seymour yelled. Hawk shrieked and rolled to the side, barely avoiding the barbs as they spat from the tentacles. They stuck out of the ground like stakes.

Hawk rolled onto her back, leaning up to shoot. The creature had already closed the distance. Already on top of her, it stabbed one of its forelegs to her shoulders, pinning her to the ground. She watched as new barbs protruded from the tentacle tips.

Terror overwhelmed Hawk. "No!" she screamed, desperate not to be left to the fate of a host.

Seymour snarled as he dashed at the creature. In one hand, he held his SEAL team knife, and a three-inch throwing knife in the other. With both knives in reverse-grip, he leapt onto the arachnid's back, and plunged the blades into the back of its head. The creatures screeched, leaning up on its back legs. With Seymour on its back, it kicked and bucked. In seconds, its movements slowed, and the creature slumped on its belly.

Blood splattered from the slits as Seymour yanked his knives free. Hawk stood up from the ground, breathing deeply through her mouth. Her heart pounded hard in her chest, and she shook with adrenaline. A smile creased her face. It wasn't fright she was experiencing. It was relief and excitement; a thrill from looking death in the face and coming out on top.

"Whoa!" she cheered, giving Seymour a two-finger salute. "That was close!"

CHAPTER
39

The sky turned a shade of grey as smoke traveled from the jungle high into the atmosphere. The air smelled of burning plants and wood, with an ammonia-like stench from the slaughtered aliens.

Terrie kept her rifle pointed low as she ran to the ShinMaywa. Seymour and Hawk stood at the starboard wing, inspecting the damage and repairs. She checked her watch. It would only be twenty minutes before the airstrike was due to commence.

"Is it able to fly?" she asked, eager to leave. Seymour stood under Engine Two, which had taken the brunt of the impact. He checked the rotors, and interior veins and shaft.

"Looks like it. The son of a bitch did most of the work for me," he said. Terrie blew a sigh of relief.

"Anything I can do?" she asked. Seymour looked over his left shoulder. He was watching Hawk, who was standing over one of the alien corpses.

"Tell her to get her stuff over here. We'll be leaving in a minute. Just gotta get some tools." he said. He walked around the nose to go into the port-side cabin entrance. Terrie started walking toward the agent.

Hawk was squatting near the dead arachnid creature, holding one of its tentacles in her hands. Embedded in the ground nearby were the two barbs it had launched at her. They were shaped like stakes, with the blunt ends attached to a small, bulb-shaped organic object.

Hawk saw Terrie looking at the barbs. "Those sacs carry the spore," she said.

"Creepy," Terrie responded.

"I think they're like shark teeth," Hawk explained. "Once they lose one, another one takes its place. It's probably something that happens with maturity. That's why they didn't use them in the attack last night. This fella may have been one of the first ones hatched on this island."

"First to live and the last to die," Terrie remarked.

"Seems that's what we all get in life," Hawk said. "A time to live, and a place to die." She unzipped her nylon pack, checking to make sure her flash-drive was intact. She held it out to Terrie. "But thanks to this little fella here...we'll have a little bit more than that." Terrie could sense a scientific monologue in development.

"You remember that airstrike?" she said. "If you don't get on that plane, this'll be your place to die." Hawk sensed the bitterness in her voice. She didn't resent it. After all, she did manipulate the team, which led to many of them dying. How would one forget that so quickly?

"You guys served an important mission today," she said. "When we get back, I'll have to recommend you guys for..."

A yellow illumination cast over them. A bright streak of light flashed over the grass plain like a shooting star. Terrie yelled and fell backward as the sparkling ball of energy struck the agent in the abdomen.

Seymour had just stepped around the tail as he saw Cassie Hawk consumed in a fierce explosion. Her torso separated from her midriff, scattering entrails about as her two halves launched in separate directions from the explosion.

Terrie scrambled to her feet and lifted her rifle. She had just pressed the stock to her shoulder as the tree line flickered with yellow. Realizing what was coming, she turned to run. After only two steps to the left, another ball of energy ripped from the trees, exploding into the earth where she had stood. The invisible force of the blast struck Terrie like a freight train, shuddering every organ in her body. Hurled several feet off the ground, she struck down hard on her stomach. Ribs crunched in her sides, and her head bounced back. With adrenaline still pumping, she rolled to her side, still attempting to run forward. Her blurry vision turned to black, and her motions slowed to a stop.

Seymour drew his revolver and began charging the trees. He didn't get more than a few feet as two more streaks of light ripped from the trees. Two explosions burst in front of him, throwing him onto his back. The impact juddered his body, shaking the firearm from his hand.

Cursing under his breath, he propped himself up on his elbow. Through the smoke, he could see the eight-foot figure emerge from the trees.

Blood dripped from the Pilot's many wounds as it moved across the plain. A jagged piece of metal, a fraction of its own armor, stuck from its left leg, causing a limp as the creature marched. Its body armor was blackened, and marked by several gashes, each of them crusted with dried blood. Electrical sparks flickered from its damaged gauntlet. Its pincer glove was also severely damaged. Much of the exterior plating was missing, revealing bio-organic material fusing the glove to the arm. The top pincer jaw was missing entirely, and the bottom wobbled in its slot.

Its exoskeleton was marked throughout with burns. Blood and other fluid crusted along its neck, arms, and face, tinging its appearance in a dark red. The bottom half of its left fang was torn away. Blood and saliva spat from its mouth as it hissed.

Seymour pushed himself up as the creature approached. Its gauntlet flickered, struggling to generate power for another blast. Groaning, the Pilot aimed its weapon at the indigenous warrior. It was careful in its aim not to overshoot and damage the ShinMaywa.

Seymour snatched his revolver from the ground and ran. The Pilot moved its arm to follow his path. With its senses in disarray from its many injuries, it had to rely solely on its visuals to aim. The gauntlet whined and sparkled as it generated the energy projectile.

The blast zipped from its arm. Seymour saw a blinding flash before his eyes. He stopped in his tracks, feeling the heat against his forehead and the high-pitch squeal in the air.

He fell to his knees as the projectile passed within a centimeter of his face. *Damn! There goes one of my nines!*

The gauntlet whined, spitting out even more sparks. The yellow lights flashed for a moment before dying down. The Pilot pulled its arm back to its face. Its fang protruded into the device, adjusting the internal veins. It extended its arm out again, aiming the weapon at Seymour. It whined and sparked, emitting several yellow flashes before failing.

With its projectile weapon dysfunctional, the Pilot marched at Seymour. It drew its left arm back as though about to pull a punch. Seeing the pointed pincer jaw, he realized the alien intended to run it through him like a lance.

Terrie coughed, spitting out several drops of blood. Daylight strobed in her eyes as her brain struggled to reactivate from the brief unconsciousness. Her stomach ached with nausea, and her chest pounded with each heartbeat. Lifting her face from the dirt, she gauged her surroundings.

Hawk's torso lay twenty feet from her. The deceased agent's eyes were still wide open, her shock eternally frozen on her face. By the time her mind registered what the yellow flash was, it was too late. Burnt entrails and blood soaked the nearby grass.

Terrie's arms shivered as she struggled to push herself off the ground. Her stomach churned with pain and nausea, and her head felt as though it was in a vice. Looking behind her, she saw two blurry images facing off. There was Seymour, with his revolver in hand, facing down the Pilot as it closed the distance on him.

It was certain death.

Terrie propped on her hands and knees, and crawled for her rifle.

Seymour extended the revolver, aiming for a headshot. Still advancing, the Pilot lifted its glove over its face as he fired. .357 caliber bullets cracked the already ruptured shell, bursting the mechanics inside. Orange blood spilled from the fused arm, mixing with a grey oily fluid.

Seymour lowered his aim for the torso and fired. Two rounds were crushed against the body armor. A third shot entered the torso, drawing a squeal from the Pilot. It bent forward, compensating the sudden rupture of internal organs. Seymour pulled the trigger again, only to hear that dreaded empty click. As he swung the cylinder open and ejected the casings, the Pilot resumed its advance.

Seymour started backing away. He dug into his vest for a speed-loader. Though the alien limped, it was still faster than him. In seconds it was less than three yards away.

Seymour pulled the speed loader from his vest.

Two yards away.

He pressed the bullets into the chambers and slammed the cylinder home. One yard away.

Seymour pointed the gun to fire. The Pilot swung its arm, knocking the gun free from his grasp. It drew its claw back. Seymour stumbled back as it slashed.

The jagged tip ripped at a downward angle, cutting through the vest and lacerating Seymour's torso. The SEAL reeled backward, bleeding from his chest and stomach.

The Pilot stood over him. The fingers on its right hand bent back, and the fleshy palm opened, giving way to a fresh stinger.

Seymour tensed, anticipating the horrific fate.

A shot rang through the air, and the Pilot jolted forward from an unforeseen impact from behind. Seymour rolled to his feet and distanced himself from the creature. He looked near the plane.

Terrie, bruised and bleeding, was on her stomach. Her hands trembled as she aimed her rifle. She sneered as she fought against the pain and dizziness.

The Pilot generated an ear-piercing hiss as another shot struck its damaged armor. Tiny metal fragments burst from the impact as the bullet landed, its impact force driving the Pilot backward. Its brain analyzed the situation, quickly concluding that the enemy would attempt a headshot.

It swiftly moved its glove over its face, just as Terrie fired off another shot. The round crashed into the glove, spewing fluid and breaking the other pincer jaw completely off.

"Come on, you bastard!" Terrie muttered. She focused her crosshairs once again on the Pilot's head and squeezed the trigger. The gun was silent, and the mag had run dry. "Damn!"

Despite bleeding profusely, the Pilot advanced in her direction. Its stinger remained protruded, ready to paralyze and impregnate the host.

A slight metallic clang turned its attention back toward Seymour. It looked, seeing his arm extended outward, palm open.

The oval object bounced along the ground toward it before bursting. The shockwave from the grenade knocked the Pilot to the ground, while embedding shrapnel into its armor and flesh.

It writhed on the ground, thrashing its barbed arm to and fro. Screeches filled the air as its sensory nerves overloaded with signals.

Seymour looked past the flailing alien at Terrie. She lay on the ground with her rifle, her head slumped against the stock.

The Pilot started to scramble to its feet. It was now bleeding from its forehead. Its body seemed to pulsate, as though it was beginning to experience organ failure. Its barb remained protruded, and it continued its advance.

Seymour sprinted around it as he rushed to Terrie's defense. The Pilot extended its gauntlet, its arm wobbly. The gauntlet whined and sparked, managing to generate a small portion of energy. Seeing the flash of light, Seymour ducked.

The projectile exploded several feet behind him. Though small, it still generated a shockwave strong enough to hurl Seymour off of his feet. He hit the ground as a meteor shower of dirt and grass rained down around him.

The Pilot abandoned its pursuit of the two warriors. The bleeding had stopped, though nerves lit throughout its body, continuously reminding the creature of its many injuries. With its instinct driving it to preserve the species, combating the indigenous creatures was not worth the effort. It elected to retreat in the vehicle and find a larger population. In time, it would be healed after an extended molting process, and would be free to stalk fresh targets and grow a new army.

The creature sprinted around the plane, ignoring the injury to its leg. It pulled itself through the cabin doorway, and limped into the cockpit.

The world spun as Seymour crawled on his elbows and knees, determined to reach his fallen comrade. After closing the distance, he stood up on his knees and rolled Terrie to her side. Blood had dried around her nose and mouth. Her uniform and skin were singed, and her head bruised where she hit it. He pulled her up, holding her head in his arms.

"Hey, we gotta move!" Seymour said. He tried picking her up off the ground. Her body was limp, completely lacking in energy. She lifted her hand and put it to his, signaling for him to stop. Gritting her teeth in pain, she collapsed back to the ground.

"Good thing I don't have a date lined up," she joked, though grimacing in pain. "I look awful."

"Not at all," he said. "And don't forget, we had an agreement." Terrie forced a chuckle through her coughing. Her eyes were shut, and her breathing grew shallow. Seymour gently tapped her face. "Hey, kiddo, stay awake! You'll be fine."

"The alien," she muttered. "Don't let that bastard…" her voice trailed off. She lay motionless in his arms.

The roaring of the four Rolls-Royce engines drew Seymour's attention. The ShinMaywa was in motion, slowly turning as the Pilot was initiating a takeoff. Seymour tensed with fury. There was no time to check Terrie's vitals and revive her.

After gently laying her down, he sprung to his feet and sprinted toward the plane. The engines rotated, spewing gusts of exhaust at him. The plane was now pointed at the ocean, and it slowly started its run.

Seymour ran as fast as he could, fighting against the gusts of wind. He was now by the tail wing, only a few meters from the portside door. The plane moved, gaining traction with each wheel rotation. Seymour's heart pounded as he forced himself to run faster than ever. His approach grew slower as the plane steadily moved faster.

He was now barely within reach.

With a final, desperate effort, Seymour leapt. His fingertips hooked around the frame. Dragging along the side of the plane, he pulled himself up. The plane was now moving at a shooting speed. Its nose began to lift, and the engines roared.

Wind tore at Seymour as he clung for his life. He saw the ground beneath him grow distant. Now, it was water. The ShinMaywa had achieved flight, and the Pilot was now on route to spread its disease to the world.

Seymour yelled for God's help. His muscles bulged as he pulled himself up against the mighty wind. He completed the chin-up motion and immediately threw his arm deeper into the cabin. His fingers clawed against the floor as he pulled himself in.

In moments, only his legs were dangling out the door. He grunted as he hauled himself completely inside. Pressing his knees against the metal floor, he slammed the door shut.

The slamming sound echoed through the cabin. The Pilot looked over its shoulder, peering through the open cockpit door. The indigenous stood in the cabin, with full access to the armory. Activating the vehicle's autopilot, the beast stood from the seat.

Seymour pushed himself to his feet as the beast stepped from the cockpit. It stopped and sized him up. In an aggressive stance, it leaned forward with its arms out and bellowed. Blood and saliva spewed from its torn-up jaw.

Seymour spat as he snatched his SEAL knife.

"Yeah, fuck you too!"

They charged at each other. With his knife high over his head, Seymour leapt at the creature's face. He thrust the knife down in a hammer-like motion. The blade plunged between the damaged glove components as the creature lifted its left arm in defense. Seymour landed down, his knife lodged in the creature's glove.

Like a raging bull, the beast rammed forward, slamming Seymour hard against the port wall. With its arm held across his torso, Seymour was pinned. He grunted as he fought to push the beast away, but its superior strength held him firm. It raised its right hand, bending the fingers back.

Not happening!

With his left hand, he reached for his vest, snatching his three-inch throwing knife. Holding it in reverse grip, he plunged it directly into the palm. The blade sliced through flesh, splitting the stinger down the middle.

The creature screamed, sensing the damage to its organic weapon. A small fountain of blood and venom sprayed as Seymour ripped the knife out. With the blade still in reverse-grip, he plunged the blade into its neck.

In a vicious, reactionary motion, the Pilot vaulted backward. Still lodged in the glove, the SEAL knife was ripped from Seymour's grasp. Blood seeped from the creature's neck as it stumbled backward. It quickly steadied itself and started for Seymour again.

This guy just won't die! Seymour snarled and ran forward, ready to plunge his knife.

The Pilot thrust its hand out. Its palm struck Seymour square in the chest as its fingers grabbed a fistful of his vest. He felt himself lifted off the floor as the creature swung him in a counter-clockwise motion. A tremor rippled through his body as it slammed him hard against the starboard wall, shaking the knife from his grip.

Pressed against the wall, Seymour felt his feet dangling two feet off the floor. The creature screeched furiously and drew its left arm back. Like a boxer, it rammed the now-blunt end of its glove into Seymour's side. Ribs cracked, and painful yells hollered as the blow landed. It struck a second time, cracking another rib. Seymour shouted as a third punch blew his air out.

It felt as though his ribcage was compressing his lungs. The Pilot stepped back, yanking Seymour from the wall. Screeching viciously, it threw him to the floor like a ragdoll. Seymour struck down hard on his stomach. His jaw clenched as his chin hit the floor, cracking two of his crowns. Blood spat from his mouth as he pushed himself up onto his hands and knees.

He looked up over his left shoulder, seeing the Pilot standing over him. It lifted its right leg and thrust its heel down on his side like a battering ram. Pain burst through his body as the force drove him onto his back.

Coughing and groaning, Seymour clutched his sides. "Son-of-a-BITCH!" he yelled out.

The Pilot stood over him, gazing at its prize. It lifted its knee again, placing its foot square atop Seymour's chest. It steadily applied pressure. Seymour felt like an air balloon being squeezed. His chest compressed tightly, and all air left his lungs as he wheezed for breath.

He tried pushing the foot off, but the creature's strength was far superior. He felt himself growing weak. His chest tightened like he had never felt before in his life. In a moment, his chest plate would crack, and be driven into his lungs and heart.

He felt the curtain closing in on his vision. With almost all energy and air depleted, Seymour's arms fell to each side.

The tip of his fingers touched something. Something metal. Solid, but loose. Looking to his right, he saw the open metal container.

Beside it was the fallen flare gun.

Seymour summoned any remaining energy and seized the weapon by its handle. He pointed up, squeezing the trigger.

A ball of flame blasted from the nozzle, striking the Pilot square in the face. Sizzling fire scorched its mandibles and ate away at its vision. The Pilot scurried backward in a frenzy. Stumbling into the back of the cabin, it clawed at its own face to rid of the embedded flame.

Relieved of its weight and pressure, Seymour pulled himself to his feet. Fighting through the intense pain, he ran for the cockpit. He stumbled inside, slamming the door shut behind him. He secured the latch, locking the creature out, then sat at the pilot's seat.

He switched off the autopilot and turned the plane around. The hisses echoed through the cabin, and he could see the red flare glinting in his peripheral vision. The nose of the ShinMaywa now pointed back toward the island.

His chest and sides throbbed intensely. The bleeding from his nose had ceased, and his vision had cleared. He ignored the pain as he quickly ran through a series of plans in his mind. He thought of splashing the plane down into the water but couldn't guarantee that it would inflict enough damage from this altitude. He quickly realized the best option was to crash the plane.

The Pilot slammed itself onto the cockpit door. Looking over his shoulder, Seymour could see its enraged face through the window. It punched the door repeatedly, denting it inward.

Time was running out. Seymour turned his eyes forward. The ShinMaywa had passed over the shore and was now traveling over a sea of green.

Seymour drew a breath, ready to smash it down; an act that would likely cost him his life. The creature would likely survive the crash, but at least it would be stranded on the island. He dipped the nose, lowering the altitude. He watched the jungle's detail grow more meticulous as he lowered. The individual details of each tree was perceptible.

One detail caught Seymour's eye.

In the sea of green, there was something out of place. Something metal. Seymour briefly pondered the new idea in his mind. A heavy blow to the door forced him to make a decision.

He turned the plane to port. He located the slight gap in the trees; the creek where his team first encountered the Pilot. The cockpit door bent inward, folding in off of the frame. The three fingered hand reached at Seymour through the breach.

Seymour leaned forward, keeping just out of reach of its grasp. He flew the plane in a tight circle, lining the nose up with the creek. He reduced the speed and began lowering the altitude.

"This would be a lot easier if they built some damn ejector seats into this thing..." he said to himself as he lowered into a descent. He ducked down and braced for impact.

Nature and metal collided. The ShinMaywa crashed down. Wings smashed simultaneously against trees on both sides, breaking off the body of the plane. The engines burst like grenades, breaking apart on their own debris. The fuselage erupted into flames, spreading fire into the jungle.

The body broke into segments. The tail broke apart completely, disintegrating in to unrecognizable fragments. The cockpit detached from the cabin, both fragments rolling through the creek like logs on a river.

The floor split apart from underneath the Pilot's feet like a fault line. Driven by the forward momentum of the crash, the Pilot hit the ground. It splashed in the shallow water as the ShinMaywa spread all over the creek.

CHAPTER 40

Smoke and vapor swirled together as the debris settled down. Burning fuel scorched the surrounding trees. Ammo and explosives fired off within the devastated cargo hold, igniting new explosions along the creek. The running water turned black from gunpowder and fuel, and the surrounding canopy turned grey from the vast smoke trail.

Soot and water dripped from the Pilot's charred face as it lifted its head. Its sensory nerves pounded through its body. Its senses were in complete disarray. The burns to its face severely narrowed its vision. Broken flaps in its armor folded inward, stabbing into its body. Its left arm was crushed within its glove. One fang was completely broken off at the chelicerae, the other chipped an inch from the tip.

It stood up to its feet. After assessing its own injuries, it looked at the wreckage. Fragments of the plane lined the crash trail behind it. Its neck throbbed, as the malfunctioning sensory nerves pounded with an overwhelming influx of signals. The Pilot turned away from the trail and looked up the creek.

The cockpit lay in the water, embedded into the gravel. There was no sign of the indigenous. Ignoring the multiple injury signals in its nerves, the Pilot marched through the shallow water toward the cockpit. Despite its condition, the creature still lived to fulfill its purpose of preserving the species. Doing so meant eliminating any threats.

It no longer saw the human warrior as a potential host, but as a fundamental threat to its existence. The species had no concept of honor or morality. Right and wrong didn't exist. All it had was instinct, and the uncompromising drive and intelligence to enact its purpose. The indigenous being was an obstacle to its purpose that must be destroyed.

Fluid coagulated over its burnt face, forming an orange-black scab. It leaned its head to the left, allowing the intact cells to provide sight. Marching through the water, it approached the cockpit. The cockpit lay across the creek, the broken end angled away from the Pilot. The windows were blackened by smoke, making it impossible to see inside from the front.

The Pilot flexed its fingers, ready to grab its enemy and strangle it to death. It marched around the nose and approached the edge of the cockpit. Mustering its strength, it increased its speed and swiftly moved around the corner. It tore into the cockpit, ready to hammer down on the seats.

It paused. Both seats were empty. Human blood marked the dashboard, though only in small streaks. Not enough to imply death. The Pilot stepped out and looked around. There were no bodies anywhere near the wreckage.

A faint sound echoed from the jungle. The Pilot froze. Standing in the middle of the creek, it allowed its damaged nerves to pick up on the signal. The sound continued. It heard another sound. Language. Its enemy!

"Hey! We're not done yet!"

The Pilot whipped its gaze toward the trees. It couldn't see the mercenary, though it was nearby. The alien knew its opponent had no projectiles and was disarmed of its edged weapons. Even with its many injuries, it would easily be the victor in another physical confrontation, as the Pilot had superior strength and ferocity.

It tore into the jungle, following the sounds. The smoke thinned out as it moved further into the terrain. It tore any obstacle out of its path, ripping bamboo and bushes from their roots.

"Come on! Come on!" the voice continued. The Pilot paused, analyzing the sound in its brain. The voice sounded somewhat different, and slightly muffled. The shouting continued. Suddenly, loud bursts sounded off. Gunshots. The Pilot knelt, ready to avoid incoming fire. Its senses heightened, realizing the human was indeed armed. It activated its gauntlet. Sparks zipped as the device struggled to generate energy.

The gunfire continued in rapid bursts. Another high-pitched sound reverberated from the same direction. Screeches. Hisses.

They were cries from its spawn. The Pilot hissed, realizing some of its spawn were still alive. That hiss sustained into a deathly snarl as it realized those spawn were being slaughtered.

It tore through the jungle in a mad fury, ripping up vines and leaves with each step. The gunfire and screams grew louder and more intense. The enemy shouted, taunting the creatures as they closed in on him.

The Pilot snarled as it leapt between two large trees. It landed in an aggressive pose, thinking it had landed in the battle-zone. It paused, seeing nothing but jungle. However, the firefight was louder than ever.

The creature stepped forward, approaching the large tree several feet ahead.

Thirty feet high, something rested in the branches. The Pilot gazed up, seeing the old Japanese WW2 plane propped high above it. It stood under the plane, looking around for the source of the gunfire.

Its nerves pulsed hard in its neck. Despite the sound being strong, there was no vibration around it. No sign of any living creatures moving about. Yet the noise seemed to be coming from here.

It looked down at the ground. There, something lay in the grass, covered in dirt and ants. Rectangular in shape, it was no bigger than six inches long. The sound boomed from this small device. It picked the object up and flipped it over, revealing a playback screen.

On the tiny monitor, it observed footage of the attack on the bunker, as Ivan repelled the horde with his M60. The Pilot hissed and looked ahead of it. A red light blinked high above the ground, attached to a small black block. That black block was strapped to a large, cigar-shaped object.

Ivan yelled in the bodycam playback audio.

"*Adios, Motherfucker!*"

Two hundred meters away, Seymour peeked from behind a large tree and watched as the Pilot stumbled into his trap. In his hand he held a detonator, its antenna fully extended.

"My sentiments, exactly," he said. He pressed his thumb on the trigger and ducked behind the tree.

The Pilot let out one final screech as the C-4 block detonated, triggering the torpedo. Dormant since World War 2, the huge explosive finally met its conclusion, erupting into a massive blast capable of devastating a battleship. The ball of fire ripped up into the tree, the vibration shaking the bomber plane free from the branches. It fell into the ball of fire, detonating the two-thousand pounds of unused explosives contained within it.

Balls of fire burst in unison as though a string of volcanos had erupted. Trees leaned outward as they absorbed the concussion of the blast. Smoke and dirt hurled outward in a massive ring, sweeping the interior of the jungle. Fire roared inside the resulting crater, reducing the lively green jungle to a hellfire netherworld.

Smoldering in the middle of it were the fragments of armor and technology: its owner completely disintegrated.

CHAPTER
41

Seymour had limped nearly a mile out before he found air clear of smoke and dust. The artillery explosion had created a mountain of smoke that hovered over the north side of the island. Debris had rained down like volcanic ash, spreading all the way to the shore.

Seymour took a deep breath as he embraced the clean air. His left arm had been broken in the crash, and he held it close to his stomach. Torn strands of his shirt served as a makeshift tourniquet. Seymour suspected a fracture in his left leg as well, as it was extremely painful to walk with. In the crash, he had turned to the right as he ducked, and the control panel smashed in against him as the ShinMaywa struck down.

A cool breeze swept inland from the ocean, indicating he was close to the shore. With pain flooding his ribs, leg, and arm, he limped his way through the jungle. Soon, he could hear the waves splashing against the shore. The sunlight grew brighter as he approached the west edge of the island.

He stood on a small ledge, which extended only a few feet from the tree line. Several large rocks marked the dirt shore. He sat down on one, fully extending his injured leg. His temples pounded, and his broken arm was swelling drastically. He didn't care. The airstrike would commence any moment, and he knew the pilots would not allow any square inch of the island to go untouched. There was no escape.

There was only one thing to do. He relaxed himself and gazed out into the endless blue. It was a beautiful sight. A perfect final note to close his lifetime on. Despite the deception surrounding the mission, he was able to conduct one final act to truly better humanity.

He watched the ocean, looking for the incoming aircraft that would bombard the island. So far, the skies were clear. But there was sound. The sound of an engine. It didn't sound distant, however. It was close, and not from two-thousand feet in the air. He gazed up, looking for the source. There was a gentle clamor to this engine sound, something a jet traveling at top speed would have. And it wasn't coming from high above…

His eyes lowered back to the Pacific.

Something was moving along the surface. A boat…a Zodiac. Seymour stood up, his eyes wide with amazement.

Terrie stood at the helm, gazing up at the enormous cloud of smoke. She lowered her gaze toward the shore, seeing her brother-in-arms waving at her. There was something on his face she rarely ever saw. A bright smile.

After boarding the vessel, he leaned back into one of the back seats. Terrie stood at the helm, driving the Zodiac as far from the island as possible.

"Good God, I thought you were dead," Seymour said. He closed his eyes and enjoyed the cool air brushing against his face.

"Well, the bump on the noggin did a number on me," she said. "But, as you said, we have an arrangement." Seymour opened his eyes, seeing Terrie looking back at him and smiling.

The resounding echo of jet engines drew their eyes to the sky. White streaks stretched between the clouds, trailing arrow shaped aircraft that rapidly approached.

Terrie looked back at Seymour. "What's in store for us after this?" Seymour shrugged, watching the jets lower their altitude.

"I don't know," he said. "Hawk's dead. We know the Agency's Top-Secret project. They don't have much use for us."

"Maybe," Terrie said, reaching into her pocket. "We'll have to see." She held her hand out, holding Hawk's flash-drive. A perfect little insurance policy.

They shared another smile, then watched the jets pass overhead. In the blink of an eye, the large green island erupted in flames as several bombs rained down. Fire ripped through the jungle, torching the plant life and any nest that remained.

"I guess you're right," Seymour said. He and Terrie solemnly watched, as a thousand balls of fire rolled from the island's center into the shore.

EPILOGUE

For several hours, fire ripped across the terrain as the bombs continued dropping. The jungle, thick and vast, was now reduced to a smoldering cinder. It was the will of the U.S. Government that no biological trace be left.

However, the pilots had strict instructions to avoid one specific area.

By nightfall, the fire had burnt away all life on the island, extraterrestrial or otherwise. The landscape was reduced to an eight-mile long ashtray.

In the middle of it all, one spot was left untouched. What remained of the Command Post after the attack twenty-four hours earlier still stood firm. The east wall remained intact, along with most of the second-floor laboratory. Dust, ash, and smoke had smothered the building, leaving the interior covered in pasty gray grime.

However, deeper in, there was an area left mostly untouched. Two steel doors, sealed tightly, protected the quarantine chamber from the burning remnants. Inside, a depleted, mushy corpse lay on the table, its identity completely erased. Protruding from its center, the pod had grown, having healed from the intrusive injury subjected to it.

Standing six-feet high off the table, its sides pulsated. Black secretion spilled from pores in its pulsating sides.

A wet tearing noise rasped from its side, as a thin layer began peeling back from the top.

THE END

CHECK OUT OTHER GREAT SCIENCE FICTION BOOKS

MAX RAGE
by Jake Bible

Genetically Engineered. Physically enhanced. Mentally conditioned.

Master Chief Sergeant Major Max Rage was the top dog in an elite fighting force that no one in the galaxy could stop. Until, one day, someone did.

The lone survivor, Rage was blamed for the mission failure and court-martialed.

With a serious chip on his shoulder, Rage finds himself as a bouncer at the top dive bar in Greenville, South Carolina. And, man, is he bored with his job.

At least until he gets a job offer he can't refuse. Now, Rage is headed halfway across the galaxy to the den of corruption known as Horloc Station.

With this job, Max Rage may have a chance to get back to what he was: an unstoppable Intergalactic Badass!

WARNING: THIS NOVEL HAS GRATUITOUS VIOLENCE, SEX, FOUL LANGUAGE, AND A LOT OF BAD JOKES! YOU MAY FIND YOURSELF ENJOYING HIGHLY INAPPROPRIATE PROSE! YOU HAVE BEEN WARNED!

RECON ELITE
by Viktor Zarkov

With Earth no longer inhabitable, Recon Six Elite are sent across space to scout promising new planets for colonization.

The five talented and determined space marines are led by hard-nosed commander Sam Boggs. Earth's last best hope, these men and women are the "tip of the spear". Armed with a wide array of deadly weapons and forensics, Boggs and Recon Elite Six must clear the planet Mawholla of hostile species.

But Recon Elite are about to find out how hostile Mawholla truly is.

CHECK OUT ANOTHER GREAT SCIENCE FICTION NOVEL

SPACE MARINE AJAX
by Sean-Michael Argo

Ajax answers the call of duty and becomes an Einherjar space marine, charged with defending humanity against hideous alien monsters in furious combat across the galaxy.

The Garm, as they came to be called, emerged from the deepest parts of uncharted space, devouring all that lay before them, a great swarm that scoured entire star systems of all organic life. This space borne hive, this extinction fleet, made no attempts to communicate and offered no mercy. Such was the ferocity of their assault upon the civilization of humanity that our own wars and schemes were made petty in comparison.

Humanity has always been a deadly organism, and we would not so easily be made the prey. Unified against a common enemy, we fought back, meeting the swarm with soldiers upon every front.

We were resplendent in our fury, and yet, despite the terrible slaughter we visited upon the enemy, world after world still fell beneath ravenous tooth and wicked claw. For every beast slain in the field, another was swiftly hatched to take its place and humanity was faced with a grim war of attrition.

After a decade of bitter galactic conflict, it was all humanity could to do slow the advance of the swarm and with each passing year we came closer to extinction. The grinding cost of war mounted. The realization set in that without a radical shift in tactics and technology the forces of humanity would run out of soldiers before it ran out of bullets.

In desperate response to the real threat of total annihilation, humanity created the Einherjar. Fearless new warriors with frightening new weapons who were sent to fight the wolves at the gate.

CHECK OUT OTHER GREAT
SCIENCE FICTION BOOKS

LOST EMPIRE
by Edward P. Cardillo

Building on their victory in the last Intergalactic War, the imperialist United Intergalactic Coalition seeks to expand their influence over the valuable Kronite mines of Golgath. Reeling from their defeat, the warrior Feng are down but not out. The overextended UIC and the vengeful Feng deploy battle groups and scramble fighters as they battle for position in the universe, spinning optics and building coalitions. Captain Reinhardt of the Resilience and the elite Razor's Edge squadron uncover the Feng Emperor Hiron's last ditch attempt to turn the tables with a new and dangerous technology. With resources spread thin, the UIC seeks to exploit Feng's weakened position through a very conditional peace accord. Unwilling to submit, Emperor Hiron must hold them off and quell the growing civil unrest of his starving, warrior people just long enough to execute the mysterious Operation: Catalyst. Commander Massa and his Razor's Edge squadron race against time to stop Hiron's plan, and a new race awakens, led by a powerful prophet set on toppling the established galactic order through violent acts of terrorism.

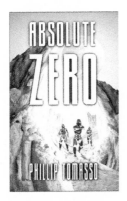

ABSOLUTE ZERO
by Phillip Tomasso

When a recon becomes a rescue . . . nothing is absolute!

Earth, a desolate wasteland is now run by the Corporations from space stations off planet . . . A colony of thirty-three people are part of a compound set up on Neptune. Their objective is mining the planet surface for natural resources. When a distress signal reaches Euphoric Enterprises on the Nebula Way Station, the Eclipse is immediately dispatched to investigate.

The crew of the Eclipse had no idea what they were getting themselves into. When they reach Neptune, and send out a shuttle party, they hope they can find the root cause behind the alarm. Nothing is ever simple. Something sinister lies in wait for them on Neptune. The mission quickly goes from an investigation into a rescue operation.

The young crew from the Eclipse now finds themselves in the fight of their lives!

Made in the USA
Las Vegas, NV
25 July 2022

52161041R00132